For Mary -
Remember for[...]
a silver linin[...]
between heaven and earth isn't that
for - God Bless you.

A Formidable Enemy

R. Gian Sante

A Novel by

R. Gian Sante

PublishAmerica
Baltimore

First printing

ISBN: 1-4241-2398-4
PUBLISHED BY PUBLISHAMERICA, LLLP
www.publishamerica.com
Baltimore

Printed in the United States of America

Dedication

Deb & Steve Sherbuk
Donald & Sheryl Ripka
J. Steven Ripka

PROLOGUE

New York City
May 13

The New York train hummed along the tracks at moderate speed to arrive at its Washington destination on schedule. The black attaché case under the window seat in the middle car went unnoticed. The man in the seat above the case was reading the *New York Times*. He glanced at the date and thought, *Oh-oh, Friday the thirteenth.* The rest of his thoughts were lost in the roar and percussion that followed. The middle car split apart like a house of cards scattered and carried off into the wind. The engineer lost control of the locomotive as the blast sent it careening off the tracks and down the embankment carrying with it what remained of the other cars. The screech of steel on steel drowned out the screams of the passengers propelled into oblivion. The roar ended as abruptly as it began with a mass of twisted steel and broken bodies strewn on the bottom of the ravine.

There was no one to hear the occasional sob or weak cry for help. The silence was broken by the rain of dirt and gray ash descending from the brown cloud raised by the disturbed landscape as it settled on the overturned cars, cutting the passage of light through the few spider-web cracked windows that remained.

* * *

Two men left the platform at New York's Pennsylvania Station. Khalil Najjar carried a black attaché case identical to the one on the train. He checked his watch, it was five minutes past seven o'clock. Neither man spoke as they walked along Eighth Avenue toward 43rd Street and the Port Authority Bus Terminal.

The scene at the bus terminal was different from the one at Pennsylvania Station. Here, women and children waited to board buses. People going to shore points or getting an early start to visit relatives for the weekend. It was more relaxed, not the fast paced, pushing hoards of businessmen and women. Najjar looked away. He didn't want to see the faces of the people he was to exterminate. Slowly, they covered the area between the entrance to the terminal and the benches where people waited. Najjar put the attaché case on the floor at the end of the bench. The two men sat down and waited. They watched the long hand of the big clock on the wall as it counted off the minutes to seven-thirty.

Abdul Shakir inserted a coin in the vending machine on the opposite side of the terminal and pulled the lever. Najjar left the black case beside the bench and joined Shakir at the vending machine and checked the change in his pockets. He put three quarters in the slot and pulled the lever for a small bag of potato chips. His eyes scanned the waiting room. No one had noticed the black bag on the floor. Najjar and Shakir left the terminal and walked east on 43rd Street. At seven-thirty-five the blast cleared away everything within a radius of two city blocks. The force from the explosion picked up buses and automobiles in the immediate vicinity of the terminal and turned them into deadly missiles that seemed to pinpoint targets thirty to fifty feet away.

It seemed like an eternity before the wail of sirens could be heard as police and fire rescue vehicles converged on the area. At seven fifty, the airwaves crackled first with news of the explosion in the bus terminal, then at seven-fifty-five, with the news of the train wreck. New Yorkers were shocked out of their apathy into a purgatory of confusion and finally into the hell of reality.

CHAPTER 1

Washington, D.C.

Waiting was something Peter Aziz did not do well. His deep-set brown eyes, partially shielded by heavy dark lashes, scanned the almost deserted cocktail lounge. He looked younger than his thirty-five years and his perpetual scowl gave him a look of petulance. He positioned himself so that he could watch the door and observe the five men sitting at the bar engaged in animated storytelling, punctuated by occasional guffaws.

He signaled the waiter for another bourbon and water. His finger tapping was a sure sign of his growing impatience. He sensed, rather than saw the figure approaching the frosted double glass doors from the street. He glanced at his watch and was surprised to find he had been waiting only twenty minutes. The door opened and the empty space was filled with the six-foot-two, one-hundred-and ninety-pound frame of Michael Redmond. He seemed to know instinctively where Peter would be sitting and weaved his way between the empty tables and sat down. "It's been a long time, Peter. How are you?"

Aziz paused until the waiter deposited his drink. "What'll you have, Mike?"

"Johnny Walker, black."

The two men shook hands. Aziz shifted his chair so that he could see beyond Redmond. "Good to see you."

Mike nodded. "What brings you to Washington? I thought you hated it here."

"I do. All this puffed up bureaucracy and pseudo-macho garbage makes me want to puke. Doesn't this shit ever get to you?"

"Sure it does but it's not going to change, so I look at it as a necessary evil and do the best I can. The money's good."

"Yeah, right, Mike. All we have to do is live long enough to spend it." He sipped his bourbon. "I ran into a friend of yours in Kuwait."

Mike Redmond's eyes narrowed but his lips were set in a smile. "Male or female?"

Aziz waited until the waiter left Mike's drink before he answered, "Antony Emerson."

Redmond's expression didn't change. He thought, *Tony Emerson was with British Secret Intelligence Service and that could mean only one thing…trouble.*

Mike downed his drink, reached into his pocket and dropped a twenty-dollar bill on the table. "It's stuffy in here. Let's take a walk."

Aziz emptied his glass and caught up to Redmond at the door, his five-foot-ten frame was dwarfed by Mike's height and massive shoulders. Aziz pulled up his collar to ward off the cold dampness that engulfed Washington like a shroud. He had difficulty keeping step with Mike's long stride. Fifteen minutes later they entered what appeared to be a boarding house and walked up a flight of stairs. Mike inserted an electronic card in a door slot. There was a faint buzzing and the door opened. They walked into a luxurious apartment.

Peter whistled softly, "Nice place. How does it feel to be Washington's playboy? You get invited to all the right parties, meet all the right people and no one suspects you're CIA. When did you move out of your condo?"

"I didn't and you know how I hate parties. The company finally broke down and got this apartment for agency people who are here on a temporary basis. I don't think anyone knows about this place yet but they still take the usual precautions. Randall Perry is assigned to you. He'll take you wherever you want to go." Mike walked to the counter that separated the kitchen from the living room and pushed a button. The countertop parted and up popped a small bar, stocked with a good selection of liquor. He took two glasses from the overhead cabinet. "Bourbon and water?"

Peter grinned. "I hate to become known by my habits. Cognac, please."

Mike Redmond handed him the drink. "Okay, let's have it. I got word you were in town from the Bossman. Since then I've been contacted by the FBI, the National Security Agency and National Security Council. Sounds like something big."

Peter Aziz swallowed some of the amber liquid. "Let's include Secret Service."

Mike studied Aziz's face and sat on the arm of the sofa. He forced his breath through clenched teeth. "Somebody's got a hit out…on the President?"

"It looks that way. The chess pieces are on the board and the opening move was made."

"Who are the players? Where did it start?"

Aziz finished his drink. "Don't know for sure. Iraq, Iran, Libya, the Sudan, certain factions of the Arab world…wherever it started, it gained momentum. They're determined to get their pound of flesh for U.S. interference, in what they consider to be internal affairs. We espouse human dignity and civil rights. They contend it's an American philosophy that is riddled with evil."

Mike sank into the soft cushions and clasped his hands behind his head. "So, the Iraqi madman is at it again and I'm sure Bin Laden has a bit of his fortune on the table along with a lot of his hatred. We should have taken them out when we had the chance. They've eliminated any opposition and there's a good probability that they've developed the nuclear weapons Hussein told the UN he didn't have. Damn! Why do we leave things half done? It always comes back to haunt us. He leaned forward and lit a cigarette. "How did you get wind of this?"

"Emerson contacted me."

"Tony Emerson's a thorough agent. At least British SIS is covering our back door." He handed the electronic door key to Aziz. "The refrigerator's stocked. If you need anything, call the office. I'll set up a meeting with the agency and get word out to our contacts. The Bossman will probably contact C in London to get Tony Emerson sent to us for a few days. We'll meet in Langley."

"Before you go…what about phone calls? Will they be monitored?"

"After you dial the number you want, press the squelch under the phone. That'll get you off the monitor." Mike laughed at the blush that reddened Peter's ears. "Don't tell me you and Laura are still an item?"

"Amazing, isn't it?"

"Laura's a fine woman." Mike smiled. "Although I'll be damned if I understand how she puts up with you."

Peter's face lit up with a rare smile. "What can I tell you? She's obsessed with my body."

CHAPTER 2

Langley, VA.

At exactly 0730 Mike Redmond entered the room. At a glance he knew there was representation from every national security agency, as well as British SIS, and Israel's Shin Beth. That accounted for everyone except for the new agent, Glenn Alexander, who had been assigned to him for this project.

Prior to the meeting, the Bossman, Clifford Ardell, handed Mike the dossier on Glenn Alexander. Redmond quickly scanned the information, satisfying himself that this agent had been with the CIA for five years as a domestic agent. Mike thought, *This poor slob's going to get his butt chewed out for being late.*

Cliff Ardell called the meeting to order, then picked up the phone. "Send in Glenn Alexander, please."

Redmond was facing the door when agent Alexander, a tall, lithe, dark-haired beauty, with long, shapely legs entered and sat in the chair next to him.

"Gentlemen," Ardell stood, "this is Glenn Alexander. She is director of Alexander International Hotels. Fortunately for us, one of AIH's hotels is in Kuwait and a new one is going up in Manama, Bahrain. Glenn is especially important to this mission because of her business connections in the Middle East as well as her visibility and recognition in Washington society." If Ardell was expecting a reaction, he didn't get one, at least not one that was obvious. He continued, "I think we're dealing with a mix of foreign and domestic terrorists. Fact-finding will be extremely difficult. We may be talking about sleepers, planted in this country several years ago. The FBI has a profile on every resident from a foreign country, so we have basic information." He turned to Duncan MacKenzie. "Mac, why don't you take over from here."

MacKenzie was the expert in counter espionage with the FBI. His close-cropped light brown hair was streaked with gray and gave him the appearance of being older than his thirty-six years. His face was angular which served to accentuate his slightly flattened nose. He was direct and to the point. "After the World Trade Center was bombed in 1993, we had a good idea where to look for the terrorists. At that time we realized that if the terrorists had placed the bombs where they had intended, the entire tower of the World Trade Center would have collapsed. The World Trade Center remains a dark looming target for any terrorist group who wanted to take on our country. Eight years later the unthinkable happened and both towers were taken out and the Pentagon was hit on September 11, 2001, and another passenger plane went down in a field in Pennsylvania. We were brought out of our apathy into harsh reality. The hit we are expecting now is a different kind of hit. We have caused a lot of havoc in the Middle East and now we are trying to rebuild Iraq and Afghanistan. Their reasoning is to get rid of the guy at the top and the contract is out on the President. They'll probably use an inside cover. The hit man could very well be an American. One thing we know for sure, he's professional, expendable and known in Washington society. They can't afford to miss." He took a cigarette from the heavy lead crystal box in front of him. "Since the information originated with British SIS, perhaps Tony Emerson can fill us in on what's happening in the Middle East."

"What information I have," Emerson began, "is sketchy. They're keeping a tight lid on this one. The code name for the kingpin in the assassination is Abd al Alim. This person probably lives in the U.S. I think there's a good possibility that the Bin Laden Organization is in this up to its eyeballs in this hit. Abu Nidal probably wrote the book on terrorism, and Osama Bin Laden fine-tuned it. He could very well be calling the shots with lots of help from other dissident groups." He walked to the wall map and picked up five plastic red flags. "Bin Laden does regular exercises to keep his hatred alive. If Bin Laden died tomorrow, the group would be just as deadly because of the tight organizational structure. It's the consensus of the field agents in the Gulf that this is a joint effort and they're getting their backing from various sources in the Arab world." He inserted one red flag in the area governed by Iraq. He inserted one flag in each area occupied by Libya, Lebanon, Afghanistan and Iran. He inserted the last flag in the land south of Egypt, in the Sudan. "It's possible these countries have put aside their personal hatreds and differences and united for a common cause, to destroy the infidels. Gentlemen, let's not forget Arabia but all of their actions are covert.

"Because no one knows how the hit will be attempted, you must consider such groups as Black September Organization based in Lebanon, the Fifteen May Organization and the Arab Liberation Front based in Iraq, and Bin Laden's suicide squads in Afghanistan. It's difficult to say where the rumor started. I heard about it in Kuwait from one of our native agents. SIS will help in any way we can."

Shin Beth's David Jabez shook his head. "Word of the proposed hit came to me in Tel Aviv through an agent who had just returned from Beirut. I believe this will be another Kennedy assassination scenario. If the plan succeeds, you can be sure there will be no terrorists alive to give testimony and point a finger. Dead men make terrible witnesses." He loosened his tie and undid the top button of his shirt. "My feeling is that this is so big it would have to come from within. It was probably masterminded from the Middle East but the kamikaze terrorist will be local. It can't be otherwise. A foreigner would be too obvious, too conspicuous. Abd al Alim was selected to carry out the hit for one reason and one reason only, Abd al Alim knows the President. That's going to make your task extremely difficult…if not impossible. They would never attempt such a coup unless they had someone who is known and accepted in Washington society."

Jabez sat back in his chair. "Shin Beth will be protecting your flanks and we'll feed you whatever information becomes available."

When the meeting ended, Cliff Ardell handed each person a schedule of meetings for the next three days. He asked Redmond, Alexander and Aziz to stay.

When they were alone in the conference room, the Bossman lit a cigarette and watched his three agents. "I think David Jabez's statement has a lot of merit. The hit will probably come from inside." He nodded to Glenn Alexander. "We've got to penetrate the inner circle of Washington society…and you're my needle. I want you to throw a party. That's when you'll be introduced to Mike Redmond. Vibes or chemistry or whatever you want to call it, must be obvious. I want the gossip columns to be speculating about the outcome." He could tell by the frown on Mike Redmond's face that he didn't like the idea.

Mike protested, "I don't do the Washington scene."

Ardell ignored the comment. "Glenn, invite my secretary, Sally Vance, to your party. Mike will escort her."

Mike repeated, "I-don't-do-the-Washington-scene."

Ardell snuffed out his cigarette. "You do now, Mike. This is not a request. It's an order." Cliff folded his arms across his chest, indicating that the discussion was closed.

When Glenn spoke, it was directly to Mike. Her voice was soft, tinged with amusement. "I'll plan a cocktail party for Friday of this week."

Mike glared at her, a frown still creasing his forehead.

She smiled and said, "It's set then. Sally will introduce us on Friday, Michael."

"My name's Mike. Michael sounds like the archangel."

Glenn smiled. "I think people could tell the difference." She closed the door quietly behind her.

Cliff Ardell coughed to conceal the grin that made its way to his lips.

Mike turned angrily on the Bossman. "You could have told me Glenn was a woman. You know damn well I don't like working with a woman."

"You had her dossier. The cover sheet clearly stated she was a female. I'm not asking you to marry her, just be her partner on this project."

"Just…be her partner? In some ways a partner is closer than a wife. Why did you do this to me?"

"I didn't do it to you. I did it for you. What better cover than a beautiful woman of high standing in Washington society. We need her. We couldn't do this without her. Time is our enemy…not Glenn. The curriculum at the academy is geared to men. The training, as you well know, is intense and brutal. If you read her dossier then you know she was at the top of her class." He pulled his glasses down to the end of his nose and studied Mike over the top of them. "You may own one of the largest chemical companies in the world but you're notorious for shying away from social events. The only plausible explanation for your sudden interest in social affairs is a love interest, which Washington will follow on the society pages. Don't judge her, Mike, just work with her."

Mike stood up to leave. "I'll work with her, but I don't have to like it."

Ardell picked up the folder from the table. "Do you want to walk away from this one? Say yes, and I'll assign someone else. I wanted her to be with you because of your past experience in the assassination attempt on Senator Leopold. But…if you can't handle it, I'll assign John Carey."

Mike reached the door before he turned around. "Over my dead body. This is my assignment and if it means escorting Alexander into hell, I'll do it." He closed the door behind him.

* * *

The Victorian house on Cardinal Drive in Alexandria was ablaze with lights. Sally Vance and Mike entered behind another couple. He recognized Senator Matthew Cameron and he surmised that the overly painted, dour looking woman with him was Matthew Cameron's wife. Glenn Alexander stood in front of a pale green marble fireplace, the perfect setting to enhance the contrast with her emerald green gown, which matched the color of her eyes. She was talking with a good-looking, dark-haired man that Mike recognized as Arabian playboy, Karim Russal. Mike took Sally's hand and they made their way to their hostess.

Glenn smiled. "Sally. I'm pleased you were able to make it."

Sally returned her smile. "Glenn, this is Mike Redmond."

He took her hand in both of his and his eyes laughingly challenged her.

Her eyes sparkled and her smile was an open invitation. She introduced them to Karim Russal.

A petite, fiery redhead invaded the circle and put a possessive hand on Karim's arm. "Che bello," she said, smiling up at Mike. "Carissima, who is this dashing man?"

"Michael Redmond, Sally Vance, this is Gabriella Russal. If I were you, Mike, I'd be very cautious. Gabi collects men and puts them on her charm bracelet."

Gabriella's lyrical laugh revealed white even teeth and an appealing dimple in her right cheek. It was evident she loved to flirt. Mike was trying to place her accent. French? Italian?

"Don't listen to her, mon chere," Gabriella purred, "I am a simple woman with simple desires."

Mike laughed. "Then why do I get the feeling you're toying with me?"

Gabriella winked at Glenn. "Hang on to him, darling, he's a live one."

A small band played slow music in the formal dining room. The furniture had been moved and the oriental rugs stored to allow room for dancing. Mike took Sally by the hand. "Dance?"

"I'd love to."

Mike nodded to Glenn. "Excuse us?" His gaze held hers.

Glenn felt Mike had just mentally undressed her. "Of course." She turned away but not before he saw the flush that started at the base of her throat and climbed slowly toward her face.

On the dance floor, Mike took Sally in his arms. "So far, so good," he breathed.

Sally said, "I'm glad you don't look at me the way you looked at Glenn, my virtue would be in serious danger."

He waltzed her around the floor. "You're marvelous." He laughed and held her close as they glided across the almost deserted floor.

Halfway through "Moonlight Serenade," Mike felt someone tap him on the shoulder. A dark-haired man, who resembled Glenn, smiled at them. "Switch partners?" he asked. "I don't want people to talk because Glenn is dancing every number with her cousin." He smiled at Sally. "I'm Brad Crawford. I know who you are because I asked Glenn." They traded partners and Glenn stepped into the circle of Mike's arms. He realized she was almost as tall as he. "When I saw you standing in front of the fireplace," he whispered, "I thought of a Botticelli painting of Venus."

Glenn pulled back slightly so that she could look in his eyes. "Oh? Which one?"

"The painting where Venus is standing in a seashell."

"*The Birth of Venus*?"

"Yeah, that's the one. Venus on-a-half-shell. That's the way you look tonight, alluring, provocative and mysterious."

"But Botticelli's Venus is a blonde."

"I don't think many men noticed the color of her hair. There are—other things to hold their attention."

She saw the amusement in his eyes and shook her head.

He pulled her closer. Her body molded to his and they moved as one. His mouth was only inches from hers. They seemed oblivious to the people around them, then the music stopped and reluctantly, he released her.

Gabriella Russal claimed him for the next dance. Her smile was friendly. She leaned back in his arms, to see his face. The top of her head was a few inches below his shoulder. "Do you live in Washington?"

"I have a place in Georgetown."

"Why haven't we seen you before? I would certainly have remembered you."

"My business takes me out of the area."

"Quel dommage. Washington is such a fascinating place."

"What's fascinating is your accent. Is it French or Italian?"

"A little of both, I was born in Rome but went to college in Paris. That's where Glenn and I met. After graduation my father and I came to the U.S. We lived on Long Island. But that was too remote for me. I needed to be where things were happening, so I moved to Washington. Glenn and I saw a lot of each other. It was Glenn who introduced me to Karim Russal."

"Karim? That's an interesting name. Arabic?

She nodded. "You must get to know Karim, he's charming and loving and," she moistened her lips with the tip of her tongue, "he has that certain…je ne sais quois. But enough about us, why haven't I seen you at Washington parties before? I think you're very enigmatic."

He looked down at the splash of crimson covering her sensuous mouth. "There's no mystery about me. I don't like parties. When Sally's friend couldn't make it tonight, I agreed to come in his place." He looked around the room for Glenn and when he found her, he smiled and added, "Now I'm glad I did."

"I think Glenn is attracted to you. In fact, I think the attraction is mutual."

Mike winked. "You may be right."

Her eyes narrowed as she scrutinized his facial features. "Yes, I can see why she is attracted to you. Your eyes make promises that I'm sure your body is quite capable of fulfilling. You could be a lot of fun. All you have to do is, how do you say…loosen up a bit?"

She liked the sound of his deep baritone laugh. He excused himself when the music stopped and he reclaimed Sally. They spoke briefly with Glenn before leaving.

On the ride back to Washington Mike wondered if the charade had been successful. Briefly, he allowed his thoughts to wander into the past and he thought about Caitlin O'Hara, then, quickly pushed the thought of her from his mind. He couldn't handle the memory of Cat just now.

At her apartment door, Sally said, "I feel good about the charade. I think you convinced the guests and the paparazzi that love, if not in bloom, is at least budding."

She turned the key in the lock and pushed the door open. "The Bossman will want to know how it appeared to me." She turned in the open doorway. "You and Glenn were very convincing. If I didn't know better, I would say you were really attracted to each other, the perfect couple."

Mike put his hand on the door. "Then I'm a good actor. If Glenn was the last woman on earth, I would die…celibate."

Sally cocked her head to the side. "Yeah. Right, Mike. Good night."

* * *

Peter Aziz got out of the car and looked up at the apartment building towering above the Baltimore waterfront. "Pick me up tomorrow morning at seven."

Randy Perry scanned the area, nodded to Aziz and handed him a card. "If you need me, call this number."

Peter grinned. "I don't think I'll need you before seven but thanks." He watched Randy pull away before he entered the building. He took the elevator to the eighteenth floor and knocked on the door of apartment eighteen-twelve. The door opened almost immediately and the young woman stood looking at him until he broke the spell and gathered her in his arms. His mouth sought hers and a slight moan escaped his lips.

She pulled him into the apartment and pushed the door closed with her foot. They moved together but their lips never parted. Her hands were busy unbuttoning, first his jacket, then his shirt. His hands were busy exploring the soft flesh under her silk robe. The path from the door to the bedroom was strewn with his jacket, tie, shirt, trousers and shorts, in that order. The last item at the foot of the bed was a midnight blue silk robe.

Sated, Peter held Laura Madison in his arms. His fingers traced the outline of her face, as though trying to memorize each feature.

"When do you have to leave?"

He shifted his position so that he could see her in the dim light from the living room. "I'm being picked up at seven."

"Are you going back to Kuwait?"

"Yes, for a while."

"Can I visit you there?"

"Not now. I'll let you know when."

Laura knew better than to ask any more questions. She pulled him closer to her. "Why am I always so afraid when you leave?"

"Because you read too many spy novels." He laughed and kissed the tip of her nose. "I'll be back before you know it."

He kissed the tears that escaped from under her closed eyelids.

CHAPTER 3

Kuwait
May 7

Tony Emerson finished dressing and was straightening his tie when the phone rang. He picked it up "Emerson, here."

"Mr. Emerson," an unfamiliar voice said, "this is Ahmed at the lobby desk. Mr. Asad al Rachid says he has an appointment with you. He will meet you in the dining room."

"Thank you. Tell Mr. Rachid I'll be down in a few minutes." He thought, *Peter Aziz, alias, Asad al Rachid, is a very cautious man.* Working on this assumption, he unscrewed the mouthpiece of the phone and smiled to himself. *Bugged.*

When he reached the dining room, Haddad, the maître d' had already seated Peter. Tony extended his hand, "Mr. Rachid, thank you for coming." He turned and spoke with the maître d'. "Find us another table, away from the band."

"Of course, Mr. Emerson, will the table in the far corner suit you?"

Tony looked over his shoulder. Seated next to the table Haddad mentioned were three men and a woman. He recognized one of the men as an active member of the ANO. He scanned the room quickly. "The one near the kitchen will do."

Haddad smiled. "As you wish, Mr. Emerson."

Tony turned his attention to his guest. "Mr. Rachid, your jewelry designs are quite unique. There will be international shops in the lobby of the new Alexander Hotel in Bahrain. Would you be interested in opening one of your design shops there?"

"Yes, sir, I think it could be profitable for the hotel and for me. I spoke with Miss Alexander on the telephone and sent her some designs. She was pleased and wants to meet with me on her next visit."

"Excellent, Mr. Rachid. We can discuss the details during dinner."

The maître d' handed them menus and signaled a waiter. "Khalifa will be your waiter tonight." He bowed and walked to the reservation desk and picked up the phone.

Emerson carried on the charade. "Mr. Rachid, would you care for a drink?"

"Please, allow me to order a bottle of wine."

Khalifa signaled for the wine steward. Rachid studied the wine list.

"Rothschild, Bordeaux."

After they ordered dinner, Rachid pulled an envelope from his breast pocket and put it on the table. Tony Emerson noted the name and address on the envelope.

Fatin Kardel Pottery Shoppe
17 Safat Square 1100

Rachid was drawing an intricate design on the back of the envelope when their food was served. He put the envelope back in his pocket and they attacked their meal. He knew Tony would meet him at eleven o'clock at the pottery shoppe.

* * *

The pottery shop was owned and operated by Rachid's uncle. Tony Emerson examined a small, handsomely crafted vase.

"Our pottery is the finest in the Persian Gulf, perhaps in the world. Are you looking for something in particular, sir?"

Tony looked into the weather-beaten face of Fatin Kardel. "Yes. I'm looking for a vase that would be reminiscent of the Rachid dynasty."

Fatin checked the front door before looking toward his office at the end of the hall. "I'm sure you'll find designs to your liking in the catalog in the back room."

Tony threaded his way through the narrow aisle to the room indicated.

Rachid was bent over a map and straightened when the door opened. "Were you followed?"

"I don't think so. I took a circuitous route to get here." He opened a catalog and stood in front of the window looking out through the opening of the bamboo curtain. Satisfied that no one was lurking outside, he turned to Aziz.

Aziz lit a cigarette. "Any news from your informant?"

"Not yet. He was called back to the desert camp."

Peter's face registered alarm. "Abd al Bari Camp? What does it mean?"

"I'm not sure. At best, it could be for more specialized training. At worst, he could have been taken to Section Sixteen for interrogation. He did manage to get a message to me. The assassination is to be carried out simultaneously with explosions in New York and Washington. The first contingency will start to arrive in New York at the end of this week."

"Does he know the identity of Abd al Alim?"

"No. I don't think anyone knows Alim's identity…except for the ones picking up the tab."

"Can you trust your informer?"

Emerson checked his watch. It was 1115 hours. "This one I can. He's a native SIS agent. He was with Fifteen May Organization. What we're seeing is cooperation between several radical groups. That would have been unheard of under any other circumstances but the baton is in the hands of the kingpin of terrorists."

"Do we have a time frame?"

"Not yet."

Peter Aziz looked out the window. "You'd better leave before anyone gets suspicious. I'll see that Ardell gets whatever information we have. God knows that's little enough."

* * *

Washington, D.C.

Gabriella Russal was pleased with her naked reflection in the full-length mirror. Her generous breasts were firm and uptilted. Her slim waist accentuated her flat abdomen and rounded appealing hips. Exercise was almost a religious ritual in her determination to keep her figure agile and fit. She got over her disappointment of being only five feet two inches tall when she convinced herself that small packages were more intriguing than large ones. She glanced at the unopened telegram on her vanity. It was addressed to her husband.

Karim opened the door and stood behind her, admiringly. His arms wrapped around her and his hands caressed the firm nipples of her breasts. She turned in the protection of his arms, sliding her arms around his neck and pressed her body against him. She enjoyed the surge of power she experienced when she felt his hardness probing the soft folds between her legs. She stood on the tops of his shoes and he walked her to the bed. The soft satin of the coverlet pleased her senses and she reacted to each stimulus caused by the intimate contact of their bodies. After seven years of marriage, she was still able to carry him to unbelievable sensual heights. Exhausted, he lay with her cradled in his left arm. The tips of his fingers made abstract patterns as they travelled along her back.

She kissed his chest. "Darling, there's a telegram for you on the vanity."

"Didn't you open it?"

"Of course not, carissimo, have I ever done anything like that? The telegram is addressed to you not to us." She lifted her head and smiled at him. "But my curiosity is aroused."

He kissed the tip of her upturned nose. "Darling, your curiosity isn't the only thing that was aroused. Let me get it and we can open it together."

She ran the tip of her tongue tauntingly over his lips. "I'll get it, my love."

He watched her move across the room. "You have a magnificent body, my Gabi."

She returned with the telegram. "You're supposed to say things like that to your wife, even if you don't mean them." She handed him the telegram.

"You know I mean every word." His fingers worked deftly to open the flap of the envelope. He scanned the contents of the single page and frowned. "Damn."

"Bad news, darling?"

"Yes and no. Boulus Qadir is coming to Washington and wants to spend some time with us."

"Use his American name, darling. Paul sounds so much better than Boulus." She saw the disappointment in his eyes. "I think it's wonderful that Paul is coming to visit. The Rumanian Ambassador is on holiday, which left a hole in my invitation list. I was getting desperate for someone to sit next to Anita Gregory." She kissed the tip of his nose. "If Paul is here, my guest arrangement is perfect."

Karim laughed. "How can you do that to the beautiful Anita? Paul is a bore. Besides, I don't like the way he ogles you."

Gabriella said, "Everyone knows I love to flirt but I will always go home with you. I go to Arabia with you every year and you know if I didn't love you, I would never put myself in that position of submissiveness. It's just not in my nature. I do it because I love you. Paul is no threat to you. Everything I want or need is right here." She caressed his face. "Men like Paul only remind me how fortunate I am to have your love."

He kissed the top of her head. "You have a way of making everything all right."

CHAPTER 4

Glenn Alexander replaced the file in the wall safe and straightened the painting that covered it.

"Come in," she said, responding to a knock on her office door.

"I'm ready to leave now, Miss Alexander, is there anything you need before I go?"

"Get Michael Redmond on the phone." She glanced at her watch. "His home number is on the card I put on your desk. Lock the door on your way out?"

"I will. Good night, Miss Alexander."

When the buzzer on her phone sounded, she picked it up, and said, "Hello, Michael, this is Glenn Alexander." Her smile turned into a frown and she held the receiver away from her ear and stared at it.

"Miss Alexander, has anyone ever told you that your timing stinks? What the hell do you want?"

"Mr. Redmond, are you always so disagreeable or is it only on Wednesdays?"

"No, Miss Alexander." His voice sounded angry as he pronounced his words slowly. "It only happens when an outside source causes coitus interruptus. Now what the hell do you want?"

"Good heavens, at five-thirty in the afternoon?"

"Small minds think sex is good only after dark. Once again, Miss Alexander, what the hell do you want?"

She stood staring at the instrument in her hand in disbelief. "Well, I'm glad you're getting your..." She hesitated, searching for the right word. "Goodies now. Beginning at Friday noon, your ass, along with the rest of you will be spending the weekend with me on Gabriella Russal's yacht. So get this lustful energy out of your system now. I don't trust animals in heat and men in heat can be an absolute comedy." The tone of her voice softened. "Be an angel and try to be on your good behavior this weekend." She hesitated. "Oh, yes, as the British would say, carry on." She hung up the phone and shook her head. Her imagination raced wildly, as she had a mental picture of Michael Redmond trying to recapture the elusive gratification with his unfortunate sex partner. She thought, *Bastard, male chauvinist. You think women are in this world only to satisfy your base instincts. Boy, Cliff Ardell wasn't kidding when he described you as a tempest, but as far as I'm concerned, you blow nothing but hot air. Well, bucko, this lady isn't going to walk on eggs just to pacify your overly inflated ego. You may have given a good performance at the cocktail party but I'm not sure you can sustain that kind of pretense. You're a disaster looking for a place to happen, a stick of dynamite with a short fuse.*

She switched off the lights, rode the elevator to the lobby and walked out through the revolving door, where Templeton Osbourne waited beside the Mercedes. At the sight of her, he smiled, tipped the brim of his cap and held the rear door open. He slid behind the wheel and watched her in the rearview mirror.

"You're upset, Missy." It wasn't a question, just a statement of fact. He looked ahead, started the car and eased his way into traffic.

"Templeton, how come you're so different from other men?"

"Different, Missy? How so?"

"You're thoughtful, considerate and kind," she smiled, "and don't tell me it's because I'm paying you." She watched his reflection in the rearview mirror; the proud set of his head, the white neatly clipped hair, the laugh lines around his penetrating blue eyes. "You were always so patient with me even when I was a spiteful brat. You were always so good to Ari and I'm sure you were faithful."

His eyes misted at the mention of his wife, Ariette. She had died on New Year's Eve a year ago. He still had difficulty dealing with his grief. "You were an infant when your father brought us over from England, Ari as your nanny and me as your bodyguard. You were always with us. You were just as much our child as you were the Alexander heiress. Thanks to you, Ariette accepted the fact that we couldn't have children. As far as my fidelity is concerned, Ari fulfilled all of my needs and desires. She always made me feel like a giant. She was the best part of me."

Glenn listened, still watching, still admiring, still loving this gentle man. She had never been close to her pianist mother. Linda Pietra Alexander was away on concert tours most of the year and when she was home, there were always parties, dinners, or recording sessions. There was never enough time for her career and her child. One of them had to suffer.

Templeton had a black belt in Karate and had encouraged Glenn to do the same when she entered her teens. Their disciplined bodies gave evidence of the training and poise of the art. In public, he addressed her as Miss Glenn. In private, she was his beloved Missy.

Being near him had a calming effect on Glenn, as it did now. She closed her eyes and relaxed on the way home.

* * *

Promptly at noon on Friday, Mike Redmond was escorted out to the veranda, where Glenn was having tea.

"Ah, Michael, would you like a cup of tea...or perhaps something stronger?"

"Bourbon on the rocks."

She picked up a glass, added a few ice cubes and poured three fingers of bourbon over them.

"Thank you," he said, his eyes compelled her to look at him. His face took on a rosy hue and he lowered his eyes. "I'm sorry about the way I talked to you on the phone the other day. It was uncalled for."

Her green eyes flashed a warning. "Yes it was. When you're sufficiently aware that I'm not one of your playmates, I'm sure your attitude will improve."

He frowned. "Ouch. You don't pull punches, do you?"

"Rarely. I call them like I see them. It's going to be difficult enough to convince others I'm falling in love with you but it'll be impossible unless your manners improve."

He almost choked on the bourbon. "I got the message. I promise I'll be the antithesis of the bore you undoubtedly think I am."

"Good. Now let me fill you in on some of the people who will be on the yacht this weekend." She looked at her watch. "We have to leave."

He downed his drink, followed her out the door and handed her his car keys.

"You drive, you know where we're going. I'll listen."

"You've met Gabriella and Karim. Senator Matthew Cameron and wife Blanche will be there, and Congressman Lyle Thomason and wife Gayle, former Secretary of State. Samuel Blanding and wife Agatha. Karim's friend Boulus Qadir, also known as Paul, and Gabriella's friend, Anita Gregory."

"I know everybody except Qadir and Anita Gregory. Who are they?"

"I'm afraid I can't tell you very much about Qadir, except that he and Karim grew up together. The Bossman put out tracers on him but so far, nothing. Anita Gregory is an actress."

He nodded. "That…Anita Gregory. What do you know about Karim Russal?"

She glared at him. "Don't you ever do your homework?"

He smiled. "That's what you're here for, love."

"Wrong, bucko. I'm not here to fetch your pipe and slippers."

He closed his eyes, and recited, "Karim Russal, born 1960. He has a reputation for being an international playboy. Receives an annual income of half a million from his father, oil tycoon, Mukhtar Abd al Bari Russal; who incidentally is one of Saudi Arabia's richest men. Karim owns the mineral rights to a dozen or so oil wells in Texas and Oklahoma. His annual income from those wells is estimated to be another half to three quarters of a million dollars. He met Gabriella Cammeo in the Persian Gulf and fell in love with her. They married and have been on a merry-go-round ever since. They make an annual pilgrimage to Arabia to visit his father and older brother, Musa. They number among their friends, senators, congressmen, White House staff, President Breckenridge and a few former presidents. How am I doing?"

She glanced at him from behind lowered lids. "See I knew you could do it. All you had to do was apply yourself." She pulled off the controlled access way and stopped at a diner. "Let's have a cup of coffee."

He carried two black coffees to a booth and sat down. "We have the perfect set-up for a hit, the means, the occasion and the opportunity. Karim Russal could easily be the hit man."

"I've known Karim for several years and I roomed with Gabi at college. They're exactly what they appear to be. Two very devoted, very social, very rich people. They wouldn't jeopardize everything they have to carry out somebody else's vendetta. Obviously, assassins are well paid. Does it look like they need money?"

"There are…reasons, other than money. Political, religious…crazy."

* * *

Gabriella Russal watched the couple approach the yacht, and waved. "I'm glad you got here, we're ready to cast off. Hurry, you're two drinks behind." Gabi looked radiant in her white silk shorts and blue and white middy blouse. Her long, red-gold hair was pulled back in a French braid and she wore white deck shoes. Glenn and Mike hurried along the dock. Glenn held Mike's hand and whispered, "Start being attentive, darling, we're on."

He looked into her eyes lovingly. "Anybody ever tell you that you have eyes like a cat?"

"Absolutely." Her smile broadened. "Claws too."

CHAPTER 5

Libya
Abd al Bari Desert Camp
Terrorist Desert Training Camp

One hundred seventy-six kilometers into the desert from Tripoli, Atsu Jobari brought the jeep to a stop at a road barrier manned by two guards. One man checked his papers while the other held an AK-47 rifle inches from his face. The guard with the papers nodded, the rifle was lowered and the barrier was raised. He had just entered the training grounds for the People's Army.

Jobari passed the village of bungalows housing the married cadres and their families and went to section eleven, training area for foreign operations. He parked under a net camouflage canopy and walked down several steps to a subterranean briefing area.

Seven men dressed in the traditional Arab garb talked in hushed voices. The fermented stench of sweat was compressed into the eight-by-ten room.

The door opened and a short, stocky man clad in a soiled khaki shirt and pants entered, adding to the already pervasive stench. He put his briefcase at the head of the table and sat down. He needed no introduction. He was Zaki, the most feared terrorist of the Arab world and commanded the Abu Nidal Organization.

Zaki and the infamous Nidal had two things in common. Both were medium height, potbellied, bald and had blue-green eyes. Both were deadly.

The single light bulb suspended from a wire above the table swayed slightly, adding a sinister note to the dark piercing eyes of the newcomer. His voice was hushed and the men strained to hear what he said.

"You are here because you are among the best in your own organizations. The mission we are about to undertake is a joint effort by Libya, Lebanon, Iraq, Iran, Afghanistan and the Sudan." He studied the faces of the eight men. "For this mission, you will be known as Husam al Din. You are, as the name implies...the sword of faith. You are the teachers, and the lesson is...fear. Paralyzing...fear."

He folded his arms across his barrel chest and continued, "Retribution is at hand for a decadent country...the United States. Our special agent is there now, ready to carry out our plan. This agent is known to you as Abd al Alim."

There was a murmur that indicated the group was impressed, and why not? Alim had managed to impress most of the world.

Zaki took an envelope out of a briefcase and tossed it to the man at the opposite end of the table. "Qasim, your new passport," he said. "For this mission, you are Abu Dawud. The authorities are looking for Qasim not for Dawud."

Gadi Qasim nodded and slipped the passport in the pocket of his grease-stained, olive drab jacket.

Zaki lit a cigarette and addressed the men to his left. "Are your passports in order?" Without waiting for a reply, he continued, "Your frequent business trips to the United States have set up an ideal situation. No one will suspect the true reason for your visit. Your contact in New York is Abu Ammar. Follow his orders. His expertise in explosives is unequaled anywhere. The thrust of your mission is to create a diversion, one that will ensure the success of our true mission."

He turned his attention to a handsome, well-dressed, pale-skinned Arabian. "Boulus Qadir, an impromptu visit to Washington to your friend, Karim Russal, puts you in a strategic place. As a house guest of Russal, you will mingle with Washington society." He paused and exhaled a thin stream of smoke that spiraled its way to the light above, blending with the cigarette fog that hid the ceiling. "It's the perfect cover and it puts you exactly where we want you. When the time is right, Abd al Alim will contact you. If anything happens to Alim, you are the backup. Our target," he anticipated their reaction, "our target," he repeated, "is Alden Breckenridge." He knew the audacity of such a mission fired the imaginations of these selected men.

The men stared at each other, proud that they were considered for such an honor.

"Unfortunately," Zaki continued, "when Mr. Breckenridge was in Kuwait last year, the plan to eliminate him failed. That won't happen this time. The American infidels will learn not to interfere in Middle Eastern affairs. Israel's friends are our enemies. On May nineteenth, the American devil is scheduled to be at a Washington political dinner." His staccato message was punctuated with venom. "When we finish with the Americans, they'll never shame us again in the eyes of the world. We'll teach them to stay within their own boundaries. Allah blesses our efforts and will reward us with victory." He pointed to Atsu Jobari. "You are in charge of the diversionary team for the Washington project. The target is the Lincoln Memorial." He looked at the men on the right side of the table. Take your orders from Atsu Jobari. He'll be in touch with you next week. Leave on separate flights. Your destination is Mexico City. One of our resident agents will meet you and drive you to Juarez. Make your way over the border into Texas. The border between the two countries is long and impossible to police. Once you're in Texas, getting flights to Washington will be no problem. All you need is picture identification and money.

"Timing is crucial. At nine-thirty p.m. Eastern daylight time, on the nineteenth of May, the explosion in New York must coincide with the explosion in Washington. At that precise time, Abd al Alim will take out the true target." His mirthless smile showed uneven, stained teeth. "When we claim responsibility for conquering the American spirit, it will be in the name of Husam al Din." He raised his fist. "We will succeed." His eyes confirmed the passion in his voice. "INSHA'ALLAH—God willing."

As the men filed out, he detained Atsu Jobari. "Remain in camp. Your credentials will be checked again and your knowledge of explosives will be tested. What you do not know, you will learn."

* * *

Atsu Jobari sat on a wooden crate at the entrance of his tent. In the distance the shadow of the Al Hamra steppe embraced the Tunisian frontier and the silhouette of the Soda Mountains were the only distant patches on the empty landscape of scrub and dunes. Anti-aircraft missiles loomed on either side of the entrance to the advanced training area. Jobari was at the end of his education in plastique explosives. He tried to block out the tortured screams that raked through the stillness of the night. Screams that emanated from the victims in the ominous, dreaded, Section Sixteen...the interrogation compound, where even the bravest men cowered and were reduced to blobs of quivering protoplasm. There seemed to be increased activity in Section Sixteen. The unfortunate victims were men inside the organization, accused of treason, suspected of being double agents by a paranoid leadership. Once accused, there was no recourse. There were no trials, no hearings, just drawn out torture, with one outcome. The scent of death hung heavy in the air.

* * *

New York City

Khalil Najjar and Abdul Shakir sat on the floor in the abandoned shack two hundred feet from the East River. A light drizzle and fog muffled the sounds from passing boats inching their way through the mist. Lack of maintenance and a leaking roof caused most of the floorboards to warp and crack. Between the river's edge and the shack was a weather-beaten *For Sale* sign. The property wasn't large enough to generate commercial interest and too commercial for residential interest. It was the perfect place for clandestine meetings.

They tensed at the grating sound of the broken door latch. Shakir slipped his hand under his jacket and wrapped his fingers around the grip of the 9 mm Marakov PM. The door opened slowly, registering a grinding protest from its rusty hinges. The bottom of the door scraped the rotting floorboards.

"Khalil..." The raspy voice was barely audible.

"Close the door," Khalil answered. He lit a match after he heard the latch slip into place.

Shakir relaxed his hold on the Russian made revolver and lit a kerosene lamp. Two trained terrorists picked their way between the splintered boards, empty beer cans and old newspapers that littered the floor. The new arrivals put their metal lunch pails down and sat on the floor.

Khalil opened a detailed map of Manhattan, while Shakir held the lantern above the map. "That's our target," Najjar said, pointing to a spot off Madison Avenue.

"Allah be praised," Shakir said, as he peered closer at the target.

Najjar continued, "The Empire State Building. This will please Allah. We'll take our orders from the authority on explosives, Abu Ammar. He'll be responsible for assembling the bombs." He lit a cigarette and let it dangle from the corner of his mouth. At twenty-nine he could have been considered good-looking, except for the six missing front teeth. Smoke from the dangling cigarette curled back on itself and settled in front of his dark brown eyes, making them water. "A small group of Husam al Din will arrive in New York. We'll know more about that when Ammar contacts us." He put the map away and extinguished the light in the lantern. "Let's meet at the garage tomorrow morning at nine. We should reach our target after rush hour. We'll get to the building through the sewer and sketch the layout of the ventilating system." He tossed his cigarette on the floor and ground it out with his heel.

* * *

The Violetta cruised twenty miles off Virginia Beach. The men fished while the women lounged on chaises and deck chairs, nursing afternoon cocktails. Glenn was staring at Mike Redmond's profile.

Gabriella sat next to her, watching her. "I think you're in love."

Glenn shrugged, then smiled. "He is handsome, isn't he?" To herself she said, *In love? With that conceited asshole? He's got the disposition of a piranha and apparently the sexual appetite of a rabbit.* She smiled as Mike walked toward her. He was carrying a bottle of sunblock. He sat on the edge of her lounge chair.

"It looks like you're starting to burn. Lean forward and I'll put sunblock on you." Reluctantly, she bent forward. He kissed the tops of her shoulders before he applied the lotion. His hands were surprisingly gentle as he worked the lotion into her skin.

Glenn knew Gabi was watching. She cooed, "Don't stop, you have a wonderful touch." To herself she said, *And you had better stop touching before I push you overboard.*

Mike smiled. "I'd better put some on your legs too, can't have you suffering with sunburn."

Deliberately, he massaged the lotion into her calves with a

circular motion, each time increasing the size of the area he covered. His fingers caressed her thighs, sending electric impulses through her body. He felt her muscles tense under his hands. His eyes reflected his amusement. "Relax, darling," he said. "Sit back and enjoy it."

Mindful that Gabi and now Anita Gregory were watching, she moistened her sensuous lips and squirmed slightly. Deliberately, she spread her legs. Not enough for it to be obvious to the others but enough for him to realize she was as good at this game as he.

Mike saw the laughter in her half-closed green eyes and moved his hands down toward her ankle.

"Mike," Karim called to him, "what do you want to drink?"

"Bourbon and water." He dried his hands on a towel and joined the other men at the bar.

Gabi leaned over. "I thought I was going to have an orgasm watching him massage your legs. Don't let this one get away, cara mia."

"Yes. Well, you know my luck with men."

Gabriella whispered, "Don't be ridiculous. Philip's death was unfortunate. He was in the wrong place at the wrong time."

Glenn recoiled, as though Gabriella slapped her. "Sure, just like Leslie Powers' death was a senseless accident. You have to admit, I have a talent for getting them killed."

"Leslie Powers was a fool. He knew the mountain was iced over. But he had to show off. He was going to ski that mountain if it killed him...and it did. You had nothing to do with that and you had nothing to do with Philip's death." She sipped her drink. "Besides, death is part of living. We start preparing for it the minute we're born."

Glenn laughed. "When did you become so philosophical? If I remember correctly, you flunked philosophy in college."

"It's strange, when we were in college, I thought death was the most frightening thing that could happen to me. I don't feel that way anymore. Since we started our annual visits to Karim's family in Arabia, I feel death is not a tragedy but a passport into a higher dimension."

Glenn studied the peaceful expression on Gabriella's face. "You're such a social person, Gabi. What do you do in Arabia? Women are so…I don't know, held down."

"I don't have to abide by the customs of the veil and all that crap because I'm not Islamic but I do have to make sure that I'm covered. I can't smoke and I speak only when I'm spoken to. That's okay for a short time. Karim and I travel while we're there, so I don't feel repressed."

"Where do you go?"

"Kuwait, and some of the other Emirates. It's beautiful country. Even the desert has its own enchantment."

Glenn looked out at the ocean. "Have you ever been to Iraq?"

Gabriella hesitated before answering. "Once. We went to Baghdad. Never again, I'm convinced that crazy Iraqi son-of-a-bitch has people put to death for his own amusement."

Glenn looked concerned. "Aren't you afraid you'll be taken hostage?"

"Never thought about it. We avoid going to Iraq, Iran, places like that; women don't fare too well there." Gabriella turned on to her stomach, her chin rested on her folded hands. "What about you? You have hotels over there. How do they treat you?"

"I was smart enough to put a man in charge in Kuwait and Tony Emerson handles the construction of the new hotel in Manama. So the Arabs don't have to deal with a woman on a day-to-day basis."

"Clever. Now tell me how clever you're going to be with Mr. Wonderful. What does he do? Why haven't we seen him before? What's his phone number?"

Glenn looked amused. "Primo: He's a chemical engineer, educated at Princeton, and he's CEO of Redmond International Chemicals. He's thirty-eight years old and a bachelor. Secondo:

He travels a great deal and has never been fond of social events. Terzo: You may not have his phone number. I've decided to keep this one for myself."

Gabriella leaned close to Glenn and whispered, "Aside from Karim, Mike is the sexiest man I've ever seen. The way he looks at you should be labeled, *erotica.* I would keep him around just to look at me…even if he was impotent."

Glenn's familiar laugh carried to where Mike, Karim and Paul Qadir were slugging tequila, Mexican style. Glenn's thoughts weren't as loving as her gaze.

She thought, *Oh, Gabi, how could you think Mike is sexy? I've seen more sex appeal in a wooden Indian. When he looks at me, with what you think is passionate desire, you're not on the receiving end of that leer. It's not passion you're seeing, my friend, it's ridicule. He's accustomed to women gushing over him, like you do, Gabi, my dear. Not me, not this baby. My true feeling for him borders on contempt. I'll be glad when this mission is over so I won't have to tolerate his conceit…on the other hand, I was beginning to enjoy the leg massage. Nonsense, Glenn, stop it! Mike Redmond is a third-rate James Bond; a womanizer first, and an agent second.* Aloud, she said, "Who is Paul Qadir? Why does Karim call him Boulus?"

Gabriella followed her gaze. "Paul is the English translation of Boulus. Paul and Karim grew up together. When Karim went to school in England, Paul chose not to go to college, but they would visit whenever Karim had a holiday. Paul's father is the right-hand man to the elder Russal. Paul's a little shy but he is an amusing dinner partner. When we got his wire saying he was coming for a visit, I was delighted. I got word that Serge Ganya couldn't come to my dinner party. To tell the truth, I was pissed off. I had already invited Anita Gregory and Serge was to have been her dinner partner." Gabi shook her head. "Honestly, you can't depend on men."

She looked around to see if anyone was listening, then leaned closer to Glenn. "I hear Serge Ganya spends all of his spare time at Virginia Beach, shacked up with a stripper."

Glenn grinned. "I can remember a time when you would have thought that was romantic."

"But, darling," Gabi gushed, "that was B.K."

"B.K.? What's B.K.?

"Before Karim, cara mia."

The chef came on deck and told Gabi lunch was ready. She pulled the chain attached to the ship's bell and said, "Lunch is served in the dining room."

The buffet was attractively arranged and featured French onion soup, Cornish hens stuffed with wild rice, zucchini Romano, baked mushroom mounds and Caesar salad. Fresh fruit was arranged in a wheel with various cheeses, with the finishing touch of orange liqueur mousse.

Seating was random. Mike sat on one side of the table and Glenn on the other, at opposite ends. Glenn thought, *What a great way to monitor conversations from both ends of the table.* It was only table talk, urbane, uninteresting, boring.

When lunch was over, Blanche Cameron tapped her glass with her fork. "Matthew and I are having a dinner party on Friday, the nineteenth. You're all invited. I'll send out formal invitations but I wanted to be sure you kept the date open."

The senator came up behind her and whispered in her ear. Annoyance showed on her overly made-up face…until she realized everyone was watching. "Matthew reminded me that we'll be at the Algonquin Club on that date. The President will be there so we really must attend." She made a shrill noise that could have passed for a laugh. "Now I'm embarrassed," she cooed. "Our dinner party will be on the twentieth."

Mike and Glenn looked at each other, then at the other guests for reactions. There were none.

On deck, Sam Blanding, Secretary of State, was involved in animated conversation with Matthew Cameron. Mike knew Blanding well enough to know that the flush on his face was generated by anger and guessed that Senator Cameron was getting chewed out. Since the failed assassination attempt on Mr.

Breckenridge's life the previous year, the presidential schedule of political and personal appearances wasn't made public. Mike wondered how many innocent slips were made about similar plans.

Mike looked for Glenn and found her sitting aft, listening to and smiling at Paul Qadir. It gave him the chance to study Qadir's body language. At this, he was an expert. He already knew Glenn's body language and that was provocative, the perfect cover for an agent. There was something about Paul Qadir that Mike didn't trust.

"Darling, don't be jealous of Paul," Gabriella gushed. "He's too shy to make a pass at Glenn. In fact, I don't think he knows what a pass is."

"You're a wonderful hostess. Thank you for your concern. I wasn't jealous, just admiring Glenn's," he raised his eyebrows, "assets."

Gabriella covered her mouth with her hand and laughed. "Now I know why I'm attracted to you. You have a superb sense of humor. It's good for Glenn to be around you. She doesn't laugh enough."

"You're right, she doesn't." Mike's eyes narrowed as he studied Glenn.

Gabriella looked at Glenn's profile. "She's got everything going for her but she thinks she's bad luck to any man who takes an interest in her. Until now, she's done a good job keeping men at a distance."

"Why?"

"You knew Glenn was married?"

Mike nodded. "She doesn't seem to want to talk about it."

"The memory is still painful. His name was Philip Meyer and he worked for Clayton Alexander, that's how she met him. They fell in love and got married. Glenn was doing a tour of the foreign Alexander hotels, to set them up for computer hookups, when she came down with flu. Philip finished the tour for her. On his way back to the States, his plane was hijacked. The terrorist, Gadi

Qasim, checked Philip's passport, thought that he was Israeli, pistol whipped him and shoved him to the back of the plane. When the plane landed, the terrorists dictated their conditions, which of course were unreasonable. To show their determination, Qasim stood Philip in the doorway of the plane and shot him in the back of the head then pitched the body onto the tarmac.

"To save the lives of the other passengers, the government agreed to allow the pilot to fly the terrorists to Iraq. A few of the passengers were pistol-whipped and two were shot but recovered. Glenn flew over to claim Philip's body. She never got over it."

Mike shook his head. He was about to say something when the captain approached.

He apologized for the interruption. "It looks like we might be in for a bit of unfriendly weather. We're moving into a squall. There's no way to avoid it. I'll have the crew batten down everything on deck. You'll probably want to get your guests below."

Mike said, "I grew up on boats, do you need extra help?"

The captain said, "Thank you, sir, if we need help, I'll call for you."

Gabi took Mike by the arm. "Help me get everybody below."

The pitch of the waves was gentle at first. Gradually it became more violent. No one panicked but the party took on a somber tone. Mike put his arm around Glenn.

"Do you get seasick?" he asked.

"I don't know. I've never been on a boat in a storm."

The boat heaved and forced the passengers to the windward side. Glenn was shoved into the corner and Mike was thrown against her. Involuntarily, his body reacted to the soft curves of her hips and her small firm breasts. Gabriella was thrown against Mike. He looked over his shoulder at her. "Getting this close to Glenn might have taken at least another month. Gabi, how did you arrange this?"

Gabriella laughed and pushed herself away. "We aim to please."

The tension was broken and everyone began talking and laughing. Glenn tried to push him away. When their bodies separated, the boat pitched again and he was pressed against her. He whispered in her ear, "You're not going to believe this but I'm not doing this on purpose."

"I know you're not." She tried to push away from the wall, which forced her hips against his. Her action was a surprise and his body reacted. This time, it was Mike who pushed against the wall…with both hands. Their bodies separated then pressed together again. Her eyes mocked him and her grin was irritating.

"You're enjoying my discomfort," he hissed through his teeth. "At least you could pretend to empathize."

The boat pitched and their bodies meshed again.

"Aren't you the guy who told me small minds think sex is good only after dark?"

"I didn't say in public."

"You could have fooled me, darling."

Gradually, the sky cleared and the only indication that the squall had passed through were the splintered deck chairs that had come loose from their moorings.

Karim put Mantovani's *Love Is a Many Splendored Thing* on the CD player. Mike took Glenn's hand and pulled her into his arms. The breeze pulled strands of Glenn's hair loose from the French braid and they curled like tendrils in front of her ears. He danced her away from the others and while he was pretending to kiss her cheek, he whispered in her ear, "Are all senators' wives that dumb, or do you think it was an intentional slip?"

"I don't know what to think," Glenn replied. "If betrayal comes from inside, she could be the source. Why wouldn't she just send out the invitations? I watched the faces of the people near me. I didn't see anything unusual. Do you think the senator or his wife would deliberately endanger the President?"

He held her closer. "Wait until you're in this game a little longer. You'll lose the Pollyanna syndrome. To this day, there are a lot of people who aren't convinced the Kennedy assassination wasn't an inside job."

Glenn saw several people watching them. She reached up and caressed his face with her fingers, then pulled his face down to hers and kissed him lightly on the lips.

"Hmmm. Nice. I take it we're being watched?"

She smiled sweetly, flirtingly. "Quite so."

The music stopped. Arm in arm they rejoined the group. When the music started again, Mike steered Anita Gregory to the bar and Glenn sat beside Karim. Paul Qadir led Blanche Cameron around the floor, in what could roughly be called a dance. He held her at arm's length because her bulk prohibited a closer alliance.

Mike watched as Blanche flirted with Qadir. He thought, *I don't like Blanche Cameron. Her makeup's too heavy, her voice too loud, her laugh too shrill.* He shook his head, a fifty-five-year-old body living in a fifteen-year-old mind. Anita Gregory's chuckle brought him out of his reverie. She, too, was watching Paul and Blanche.

"It looks like Jimminy Cricket dancing with Dumbo." She blushed. "I'm sorry, that was very unkind."

Mike laughed. "I don't envy him. He's a true gentleman. He even looks like he's having a good time. Is Paul always like that?"

"I've only known him for a week or so," Anita said. "I don't know very much about him. He's charming but he seems secretive."

"You can get to know someone fairly well in a week," Mike said. "It all depends on how you feel about him."

"He's not spending time in my bed, if that's what you think. He's charming but too *old world* for me. I wouldn't put myself in a position where I'd have to walk two paces behind any man."

She glanced at Gabriella. "I promised Karim I'd keep Paul occupied." Anita winked. "It seems that shy, quiet Paul has the hots for Gabriella. That makes Karim very unhappy."

CHAPTER 6

Kuwait

Fatin Kardel's Pottery Shop was, as the owner stated on Tony Emerson's last visit, the finest in the Persian Gulf.

"Ah, Mr. Emerson," Kardel said, bowing, "how may I be of service?"

"I'm looking for planters for the lobby of the new hotel, under construction in Manama. A design that's descriptive of the area, in a shape that's unique."

Fatin Kardel nodded. "Perhaps you would like to talk to the designer. You're aware that it will be several months before the pottery is completed?"

"That's not a problem," Tony said.

"The artist who does most of our designs is in his office. Perhaps you would like to discuss your needs with him. It's the last door on the left."

Emerson walked to the back of the shop, knocked on the door and entered.

The man sitting at the desk looked up from the piece of parchment he was working on. "It's been quite a while since we played cloak and dagger," Peter Aziz said, and put aside the pen he was using. "Were you followed?"

"Yes. I'm almost certain I was."

"No matter," said Aziz. "When you leave, you'll take this design with you." He checked the monitor on the desk. The only person in the shop was his uncle, Fatin.

"Has your agent contacted you?"

"No. He's still at Abd al Bari." Tony Emerson looked worried. "Either he's taking advanced training, or his cover got blown. They're keeping a tight lid on this one."

Peter Aziz shook his head. "They can't afford a leak. Their target is the biggest ever attempted. You don't make a hit on the president of the most powerful nation in the world, without a game plan. It has to be elaborate, well timed and diversified. The propaganda value alone could carry them for years."

Emerson lit a cigarette. "Has the President been told?"

"Probably," Peter said. "That was the Bossman's job. You can bet Mr. Breckenridge will get his back up on this one. Last year, when the attempt on his life failed, Secret Service put a stop on making the President's schedule public. That upset him. With this new threat, they'll try to put more restrictions on him and they'll find out how irascible he can be."

Tony Emerson turned the corner and walked toward the hotel. He sensed rather than saw anyone. Too late, he saw the shadows of two men on the wall of the building just before he lost consciousness. When he opened his eyes, he felt the lump on the back of his head and winced. He was in an alley that separated two buildings. His billfold was gone and so was the design from the potter's shop. When he got back to the hotel, he sent a wire to Glenn Alexander, telling her about the loss of the design. The coded message informed her that there was no new information on the plan for the assassination. He would keep her advised.

* * *

Washington

The private phone in Clifford Ardell's office rang. He picked it up on the second ring. A male voice identified himself as *Goliath*. Ardell listened as David Jabez, of Shin Beth, spoke quietly into the phone. "It appears the time frame is set for the nineteenth of May. Four men are coming in through Mexico. Contact person for the New York contingency is Abu Ammar. His work with explosives is identical to that of the terrorist Abd al Jabbar. Too identical, I'm afraid. The Aman claims to have killed Jabbar in Gaza. Seeing the work of Ammar, I have to wonder. Checkmate has been in touch with Blue." There was a click and the phone went dead. Ardell replaced the receiver in the cradle. Checkmate was Tony Emerson, and Blue was Peter Aziz. He pressed the intercom button.

"Yes, sir?"

"Find Duncan MacKenzie and ask him to meet me here."

The pleasant female voice answered, "Mr. MacKenzie is here waiting to see you."

"Mac," Ardell said, "I got a call from Goliath. The guy heading up the New York group is Abu Ammar. What do you know about him?"

"He has quite a reputation," Mac answered. "His M.O. is identical to that of another terrorist."

"Abd al Jabbar?"

Mac nodded. "It can't be coincidence." He stood at the window looking out at the traffic below. "What if…Jabbar is alive? What if…he's in the States? Nobody looks for a dead man. Hell, he could have come in, any number of ways."

"Could he have masterminded the attack on the World Trade Center?"

Mac shook his head. "No. Too clumsy. Jabbar ties up all his loose ends. He's an obsessive compulsive. It must be a blow to his pride to have Abd al Alim in the limelight."

"It just makes him more effective," Ardell said, taking a bottle of antacids from his drawer, he popped two in his mouth and chewed them. "He enjoys being the decoy and he can create a lot of hell out there."

Mac walked to the door. "I'm going back to New York…while it's still there. I've been in touch with my men and there's not even a rumble on the streets. That…concerns me because it's typically Jabbar. He's called the Scorpion for a reason. He's fast, silent and deadly."

* * *

New York City
Friday, May 6

Khalil Najjar sat at the kitchen counter talking to Shakir on the phone and eating sliced peaches out of a can. "I got a call from Abu Ammar telling me to stay by the phone for instructions. So, I sit here waiting. After I talked to him, I had a strange feeling that I knew him. A page out of a lost book, like the voice of a dead man, surely, I would remember if I had met Ammar, yet there was something…" He skewered a slice of peach on the tip of his knife and carried it to his mouth. "The schematics are done. We'll meet at the shack tonight at eleven-thirty, with the plans." When he hung up the phone, it rang immediately. He picked it up.

"Idiot. When I told you to stay by the phone, I didn't mean for you to be talking on it."

Najjar began to sweat. "I beg your pardon, I did not think."

"Precisely my point, you do not think. Is everything ready for our meeting tonight?"

"Yes, Abu Ammar. We'll meet at the shack at eleven-thirty." He heard a click.

* * *

Khalil Najjar was the last of the four men to arrive. In the dark, they sat in a circle on the floor waiting for their leader. There were no sounds, other than the friction of the door as one edge dragged along the floor. No one moved. The beam from the flashlight held by the intruder was directed to each of the men in turn.

"Light the lantern," the voice said, in a raspy voice.

Once again, Khalil Najjar felt chills coursing through his body. The voice…he knew that voice.

Abdul Shakir struck a match and lit the kerosene lantern.

Najjar's eyes widened when he looked into the face of Abu Ammar. Without realizing it, he spoke the name, the forbidden name…"Abd al Jabbar."

He stood over Najjar like an avenging specter. "Abu Ammar," he hissed through his teeth.

"Yes, of course, Abu Ammar." Najjar broke out in a cold sweat. He was looking at a ghost.

The light from the lantern caught the side of Abu Ammar's face. A long jagged scar ran from his left temple, catching and pulling at the corner of his left eye. It continued through his left cheekbone, cutting diagonally across the left side of his lips, over his chin, down the right side of his neck, and disappeared beneath his shirt.

The men had to strain to hear his words. "Show me what you've done."

Shakir produced the drawings, smoothing them with his hands on the bare floor. He picked up the lantern and held it over the parchment-like paper. Ammar traced the path he would follow with his finger. When he was satisfied, he put both hands on the translucent paper, flattening it. His manicured nails emphasized the long fingers that looked oddly delicate in contrast to the broad, muscular, scarred body. He nodded, slightly. "Good."

He looked to the smallest of the four men. "What about transportation?"

"We have two vans that cannot be traced. They were stolen, repainted and the serial numbers filed off. The windows are darkly tinted. It's almost impossible to identify anyone sitting in the van. They are garaged and two hundred and fifty dollars rent is paid in cash each month. I never saw the owner, nor has he seen me. The arrangement was made through my brother-in-law, Sam Bentley, who has since died."

Ammar touched the smaller man on the shoulder. "You've done well." He turned his attention back to the drawings. "How and where do we get into the sewer system?"

Najjar opened the map of Manhattan and spread it beside the drawings. He said, "One block west of the building is the point of entry. Last year, we stole equipment from the department of streets, piece by piece. We have everything we need to open a manhole and enter the system, including regulation hard hats. We even have the sign that says *Caution: Men working*. We converted one of the vans to look like a paneled city truck. We covered our tracks."

Ammar folded the drawings and handed them to Najjar. He said, "When are the three men due to arrive from Kuwait?"

"Tomorrow, I will meet them at the airport."

Ammar said, "That won't be necessary. Other plans will be made. In the event something goes wrong, then you will pick them up and deliver them to Central Park. Direct them to the lake. They must be there by five o'clock. Tell them not to look for me. I'll find them." He watched Najjar through half closed eyes, the trace of a sneer played at the corner of his mouth. "I don't think it will be necessary for you to pick them up." Ammar paused. "However, stay by the telephone in the event you are needed." His eyes met those of Najjar. His voice was barely audible. His words were for Najjar only. "I have special plans in mind for you…Khalil."

* * *

Washington, D.C.

Gabriella lay in Karim's arms listening to the night sounds and the ocean as it lapped against the hull of the *Violetta.* She turned her face to him. "I think Glenn has finally found a man she is not running away from."

Karim's arms tightened around her. "I don't think Mike is good for Glenn. I don't trust him. There's something about him that's cold and unyielding. When he looks at her with what you call sexy eyes, all I see is amusement, maybe even contempt."

"Darling, how can you say that? He's so attentive."

"He's as attentive as a cat playing with a mouse. I think he considers women as playthings and then he discards them when they cease to amuse him."

"Karim, I hope you're wrong."

"So do I, my love. So do I." He smiled down at her. "If it doesn't work out, there's always Paul."

Glenn groped her way to the deck, her eyes not quite open but not quite closed either. Mike stood with his back against the rail watching her limited progress.

"Good morning," he smiled, "I believe every young couple should have the advantage we have now. Seeing how the person you intend to spend the rest of your life with looks in the morning."

"Oh, shut up." She winced when she moved her head.

"Too much champagne?"

"Do you have to shout?" she whispered and held the sides of her head, certain it was ready to fall off.

"Stay here," he said, "I'll get you a morning-after cocktail."

Glenn waved him away. He returned in a few minutes with two glasses. One held a brownish fluid and the other some white crystals. He poured the fluid onto the crystals and the whole concoction fizzed, tickling her nose.

"Drink it while it's fizzing."

She did. Not because she thought it would work but to stop him from talking, thereby easing the pounding in her head. She handed him the empty glass and closed her eyes against the glare of the morning sun. "What time do we dock?"

"Not until this evening," he said.

"I'm not going to survive until then."

"If you're going to imbibe, why choose champagne? That stuff's deadly."

"Somebody must have put something in it to make me feel like this." She grabbed the rail. "Oh, God. Can't you stop the boat from rocking? I think I'm going to puke."

He laughed. "Nobody put anything in your champagne but you drank enough of it to float a battleship."

She opened one eye, squinting at him. "Did I do anything foolish?"

A smile tugged at the corners of his mouth. "It depends on what you call foolish. You insisted on going to my cabin. You said you would show me…and you did."

She opened the other eye, slowly, studying the expression on his face, which told her nothing, until she detected a trace of amusement in his eyes.

"You sonofabitch," she hissed. "Maybe I was drunk but I wasn't crazy and I sure as hell didn't…" She paused. "Do what you intimated." She pushed him away. That was when she saw Karim standing aft. She smiled and backed into Mike's arms. "Good morning."

"Good morning, Glenn," he answered. "Are you feeling better this morning?"

She looked away. "Wasn't I feeling well last night?"

He laughed. "I think the expression is, you were feeling no pain. But you were a riot. You insisted Mike had to show you his cabin. You were convinced his cabin was twice as large as yours." He winked at Mike. "Breakfast in ten minutes."

Glenn pushed Mike's arms away and turned to face him. Her eyes seemed to be sending out green sparks. "You bastard!" Her voice was barely a whisper. "You're really enjoying this."

His mouth opened in mock shock. "Moi?" His hand touched his chest. "Jamais de ma vie, mon cher." The amusement returned to his eyes.

"Screw you, Michael Redmond."

"Again? My goodness, you are insatiable." He walked to the dining room.

She turned her face into the wind, angry with him but angrier with herself. She turned and leaned against the rail looking at the choppy ocean.

"I know that posture. It means Glenn Alexander is on the warpath. What happened?" Gabriella's bright smile greeted her.

"Gabi, did I make an utter fool of myself last night? Should I be embarrassed when I go in for breakfast? Did I…?" She let out an exasperated sigh. "Well…did I?"

"Did you what? Cara Mia."

"Did I insist on going to Mike's cabin last night?"

Gabi bit her bottom lip. "Oh, that!"

"Oh, shit. I did, didn't I?"

Gabriella tried, unsuccessfully, not to laugh. "Darling, you have nothing to be ashamed of. You and Mike got into a discussion about the size of your cabins. You started leaning all over him. You insisted his was bigger and you wanted to measure it." Tears rolled down Gabi's cheeks and she shook with laughter. "I think…you were talking about his cabin. Anyway, you had the good sense to come to me and ask me to take you to your cabin. We got inside and you passed out cold on the bunk."

"That's it?"

"You sound disappointed. Yes, that's it."

She hugged Gabriella. "Gabi, my wonderful friend, thank you." Glenn thought, *That weasel, that Machiavelli. So, Mike Redmond, you want to play games? Okay, I can play those games too. Watch out, bucko, before I'm finished with you, you'll be saying, uncle and spelling it G-L-E-N-N.*

She put her hand on Gabi's arm. "If anyone asks, you didn't tell me it was you who brought me to my cabin."

Gabi said, "It's as if we're back in college, co-conspirators to the end." She patted Glenn's shoulder. "Go get him, tiger."

When they reached the dining room Glenn was feeling much better. Mike was talking and laughing with Paul Qadir. She went to the buffet, selected a piece of French toast and a cup of black coffee and then joined Mike at the table.

"Good morning, Paul, lovely day, isn't it?" She put her food and coffee down and turned to Mike. "Again, good morning to you, my darling." She put her arms around his neck and kissed him on the mouth, sliding her tongue between his lips as she did so.

He raised one eyebrow and looked into the cool, calm green of her eyes but all he could see was his own reflection. He whispered, "I think…I'm in trouble."

* * *

Kuwait

Tony Emerson watched as an envelope was pushed under the door to his suite. He listened for movement in the corridor before picking it up. The envelope contained a single sheet of paper with a brief message.

Jahara - 10 - Bengal

He struck a match and lit the paper. When it was almost consumed, he flushed it down the toilet. Bengal was Atsu Jobari, British SIS agent. Tony was to meet Bengal at the Jahara boat yard at ten o'clock. He looked at his watch; it was seven-thirty. He followed his normal routine and had a drink at the bar before going in for dinner. It was his habit to go for a walk after dinner so it wouldn't arouse suspicion when he left for his meeting with Bengal. During dinner the waiter brought a phone and plugged it into a wall outlet.

"Phone call, Mr. Emerson."

"Emerson, here." He smiled. "Glenn, how nice to hear your voice." He had to let her know the call was being monitored. "Sorry, old girl, but time just got away from me. I said I'd send a progress report before the end of last week. I didn't get it finished." It was enough to tell her the phone was bugged. "Yes," he continued, "we're right on schedule." He listened again. "Great. I'll pick you up at the airport, tomorrow at three."

He finished his dinner, signed the check and left the hotel. He took a circuitous route to Jahara, checking his rearview mirror at frequent intervals. He walked along the waterfront. It was nine fifty-eight. He lit a cigarette and waited. A tall figure of a man walked toward him. Tony ground the cigarette into the dock. Both men stepped into the shadows.

Bengal spoke softly but quickly. "I'm going to Cairo, then to Mexico. My destination is Washington. I'm to create a diversion by blowing up the Lincoln Memorial. The precise time is nine-thirty in the evening of the nineteenth. A New York target will be hit simultaneously. Until then, there will be other explosions in New York. No one that I talked to knows Alim's true identity so we drew a blank there. The main target is definitely Alden Breckenridge."

Tony said, "We're working closely with our cousins. You may have to contact them. When you cross the border, take the first available flight out of El Paso to Baltimore, Maryland. You have a reservation in the name of Paki Younes." He handed Bengal a packet. "Paki Younes' passport. During the flight, order Moet champagne. The attendant will tell you they don't carry that brand. Change your order to bourbon on the rocks. She'll give you two bags of peanuts with your drink. Put them away. One contains the key to a locker in Baltimore's Amtrak Station, the other contains identification for Younes." They stopped talking when they heard footsteps. A young boy boarded a dhow and went below then Tony continued, "Go to the Amtrak station in Baltimore. In locker number twenty, you'll find instructions and names of people to contact. Memorize them and destroy the paper. Take the train from Baltimore to Union Station in Washington. Rent a car. Make a reservation at the Midway Motel, just outside Washington. It's a popular motel for tourists. How will you make contact with other agents?"

"We'll meet at the Vietnam Veterans Memorial on the sixteenth and do what tourists do...see Washington. Boulus Qadir is backup for Alim. He'll be visiting his friends the Russals. I have no idea what Karim Russal's part is in this, if any but I suspect he is important to the mission."

"Who's orchestrating the program?"

Bengal kept his eye on the dhow where the boy had disappeared. "I think it's safe to say the conductor is in Afghanistan but I think the cost is being shared by others.

Tony said, "It's what we suspected from the beginning."

They shook hands. Tony said, "I was concerned that something had happened when I couldn't get in touch with you."

Bengal smiled. "The bald one decided I needed a little more instruction in the handling of explosives. I'll say this for them; they're thorough. They leave nothing to chance. Every step of this hit was planned and when it fails, I don't want to be around."

CHAPTER 7

New York City

The twenty-five watt bulb suspended from a bare wire swayed slightly, casting eerie shadows on the peeling painted walls and ceiling of the sparsely furnished room. Outside, the flashing sign from Murphy's bar across the street gave a psychedelic glow to the brooding figure lying across the bed and highlighted the edges of the scar across the left side of his face, adding a sinister element to his malevolent features. He walked to the bureau and stared at his reflection in the mottled, cracked mirror. Old memories flooded his consciousness and he was transported back in time.

It was January 17, 1991. He was a young Iraqi army officer filled with the spirit of Allah. Invincible. Unfamiliar sounds woke him from a sound sleep. He looked at the luminous dial of his watch. It was one o'clock. His wife got out of bed and struggled into a robe. "No, Rasha," he said, "stay with the little one. I'll see what's happening."

He hurried into the street outside his home in Baghdad. Khalil Najjar darted out from an open doorway, fifty feet away. He saw Jabbar and pointed overhead at an unfamiliar, low-flying F-117A Stealth bomber. The aircraft released a missile a short distance from where Jabbar stood. It was a direct hit on his house. The percussion tossed him into the air, like a leaf in an updraft then pitched him down again, battered and dazed. Searing pain tore at his body as he felt himself being dragged along the ground. When he opened his eyes, Khalil Najjar was pulling him away from the flames and falling debris that was once his home.

He lay in a pool of blood. The left side of his face and the right side of his neck and chest were torn open. His right leg was bent under him at an unnatural angle. Jabbar tried to talk but blood gurgled inside his throat and chest. He heard the screams of his wife, Rasha and their five-year-old daughter, Alula. He reached for Najjar's hand, silently begging him to help them.

Najjar pulled his hand free. "The fire is everywhere. Nothing can be done for them." A second bomb hit at the end of the street and Najjar was thrown to the ground, inches away from his friend. Blood gurgled out from Jabbar's gaping wounds and Najjar pulled away in horror. Jabbar's bloody hand took hold of Najjar's sleeve. His mouth formed the words...*help me.* Najjar scrambled to his feet, pried Jabbar's fingers from his sleeve and shouted at his friend. "You're a dead man. No one can help you." He stumbled backward, turned and ran. He never looked back. The screams from the burning wreckage that was once Jabbar's home were silenced.

That night, in a field hospital, Abd al Jabbar died, and Abu Ammar was born. His anger turned to hate. He vowed he would survive and reap his revenge on the infidel nation that robbed him of everything. The day would come when he and Najjar would meet again. Najjar would learn how it felt to face death, alone, abandoned, in despair.

He couldn't remember how long he was hospitalized. There were periods of agonizing pain interspersed with brief periods of blessed unconsciousness. Slowly, his body mended but his heart and mind remained fatally wounded. He joined a terrorist organization. He was astute and cunning. He acted and reacted without fear. His plan to avenge the deaths of Rasha and Alula took form.

Abu Ammar's thoughts returned to the present. Once again he saw his disfigured face. His fingers traced the scar. Gone was the handsome young Iraqi soldier. Gone were the days of laughter. Gone were the nights of lovemaking. Gone was his ability to feel, his desire to care. His new life provided him with a compulsion to inflict pain and a blind hate for anything American. Revenge was his savior. Only once did he hesitate and that was because his would-be victim was a woman, a beautiful woman but the hesitation lasted only a few moments until he reminded himself that she was an American agent. Caitlin O'Hara was a counter-espionage agent with the CIA. She was also the only one who knew his true identity and he silenced her before she could share that knowledge with anyone.

A gnawing pain in his right leg brought him back to the present. Abu Ammar walked two blocks to Christopher Park. From a park bench, he looked beyond the statue of General Philip Sheridan, across the street to the Lion's Claw Tavern, a favorite meeting place for actors, artists and journalists in Greenwich Village. Once his plan went into action, he would go into the tavern to hear the comments of journalists, the reactions that would echo the terror of the American people. The taste of success would be sweet on his lips.

CHAPTER 8

Kuwait

The SST glided to a near flawless landing. Each time she came to Kuwait, Glenn marveled that a culture so old could mesh with modern times and not lose its identity.

She was first to deplane. Her eyes searched the waiting area for Tony Emerson. He was beside her before she realized it. He smiled and handed her a single long stem yellow rose.

She laughed and embraced him. "My favorite flower, you remembered. Thank you, it's lovely."

He held her at arm's length and looked into her eyes. "I believe you've gotten more beautiful." He smiled. "I'm sorry we didn't get to talk in Langley. You know, I think I could fall madly in love with you just as I did when we were children."

She inhaled the fragrance of the rose. "You never told me."

"I was in love but I wasn't crazy. You were such a tomboy. If I told you about my plight, I would have ended up with a black eye."

She embraced him again and noticed someone watching them. "I think we are being scrutinized."

He picked up her overnight bag and they walked toward the parking exit. Tony asked, "Did you get a look at him?"

"When I looked at him, he looked away too quickly so I couldn't see his face but he wore a camouflage shirt and pants and the typical Palestinian kaffiyeh covering his head."

Tony put the top down on his white Mercedes convertible and put her luggage in the trunk. She settled down next to him and directed her attention to his profile. It was a nice face, a handsome face. His tranquil brown eyes lit up when he smiled. His mouth was soft and sensitive but his chin hinted at a stubborn determination. Glenn was comfortable with him...always had been. She said, "When I called yesterday, I got the impression your phone was tapped. Does anyone suspect you are SIS?"

"I'm not sure. Somebody was certainly suspicious of something, or I wouldn't have been mugged near the pottery shop. They were probably after the sketches. Maybe now, they're satisfied."

He glanced in the rearview mirror. A white sports car followed about a quarter of a mile behind them.

He said, "I asked Peter to meet us in Manama. Ostensibly the meeting is to get your approval on his jewelry designs. It'll be difficult to talk at the hotel. Your phone could be bugged but I doubt it. After all, to them you're nothing but a woman...a rich one but nonetheless, a woman." He grinned mischievously.

"You sure know how to bolster a gal's ego."

He turned serious again. "Peter has some information. Unfortunately, not the vital piece you want. When you get back to the States, a SIS agent working on the inside will contact you. He was assigned the honor of blowing up the Lincoln Memorial."

"Why the Lincoln Memorial?"

"They want to be sure the Americans get the message. Make them aware of their personal vulnerability. Diversionary explosions are geared to unsettle and terrify."

Tony glanced at the rearview mirror again. The white car was still following. He said, "Our agent's code name is Bengal. Unfortunately, the identity of Abd al Alim is a mystery. My feeling is that it's somebody in the inner circle of Washington society. It could be a senator or congressman…someone powerful. Hell, for that matter, it could be one of Mr. Breckenridge's cabinet members."

"Nasty thought," Glenn said. "One of his trusted staff, who tells him when to do what."

"Speaking of telling, has the Old Boy been told yet?"

"Not yet. The Bossman will tell him and I get the feeling he's not looking forward to it. I know the *Old Boy*, as you call him and he won't lie down and play dead. Alden Breckenridge is nobody's fool." She paused. "Is the hit scheduled for May nineteenth?"

"That's the scuttlebutt." He turned to look at her. "But how did you know that?"

"You wouldn't believe me if I told you." Glenn thought, under the best of circumstances, Blanche Cameron wasn't very believable.

Tony checked the rearview mirror again. The white car was still behind them. He turned into the construction site, spotted Peter and pulled up beside him. For the benefit of observers, Tony formally introduced Glenn to Asad al Rachid. They talked for several minutes and Rachid's animated conversation seemed to be innocent enough. He handed her some of his jewelry designs. Tony watched as the white sports car pulled up behind the construction trailer. Glenn studied the designs and put them on the seat of the convertible, under her handbag.

The construction foreman met them and handed each a hardhat. Together they moved closer to the long span steel structure that was beginning to look like a building. Tony hung back to observe the man from the white car. The intruder approached the convertible cautiously; checking the area, then took a camera out of his pocket and copied each sheet of paper, then replaced the handbag on top of them.

When Glenn, Tony and Rachid returned to the car, Glenn lifted her purse and put the papers inside. She said, "Somebody moved the papers." She smiled at the two men.

Tony said, "Our man at the airport followed us in a white sports car. He pulled up behind the construction trailer. While we were doing our thing, he was doing his thing, namely taking pictures of Rachid's sketches." He winked at Glenn.

She said, "They're anxious to know if we suspect anything. So far, I think they're convinced that everything that has happened here is linked to the construction of the new hotel."

Tony opened the car door for her. "Never underestimate these people because that would be a serious, even fatal mistake."

They waved as Peter Aziz drove away.

Tony took his hand off the ignition key and turned to her. "A couple of years ago one of your agents made that mistake." He turned on the ignition. "Do you have time for dinner?"

"Sure. I leave on the midnight plane. Why don't we invite Peter?"

Tony said, "He's returning to the States on the seven o'clock flight."

"So soon after our meeting? Is that wise?"

"It would be unwise to do anything else. He made reservations before the leak of the assassination. He usually makes six to eight trips a year to the U.S. He doesn't want to arouse suspicion by changing his habits. If the enemy is watching Rachid, I think they would laugh at the idea that he could possibly be involved in anything as gauche as spying. He reminds me of the Scarlet Pimpernel. He bathes too often to suit them; his suits are never wrinkled; his hair is always perfectly styled; his fingernails are meticulously manicured and he always looks like he stepped out of a clothing ad. His designs for jewelry are recognized worldwide and he commands top dollar for them. He has designed jewelry for the wives of Emirs." Tony studied her profile; then dropped his own bomb. "What do you think of Mike Redmond?"

Her cheeks flushed at the mention of his name. "I've always believed that nothing on this earth is perfect, everything is flawed in some way. I was wrong…I finally found the perfect ass." Her eyes shot warning sparks. "I have to work with him but I don't have to like him. He's the most conceited, overbearing, pretentious, egotistic, arrogant, puffed up peacock it has ever been my misfortune to know. In short, he's a sonofabitch."

Tony kept his eyes on the road. "He's an excellent agent. I've worked with Mike and I can tell you, there's not a better agent anywhere in this whole bloody business. He is resourceful, crafty and cunning. When the chips are down, he'll push you out of the way and take the blast himself."

Glenn looked doubtful. "If that's true, I haven't seen that side of him."

"I know Mike. He's probably not happy about working with a female agent again. A few years ago he was paired with another agent, Caitlin O'Hara, on a mission in Lebanon. Mike called her Cat. I was part of that mission, assigned by SIS. We tracked down an international terrorist, known to us only as *Le Rongeur*, the rodent. He had just bombed the U.S. Embassy in London. He started with the PLO; then joined the Black September group. His specialty was explosives. His favorite targets were the U.S. and European embassies. He had a unique style of wiring explosives. That style became his signature. He generated a lot of fear. His focus was deadly."

Tony studied Glenn's face, uncertain if he should continue. He decided she should know. "Mike was in Syria. I was in Cairo. Cat followed a lead in Beirut. She teased us, saying that she would be the one to find Le Rongeur. When Mike returned, he found Cat's body on the balcony of her hotel room. She didn't find him, Le Rongeur found her. She was shot at close range. She wasn't pretty anymore."

He shook his head as if to dispel the memory. "She didn't die right away. She wrote the name of her executioner, in her own blood, on the floor, *Chisisi Badru*. As you can imagine, in Lebanon, all our leads ended in a blind alley. We had a name but that was all we had. Later, we learned that Chisisi Badru was one of many aliases used by Le Rongeur. We've never found him."

Glenn bit her bottom lip. "I had no idea."

Tony continued, "They had been intimate before they worked together. Mike loved Cat but didn't like working with her. He thought she took unnecessary chances. When he left for Damascus, Cat told me she was getting out of the business. They were planning to get married."

Glenn nodded. "That explains a lot." She also understood Tony's message. In this business, you have to call the shot right the first time…you rarely got a second chance.

* * *

New York City

The setting sun looked like a ball of fire sitting above the East River and the somber face of Khalil Najjar was reflected in the tinted water.

"Why are we still on this project? We are experts in firearms, not explosives." Shakir's impatience put an edge to his voice.

Slowly, Khalil raised his head, his doom foreshadowed on his face. He thought, *If only I had the courage…*Aloud, he said, "Our instructions were to follow Ammar's orders. If we learned nothing else at Abd al Bari, we knew orders were to be followed, even if it meant our own lives. We have no choice; we must follow his orders. Soon we'll know what he has in store for us." He glanced at his watch. "He'll be here in twenty minutes. He's never late. Where are the others? Ammar doesn't like to be kept waiting."

Shakir said, "I think we should tell Ammar to go to hell. He walks with the devil and that is where he belongs. I don't like what's happening. I don't trust him. Especially, I don't like what he's doing to you."

"After this project, Abdul, there will be no need for further communication with him. You and the others will be free."

"But you will not be free?"

"A debt is owed to him and he will not rest until that debt has been satisfied."

The sun was on the horizon. The man walking toward them cast a mighty shadow that darkened the area where Khalil was sitting on the dock.

Shakir shielded his eyes from the sun. "It's Ammar."

Najjar's superstitious mind sent waves of panic through him. "A man who casts such a shadow will possess or destroy everything touched by it. Abdul, my friend, I am doomed."

"Nonsense, that's superstition. Look," he pointed to a spot behind the long shadow, "see our two friends are behind him."

"Superstition you say? Look at their shadows. Why is it their bodies do not cast long shadows like his? Yet they walk the same pier, in the same sunset." He shook his head sadly. "Karma. Fate has written my end and pronounced sentence."

* * *

Ammar waited until the four men gathered around him. He looked directly at Najjar. "We will assemble more bombs. The train bomb and the bomb at the Port Authority are only the beginning and they were quite successful. They achieved the purpose for which they were intended. Americans are beginning to know what it is like to have a war brought to their front door. After each bombing, we will meet at the Cloisters Museum at Fort Tryon Park. We'll meet on the parapet at noon on the day of the explosions." He watched the men, pleased that their faces were expressionless.

Abdul stepped forward. "We're specialists in firearms. Why are we handling explosives?"

Ammar's eyelids were lowered and he looked down at the five foot five frame of Abdul Shakir. There was obvious contempt in his voice as he answered, "Because I gave you an order. Until this mission is completed, you'll take any and all orders from me.

It's not necessary that you know about explosives. All you have to remember is to put them in place. Is that understood?"

Shakir stepped back, his head lowered submissively.

Ammar said, "The long overdue punishment of the infidels has begun. Allah be praised." He turned up the collar of his coat and walked toward his car. Four pairs of eyes bore holes of hatred into his back as they followed him.

* * *

Washington, D.C.
May 13

Mike Redmond rolled over until he felt something silky and soft. His hand came in contact with a round, firm breast. His eyes still closed, he moved closer to the allure of the flesh. His body responded instinctively to a naked female body. Slowly, he opened his eyes and began to peel the sheet from the delightful form beside him. Her dark auburn hair cascaded around one shoulder and down her back. He knew she was a true redhead because she had the freckles scattered across her shoulders that seemed to be so typical of females with red hair. He put his arm across her body to the far shoulder and turned her toward him. Her green eyes startled him and she reached out her arms toward him just as the phone rang. He toyed with the idea of ignoring it then realized he was on assignment. Convinced it would be Glenn He frowned and picked up the receiver as he murmured to himself, *Damned woman is determined to frustrate all my efforts at leading a normal life, what the hell is she doing, monitoring my sex life? That goddamn woman never sleeps.* He scowled at the receiver and barked into the mouthpiece, "What?"

"Helix," a baritone voice barked back at him. The Bossman rarely used Mike's code name on home territory. "Get your ass down to my office. Now!"

Mike hung up the phone and looked at his watch. It was eight-thirty. He looked at the petite redhead in the bed beside him and realized he didn't know her. "Sorry, baby, but I've got to go. I hate to rush you, but—" He threw the covers off and patted her butt. "By the way, what's your name?"

"Kathy. Kathy Mason. You don't remember much about last night, do you?"

"I think I got sloshed. Did I behave badly?" He turned on the shower and stepped on the cold tile floor. When he came back into the bedroom, she was fully clothed, leaning against the doorframe, a smile playing at the corners of her mouth. "As a matter of fact, you behaved quite well, performed well too. I'm not flattered that you don't remember what happened. You dumped the lady you were with because you wanted a professional to do all the things nice ladies won't talk about."

He stopped shaving and watched her through the mirror. "Are you telling me you're a hooker?"

"Oh, honey, not just a hooker, I'm top drawer."

"M-m-m-m-m." He looked at her from the corner of his eye. "Did I have a good time?"

She laughed. "You said you did."

He put his shirt and pants on and selected a dark blue tie from an expensive assortment. "If I said I had a good time, then I did. I never lie. Have I paid you?"

"Not yet."

He pulled his wallet out of the inside pocket of the coat draped over the chair. "What did we agree on?"

"Five hundred will cover it."

"If I had that good a time, it's worth at least a grand." He pulled two five hundred dollar notes out of the wallet, walked to where she was holding up the doorframe, lifted her dress, pulled the top of her bikini panties out, to reveal an auburn triangle of pubic hair and dropped the two bills inside. He smiled. "There aren't very many true redheads these days." He picked up the coat to the suit he had selected, led her to the door and held it open. He handed her another fifty dollars. "Cab fare."

"I'm available, stud, any time you want me." Her voice was breathy, sexy. "Any time." She dropped her business card on the table with his unopened mail.

They rode the elevator together. She got off on the main floor and he continued to the garage below. He drove the red Ferrari to the street level, only to find traffic at a virtual standstill. He put a CD on the player and listened to jazz. He picked up the cell phone and dialed Ardell's office. "Sally? Let me talk to the Bossman, it's—"

"I know who it is," she interrupted, "where are you?"

"About a mile from the office, traffic is horrendous. I'll get there as soon as I can. Is everybody else there?"

"All except Glenn. That flight from Kuwait just got in. She'll be here soon."

"Sally…" He hesitated. "Let's get a background check on Gabriella Cammeo Russal. Everything we can dig up." He labored his way through the traffic, impatient, angry and frustrated. As he reached the office, he saw Glenn hurry into the building.

He entered the inner sanctum, shut the door and took his seat beside Glenn.

Clifford Ardell studied each face before he spoke. "New York City got hit this morning by terrorists. One of the buildings was the Port Authority Bus Terminal. It was hit hard. Casualties are mounting. The other bomb exploded on the Washington-New York express. There aren't many survivors. The FBI is questioning people at Penn Station but so far…nothing." He picked up the carafe from the table and poured hot coffee into his cup. "As soon as we got word, Duncan MacKenzie flew back to New York. If there's anything to find, Mac will sniff it out. We're anxious to see if the blasts have a familiar pattern and what type of explosive was used. We're sure it wasn't a car bomb. The FBI is faxing information to us on Middle East immigrants residing in the metropolitan New York area." He turned to Glenn. "What did you find out in Kuwait?"

She related everything Tony Emerson told her. When she finished, she realized why both she and Peter were in Kuwait at the same time. If he didn't make it back, she would have the information.

Sally Vance opened the door and handed Ardell an envelope then she distributed folders with information received from the FBI.

The Bossman took a single sheet of paper out of the envelope and scanned it.

"And so it begins…"Ardell adjusted the glasses on his nose. "The unofficial number of dead at the bus terminal is seventy-five. Fifty-eight were injured, fifteen of them, critically. We don't have a number yet for the victims on the train. These were not random hits. These were planned by pros. They knew the premeditated use of violence would generate the greatest fear. Unfortunately, the mass media will do exactly what the terrorists want and that is to give them maximum exposure in all phases of journalism. I think it's safe to say the plan originated with Osama Bin Laden but his organization was not acting alone. Others are sharing the tab." He put files of suspected Middle Eastern sympathizers on the table. "When you finish with the folders in front of you, pass them along to the next person. I want each of you to review every file. If you have any knowledge of the subjects, share it with the rest of us."

The afternoon was unproductive until Peter Aziz opened the last folder in front of him. A photograph caught his unconscious awareness. He said, "The name doesn't fit the face." He repeated the name, "Lamen Abd Sakhim." He looked around at the group. "Ring a bell with anyone?" He pulled his pen out and sketched the face before him, eliminating the mustache and beard. He stared at the face; then inserted a jagged scar from the left temple, down to and across the chin, and continuing down the right side of his neck. He showed it to Ardell and said, "This is Abd al

Jabbar. I'm certain of it. He was the Iraqi Madman's top explosives expert. Supposedly, the Israeli Aman took him out. Obviously the rumors were false." He put his pen back in his pocket. "When it comes to explosives, Jabbar wrote the book and the New York City bombings are his style." He saw the excited look on Ardell's face, and said, "He's not the guy assigned to make a hit on the President. With a scar like that, he would be spotted too easily. Probably he is in charge of the New York project."

Ardell studied the sketch. "Goliath said it was him. He and Jabbar were old adversaries. I'll get the lab to do a computerized composite for distribution to everyone connected with this project."

Glenn looked at the sketch. "Tony Emerson said New York would share the stage with Washington in the assassination plot. Looks like these bombings were only a warm up, and today is only May thirteenth.

* * *

New York City
May 13, 12:00 p.m.

The view of the Hudson River from the parapet of the Cloisters Museum had a calming effect on Abu Ammar. Things were going as planned. He was satisfied. The men performed well. The bombs detonated as planned and the men escaped. He thought, *I have much to do before the ultimate target on the nineteenth.*

As tour groups passed him, there was an excited buzz about the bombings. Their fear added to his sense of accomplishment. Before the end of the month, he, Abu Ammar, would bring the U.S. to its knees.

He watched his four disciples approach. All wore casual clothes and all, save one, smiled. He praised their courage. He said, "Your next hit will be on the nineteenth. I will meet you at the sewer entrance to our objective on the seventeenth. If needed, I'll contact you by phone." He smiled. "America will remember."

He started to leave and then turned back to them. "Go inside and join the guided tour. Ask the guide questions, so he remembers you."

Ammar went to the reptile house of the Central Park Zoo. He met Asfour Riyad and Kaliq Fatin, an American whose real name was Edward (Moose) Morrison. Fatin's coal black hair and olive complexion helped assimilate him into the terrorist group but his pale blue eyes also set him apart. The three men walked outside in the pleasantly cool, bright day.

Ammar smiled and handed Fatin an envelope, which he opened immediately. The envelope contained a thousand dollars, an identification tag for Montgomery Stationers and Office Products and a slip of paper with the address of the garage where the vans were kept. He said, "Pick up the van at eight o'clock Monday morning, at that address."

Fatin replaced the I.D. and the address in the envelope. "That's not the amount of money we agreed on."

"It's not meant for you. Your payment comes later," Ammar said. "The money is for you to purchase office supplies from Montgomery Stationers. It must be done today. They'll be closed for the weekend. We'll need the wrappers and the boxes with the name of the company on them. Bring them to me at Christopher Park on the night of the fifteenth. I'll wrap the bomb in that paper and secure it with string. Attached to the string will be a very fine wire. When you attach the package to the underside of the elevator, pull out the wire. That will activate the timer. It'll be set to go off on Monday morning at ten-thirty. Your target is the Kryler Building. When your job is done, leave by the Lexington Avenue exit. Riyad will be waiting outside to pick you up. He'll take you to the subway and he'll follow his orders to dispose of the van."

He didn't add that the van would be wired to detonate if anyone tried to gain access to it once it was locked with the key.

If no one found the van, it would be set to self-destruct in forty-eight hours. The location of the van would be strategic, in that when it self-destructed, the largest and longest bridge in New York would go with it.

"When our mission is complete, the money we agreed on will be deposited in your account in the Bahamas, on the first of June." Ammar nodded. "We deal honestly with our friends. Payment…is always made in full." He checked his watch. It was time to meet with the other two men. "Go to the Kryler Building and familiarize yourself with the target."

Ammar went to the monkey house to meet with the others. When he saw Abu Dawud, they embraced, laughing and slapping each other on the back. It had been ten years since they were together in Baghdad. Ammar said, "I wondered who Abu Dawud was. Allah has been good to you, my friend, just as he has been good to me by sending you. This is one job I won't have to be concerned about. It's good to have my old friend, Gadi Qasim, working with me again."

Dawud kept his arm around Ammar's shoulder. "The irony of our situation is almost comical. The U.S. counter espionage teams are looking for us all over the world…and here we are, in their back yard." He introduced Saqr Kharouf. "This is his first trip out of the Middle East but he has earned himself a fair reputation for the damage he caused in Israel." He wrinkled his nose. "Can we talk outside? The smell of monkeys does nothing for my appetite."

Ammar laughed and they walked outside together. The sound of his own laughter was strange to his ears and he realized he had not laughed since the death of his wife and child. They walked along one of the paths, until they found a bench and sat down.

Dawud asked, "What is our target?"

"The American Post Federal Building."

"Wonderful, at last, a target worthy of my talents. Do I use a car bomb?"

Ammar frowned. "You know better than that. Car bombs are clumsy and uncertain," he scoffed. "Always remember, our work is classic. Kharouf will drive a cab, which I've already acquired. The driver won't protest. He's at the bottom of the East River. The bomb is already in place; I've done it in sections. It's in the basement. You will need to activate the timer." He handed Dawud identification of a federal inspector. "You have less than forty-eight hours to replace that picture with yours. Our contact in the Manhattan Photo Laboratory will do a good job."

"What am I going to inspect?"

"They just replaced the main boiler in the basement. Your job is to inspect it."

He handed Dawud a key. "The bomb is connected to the back of the boiler. There's an opening at the bottom. Insert this key and turn it counterclockwise to activate it. You'll have fifteen minutes to get out of there."

Ammar spoke to Kharouf. "He should be inside about fifteen minutes. Drive around and time it, so that you'll be there to pick him up when he comes out. After the job is done, drive the cab to Pier One's parking lot. Lock it and leave it there. Someone will pick it up and drive it to its final destination." Again, he didn't tell them about the incendiary device planted for the cab to self-destruct.

Kharouf watched Ammar walk away. He turned to Dawud and in hushed tones said, "Ammar knows his business and has honed a fine edge on his awareness. He's like a wild stallion. The wildness…the insanity, is reflected in his eyes. He is a purveyor of death."

Dawud studied Kharouf. "Not without reason, my friend. Not without reason."

CHAPTER 9

Washington, D.C.
May 13, 5:00 p.m.

Clifford Ardell's somber voice reflected his growing concern about terrorism on American soil but particularly because it involved the President. "I want you to be together all the time. Mike, you'll start by staying at Glenn's house. In light of what's happened, I must know where I can reach both of you at the same time. What happened today in New York is only the beginning. Let Sally Vance know where I can reach you at a moment's notice. Sally said you looked like the ideal couple, on the verge of falling in love. Good, keep it that way." He waved his hand. "Now get out of here and go do whatever it is lovers are supposed to do." He took a few steps, turned around, and smiled. "At least when you're in the public eye if you want to kill each other in private, that's your affair." He winked. "Pardon the pun."

Mike turned to Glenn. "Looks like we're an item, got room for me?"

"Sure. There's lots of room. You can have the bedroom next to mine."

"Aren't you concerned that I'll compromise your virtue?"

"Not really." She smiled. "Templeton Osbourne's my self-appointed guardian."

He picked up her coat from a chair and handed it to her. "Lucky me, now I don't have to worry about being sexually molested by you in the middle of the night."

She laughed as they left the office. "You should be so lucky."

Glenn left their schedule with Sally, and said, "During the empty time slots, we'll call and let you know where we can be reached in case anything comes up."

Mike's arms encircled Glenn's waist from behind. "You really should choose your words more carefully, darling."

Sally tried unsuccessfully to hide her amusement. She turned away but her shoulders shook with silent laughter. Glenn glared at Mike. Slowly she turned to Sally. "Don't encourage him." She hurried to the door.

"We'll go to my apartment first. I'll change into something more suitable for golfing and pack some clothes for," he smiled, "whatever comes up?"

She arched her right eyebrow. "You're very funny," she said with a frown.

Glenn put her head back and closed her eyes. Mike studied the quiet elegance of the woman next to him. He thought, *She's nothing like Cat. She has none of Cat's effervescence, none of Cat's joie de vivre. I'll bet Glenn has never had a belly laugh in all of her twenty some years. What a shame.*

"Penny for your thoughts?"

He realized Glenn had been watching him. "Not really worth a penny. I'm wondering when Bengal will contact us."

"When he feels it's safe, he knows how to reach us and Sally knows where to find us when the call comes in.

Mike scanned the books in the library of Glenn's house as he waited for her to change her clothes.

Templeton Osbourne watched discreetly from the garden where he was conveniently trimming a hedge. Mike noted the presence of the tall lean man.

Glenn saw Templeton when she came downstairs and smiled to herself. *Good old Templeton,* she thought, *always there to protect me.* "I'm ready." She dropped her golf glove and stooped to pick it up.

Mike didn't miss the charming angle of her derriere or the tight fitting shorts that moved with her. When she stood up, his eyes surveyed her from head to toe. "Damn," he said, "you even look the part. I'll bet you even know how to hit a golf ball."

"Yeah, sometimes, when I hit that little white ball with my bat, people all over the golf course start yelling, 'Fore!' I wonder why." She waved at Templeton through the French doors and they were off to the country club.

Glenn liked the way Mike handled the Ferrari. There was nothing tentative about him. His hands on the wheel were sure. He had confidence, a kind of control that she lacked.

He caught her looking at him. "Was that Templeton Osbourne out in the garden?"

"Yes."

"He looks like a good man to have around. God knows he'll protect you with his life, if necessary."

"How could you possibly know that?"

"He has the look of a Doberman pinscher. If anybody comes to within five feet of you, he looks like he'll tear their throats out." Mike pulled into the parking lot and took their clubs out of the trunk.

A tall, dark-haired man in white slacks and shirt waved to Glenn and hurried over. "Glenn, it's good to see you. I was beginning to think you gave up playing golf."

She smiled at him. "Mike, this is George Davet, the club's pro. George, this is Mike Redmond."

The men shook hands. Mike didn't miss the once over Davet gave Glenn. He thought to himself, *This broad has no idea how attractive she is to men.* Aloud, he said, "She'll probably beat me, so don't laugh when you see our score cards."

George Davet laughed and said, "Gabriella and Karim pulled in about five minutes ago. They're waiting for you at the Nineteenth Hole."

"Thanks, George. On the way out, I'll leave my wedge with you. I think the handle is beginning to ravel. Will you have it fixed for me?"

"Sure. If I'm not here, just give it to Austin. He'll take care of it for you."

As they walked toward the bar, Mike turned for another look at Davet. "I've seen him before."

"I'm sure you have. It was probably on television. He's a member of the PGA Masters circuit."

"That's not where I saw him. It'll come to me. Davet…what kind of name is that?"

"I believe it's French. He was born in Morocco but I understand his family now lives in Arabia. He's extremely popular with the ladies."

"Of course." Mike made a mental note to have Davet checked out.

Mike was pleasantly surprised to see how well Gabriella and Glenn played golf. There was none of the giggling and gossiping that he saw so often when he played behind groups where women and men made up the foursome. These women took the game seriously. At the end of the game, Gabi was four strokes over, and Glenn was two strokes over par. He struggled to come in one stroke under par. His admiration for Glenn was taking on a new perspective. Unfortunately, Karim wasn't equal to the skill of his wife. He was fifteen over par, but it didn't seem to matter to Gabriella. They sat at the outdoor bar and drank cocktails. Mike was aware that Karim was watching him and Glenn.

Karim said, "What are you doing these days, Glenn? Still top dog at AIH?"

"Of course, you don't think Clayton is going to do all that work, do you? I just got back from the Middle East. I was checking out the construction progress on the new hotel in Manama. In a few months, the hotel should be ready to open. I met with Asad al Rachid, and he agreed to open one of his fabulous jewelry shops in the lobby of the new hotel."

"Karim bought me several pieces of his jewelry. Really unique, I haven't seen any jewelry to compare with his designs." Gabriella squeezed Karim's hand.

Karim shook his head. "You're a fascinating woman, Glenn. You have beauty, poise and a business sense to rival that of any man I know." Karim's eyes took in her sensuous body. "Yet, you're completely feminine. Even your relationship with Gabriella is unusual."

Gabriella raised her eyebrows. "How do you mean, unusual, darling?"

"I don't know how women view their relationships with other women but my observation, strictly from a man's point of view, understand, is that most attractive women surround themselves with less attractive women as friends, thereby eliminating any possible competition. That theory got shot to hell by your relationship with Gabi. Both of you are beautiful, talented, and clever in ways men can't even imagine and yet you remain the best of friends. I find that very unusual." He looked to Mike for confirmation. "What do you think?"

"Agreed. Genuine friendship between two beautiful women is rare. The nicest part of your relationship is that there doesn't appear to be any jealousy between you. I find that extraordinary." He was watching Gabriella. "I'm getting to know about Glenn, but I know nothing about you, Gabi."

Gabriella laughed and her eyes sparkled. "Darling, my favorite subject is Gabriella Cammeo Russal. I can talk about me for hours. Just ask Karim. What do you want to know?"

"You have a charming accent. I know you lived in Rome, but I detect a tinge of something else in your speech."

"We lived in Rome, but we spent a great deal of time on the French Riviera. My mother was Roman by birth. My father was an American businessman. When they married, he knew my mother would never leave Rome. So we lived in Europe until she died. My father never got over the loss. Then he died just before

I met Karim." She smiled at her husband and reached for his hand. "My wonderful Karim."

"It must have been lonely for you, being an only child."

"I wasn't an only child. I have a brother. Salvatore and I never got along. He was always involved in some kind of cause. Save the children...save the whales. Any cause where he could carry a banner. He was always being arrested and poor Papa was always down at the police station getting him out of jail. When Papa and I came to the States, Salvatore stayed in Rome. I never hear from him. As far as I know, he still lives in the piazza that belongs to our family. Papa left him with enough money so that he doesn't have to worry about lowering his standard of living." She laughed. "Believe me; Salvatore enjoys money and good living."

"How do you get along with your brother-in-law, Karim?"

"I've never met him. Gabi goes back to Rome occasionally, but I always seem to be inundated with work and can't go with her."

"Doesn't your brother want to come to the States?"

"I don't think so. I haven't seen him in the last four years. When I go back to Italy, it's to see my grandmother. She's not well and has been in and out of the hospital. I begged her to come live with us but she wants to live out her remaining days with her own people. I can't argue with that."

Glenn looked at her watch. "We had better be going. We have to be at the Cameron's tonight. Will you be there, Gabi?"

"We were invited but I had to refuse. We had agreed to have dinner at Aux Beaux Champs with Paul and Anita."

"Mike and I are playing tennis with them tomorrow morning."

Gabi laughed. "I hope her tennis is better than her golf. The last time she played golf with us, she spent most of her time in sand traps or behind trees. Her ball was everywhere except on the fairway."

"Fortunately," Mike said, "there are no trees or sand traps on the tennis court."

Glenn picked up her scorecard. "Are you going to the Thomason's cocktail party tomorrow night?"

"We wouldn't miss that. They have such interesting guests at their parties."

"Great, we'll see you there." Mike put his arm around Glenn as they walked to the parking lot. His head was close to hers as he whispered, "Did you know she had a brother?"

"No. Yes. Oh, damn, I don't remember. She could have mentioned it. Is it important?"

"Everything's important. Something about Gabi and Karim doesn't add up. It's a given that she's a flirt but I think she's really in love with the guy."

Glenn snapped her fingers. "Yes. Gabi does have a brother. She told me they went to Africa together, just before she started college. He was older than she, by about seven or eight years. I was under the impression she had a kind of hero worship for him but that's just my impression. She never talked about him. She was wild about some guy named Tory. As far as she was concerned, he was the alpha and the omega."

Glenn cocked her head to one side. "I was just thinking about what you said, concerning Gabi and Karim. You're right, there's something peculiar going on. Karim never goes with her to Italy. Why? She wouldn't think of letting him go to Arabia alone. She always goes with him. That poses an interesting question. When she is in Italy, where is he? What does he do while she's gone? I've heard her say that Karim has top men in his organization that could run his company without Karim ever making an appearance in the office. I never gave it much thought before. If his office runs so well without him, why doesn't he go with her to Italy?"

Mike held the car door open and admired her shapely legs. He thought, *Those beautiful legs don't fit with her steel-trap-mind. With that kind of mind, she should be short and dumpy and have warts on her nose.*

When he climbed in behind the wheel, she said, "What do you think about it?"

He winked at her, and said, "It gets curiouser and curiouser."

"I'm impressed, Michael. You've read *Alice's Adventures in Wonderland*."

"I'm glad you're so easily impressed." Mike looked at his watch. "Let's see if we can get a guest list for the Thomason's party tomorrow night. I'd like to see who will be there. I had a tail put on Paul Qadir. It might not be a bad idea to do the same to Karim." He watched her profile for signs of resentment. There were none. "I hate to do that to your friends," he said.

"I understand," she said, without looking at him.

His phone buzzed and he picked it up. "Yes?" He listened for a moment, and said, "Patch him through." He covered the mouthpiece with his hand. "It's Bengal." He waited. "This is Helix. Raven is with me. Where should we meet you? That's fine." He hung up and looked at Glenn. "Bengal will meet us tonight at eleven-thirty, in Georgetown, at the After Hours Bistro. He'll be wearing a Detroit Tigers pullover sweatshirt. I'll ask him what kind of tiger it is, and he'll tell me it's a Bengal tiger."

* * *

The gray Lincoln Continental turned onto Interstate 95 and headed north toward Baltimore.

Randy Perry checked his rearview mirror. "Are we going to the waterfront apartment in Baltimore?"

Peter smiled to himself. "Yes. Do you still remember her phone number?"

"Yes. When should I pick you up?"

"Just wait for me. I won't be long."

The car glided to a stop and Peter Aziz checked the area before getting out; then hurried into the lobby and pushed the button for the elevator.

Laura Madison opened the door. "Why didn't you use your key, sweetheart?"

"Because I love to see the expression on your face when you open the door and see me standing here."

She reached for his hand and pulled him in. Before the door closed she was in his arms accepting and giving kisses in return. Between kisses, she whispered, "How much time do we have?"

"None, right now."

She pulled away from him so she could see his face. Her face bore all the markings of disappointment.

"I'll be back tonight." He reached into his coat pocket and pulled out a long slender box covered with black velvet. "I couldn't wait to see you, even if it was only for a few minutes. Besides, I wanted you to have this." He put the box in her hand.

"Oh, Peter, how absolutely lovely."

He took the bracelet out of the box, opened the clasp and put it on her wrist. She stared at the sparkling circlet on her wrist. Each link formed a scroll and each scroll was studded with two diamonds on either side of a marquis cut emerald.

When she looked into his face her eyes were moist with tears. "I love it, Peter. I've never seen anything like it." She was in his arms again seeking his mouth with hers.

His arms tightened around her in response to the urgency boiling within him. "Tonight," he whispered as he pulled himself away from her. Her eyes searched his face, pleading. He pulled her against him, pulled down the zipper on the back of her dress and slid it off her shoulders. The only sounds were subdued moans of pleasure.

* * *

Mike pulled his car into the parking lot of the After Hours Bistro. Glenn checked her watch. It was eleven-twenty-seven. They walked into the dimly lit cafe and quickly scanned the room. At the end of the bar, stood a tall lean man in jeans topped with a Detroit Tigers sweatshirt. They headed for the bar.

"What'll it be?" Smiled the pert, blond bartender.

Mike glanced at Glenn. "Remy XO?"

She nodded.

"And I'll have a bloody Mary on the rocks with a generous dash of Tabasco."

Glenn smiled as she watched the bartender whirl a shaker with the blood Mary, set out the brandy snifter and expertly pour the drinks.

"You're pretty good at this."

"Yeah. It's fun for now, but I don't intend to make it my career. She smiled as she put their drinks on the bar. Mike was sitting next to the man with the tiger shirt. He turned and purposely bumped the man, spilling some of his drink on the man's shirt. He pulled out his handkerchief and began wiping the moisture from the shirt. "That was clumsy, I'm sorry." He turned to Glenn. "Hey, honey, look at this shirt." He addressed the man inside the shirt. "What kind of tiger is that?"

"It's a Bengal tiger."

"I thought so." He put an arm around Glenn. "We were in India once and nobody would take us on a hunt so the nearest I came to a Bengal tiger is your shirt." He looked around. The bartender was at the other end of the bar having an animated conversation with one of the customers.

"I'm Helix and this is Raven. What's your pleasure?"

"I shouldn't be seen talking to you. It's too public. Where can we go?"

"Let me make a phone call." Mike searched in his pocket for change, picked out a quarter and disappeared for five minutes. When he returned Bengal was finishing his drink. Mike stood beside the British agent and gave him an address.

"We'll meet you outside that address in twenty minutes."

The bartender came up to Mike. "May I get you another drink?"

Mike smiled at her. "Good idea."

She cleared away Bengal's glass, wiped the bar, and picked up a fifty-cent tip. When she turned away, Glenn heard her mumble under her breath, "Cheap bastard."

They finished their drinks and Mike dropped a twenty-dollar bill on the bar. When they neared the door, Glenn looked back and saw the bartender smile when she picked up the money.

"Where are we meeting Bengal?"

"I called the office and they patched me through to Peter. He's not at the apartment and probably won't be back tonight. I have a key." Mike parked his car around the corner from the apartment and they walked back. When they approached, Bengal stepped out of the shadows. They walked up the flight of steps to the apartment. Glenn quickly glanced around and nodded her approval. French provincial was not her favorite decorating scheme but it suited the layout of the apartment. They sat in the living room and Bengal told them all he knew about the hit. He described the type of charge he would be using to blow up the Lincoln Memorial. He stressed that the charge would be set to go off at nine-thirty on the night of May nineteenth.

Mike nodded. "How many men will be with you?"

"There will be four others. One will be with me, two will be setting the other charge in place and the last man will be posted as a lookout. We'll set the charges in place at eight-thirty." Bengal took out a sketch of the memorial and made two crosses on the paper. "This is where the charges will be placed. I'll be using mercury fulminate with an electric blasting cap and a booster. It'll be booby-trapped." He drew a configuration on the diagram. "The white wire will be the bridge wire to the bead. I'll be using a high explosive, pressed charge of RDX."

Mike was pensive. "I'll have the bomb squad ready to move in. The call about the bomb will come from a couple of teenagers on holiday. The FBI will be the ones to take all of you into custody. If there is gunplay and I feel certain there will be, we may not be able to take prisoners. In that case we will report to the news media that all five of you were killed in a shootout. We'll get you out on a flight to England. What do you know about Boulus Qadir's part in all this?"

"Qadir was assigned as backup for Abd al Alim. I don't know if he has any other function. We weren't told the functions of any other members of the group. The only thing that's certain is that every man is expendable. If this project fails, each man forfeits his life, so you can be sure there'll be a fight. When they go to meet Allah they're going to take as many infidels with them as possible. They think that will impress Allah. At least death in a gun battle is merciful compared to death at the camp where I trained. If these men fail and they manage to get back home, they would be taken to the camp, interrogated, and then tortured. I'm afraid the son-of-a-bitch who runs this organization loves the sight of blood. Everybody's blood, that is, except his own. He sits back and gets satisfaction while everybody else risks life and limb. I'm sure he's being well paid."

Glenn said, "What will happen when the plans go awry?"

"He'll suspect there's a traitor in the group and since all five of us will be dead, the only logical suspect would be Boulus Qadir."

Mike grinned. "I don't think that will be such a great loss to the cause."

"Actually, Qadir is one of the kingpins and the head man is always suspicious of the top men in any organization. He's extremely paranoid and thinks they're trying to usurp his power. The bearded madman couldn't afford to do this on his own so he selected some individuals and put them under the bald headed man's command. In that way if anything goes wrong, he holds up his hands to show they're free of blood. At the same time, the baldheaded man loses face, which lessens his power. The madman uses him...but I think in a way he also fears him. It's strange to be working for two extremely powerful men, both of whom are essentially cowards." He stood up. "I had better get back in case somebody is checking on me."

Mike said, "Wait until I make sure there are no surprises waiting for you out there." He picked up the phone and pressed the pound key. "What's the weather like?" He listened, nodded and replaced the receiver in its cradle. "It's clear. Good luck, Bengal."

* * *

New York City

Abu Ammar read every newspaper published in New York. He smiled because the media was doing fifty percent of his work for him. They were instilling terror into the minds of the people, which was what he knew they would do. He walked to the mirror and traced the outline of the scar on his face. "My Holy Grail, the cause that kept me alive when all the odds were against me." He walked to the Lion's Claw Tavern, ordered a beer and listened to the comments about the bombing of the Port Authority Bus Terminal and the strange train wreck that the newspapers were speculating was caused by a bomb.

There were two men sitting beside him at the bar discussing the bombing.

"It had to be a crazy amateur. What other screwball would walk into a bus terminal carrying a live bomb for chrissake?"

The man called Harry disagreed with the hypothesis. "I think it was a goddamn A-rab," he said, stressing the A. "Who do you think could have done it, Sean?"

Sean was watching Ammar and saw him smile as he strained to hear the conversation. "I think it might be another one of those A-rabs, you know like the ones that brought down the World Trade Center." To himself, he said, *Like the one sitting next to you, Harry, old boy.*

"You're crazy. Don't you think those guys from Immigration are keeping tabs on them?"

Keeping an eye on the scar-faced man, Sean said, "Do you know how many immigrants from the Middle East are in New York City alone? It's impossible to keep tabs on all of them. The guys from immigration are too busy covering our borders…and they don't even have enough people for that." Sean marveled at how the man got the scar that disfigured his face.

Ammar finished his drink, left a dollar tip on the bar and walked out. Sean Cleary watched Ammar leave the bar. "I'll be right back," he said, walked outside and watched as Ammar entered Christopher Park. He bit his lower lip, which was what he usually did if he was trying to make a decision. *What the hell, Sean, it's none of your business. Stay out of it. Do you know what could happen to you if you get involved? No, sir, it's not worth it.* He turned and walked back into the bar.

Ammar paced impatiently, waiting for Kaliq Fatin and Asfour Riyad. When they were a few feet away from him, he turned and began walking. The two men followed.

Sean Cleary waved to the bartender as he walked out. He knew he had to hurry or he would be late picking up his wife Ellen, at the Fast Food Shack where she worked on Eleventh Avenue. He looked across the park and saw the strange man from the bar; he was met by two other men. One looked like an American but the other had the look of a foreigner. He saw them turn and walk, not together, but each following the other. His curiosity won out over the mission to pick up his wife and he followed at a distance. He watched as they entered a small hotel. *Oh, shit,* he thought, *they're probably gay and they're going into that flophouse to do their thing.* He looked at his watch and decided a few more minutes wouldn't hurt. He was late already. Ellen would just have to wait.

Ammar led the two men up a flight of stairs and to the right. He unlocked the door and they followed him inside. Kaliq looked around the room. He saw nothing personal; nothing to indicate anyone lived here. He thought, *This guy is really cautious, probably rented this room just to distribute his goodies.* His gaze met that of Ammar and the steel gray eyes seemed to penetrate to his very soul, adding a contaminant that was sure to destroy.

"When you complete your job, Riyad, drive to Texas. Go over the Mexican border and get a plane for home. Your money will be waiting for you on your arrival. Fatin, return to your home in the Bronx. Money will be deposited in your bank account before the first of June."

"But," stammered Riyad, "I already have my return ticket leaving from John F. Kennedy Airport."

"Idiot," Ammar spat the word out, giving it the venom of a deadly snake. "Don't you think the authorities will be covering the airports?" He shrugged. "Why do they always send me the stupid ones?" He looked at Riyad. "Do you have enough money for the trip to Texas?"

Riyad lowered his eyes. "Yes, I have enough."

He followed the men out of the building. Ammar scanned the area and then returned to the park to meet his friend Abu Dawud.

Sean Cleary saw the package in the hands of Asfour Riyad and noted the two men went in a different direction from the man who was in the bar. He made a mental note of the address; then went to pick up his wife.

* * *

Washington, D.C.
May 15

Laura Madison fell asleep, curled up in Peter Aziz's arms. His eyes caressed the upturned nose and petal soft lips. He shifted his position slightly and closed his eyes. The phone beside the bed buzzed gently and he awakened Laura. "Your phone is ringing."

She opened one eye. "Let it ring." She closed her eyes again.

"No, darling, I'm afraid you'll have to answer…It could be for me."

She sat up. "That's precisely why I don't want to answer it." She picked up the receiver and yawned. "Hello." She listened, made a face and handed the phone to Peter.

"Yes?" He listened. "Okay, Randy, when you get here call from the car phone." Peter got out of bed took a quick shower and dressed. She waited for him with a cup of fresh coffee and handed it to him. There were so many questions she wanted to ask but knew she couldn't. He sipped the hot liquid and pulled her into his arms.

"I'm sorry. I thought we would have more time. I'm leaving for New York in two hours." He saw the fear in her eyes before she turned away. It was that precise look that always turned him inside out. The phone rang once. "That's my driver." He kissed her lightly on the mouth and cupped her chin in his hand. "I'll call you when I get back."

He climbed into the front seat beside Randy Perry. "Anybody ever tell you that your timing is rotten?"

Randy grinned. "Just about everybody I know."

"Are you taking me to the Baltimore-Washington airport?"

"I'm taking us…to the Baltimore-Washington airport."

Peter saw the pleased look on Randy's face. "Well, welcome aboard, old buddy."

* * *

New York City

LaGuardia airport was bustling with activity at that hour and they walked toward the ground transportation area to get a helicopter into the city. When they approached the area, they were met by Duncan MacKenzie.

Peter smiled at him. "Well, I guess I don't have to worry about how we're going to get to the city."

They went directly to the FBI office in Manhattan. Peter pulled out the sketch he made of Lamen Abd Sakhim and handed it to Mac. This man masquerading as Lamen Abd Sakhim is really Abd al Jabbar."

Mac nodded. "I was sure the bomb was his signature. None of us imagined he was still alive. He must be part cat, the bastard seems to have nine lives." Mac looked out the window at nothing in particular. "I can't believe that two bombs were set off and nobody saw anything. Even the explosives tell us nothing, other than the signature of the composer. The explosives and the caps definitely come from the Middle East. We have six days until the big hit and fireworks. In the meantime, they're out there making plans for the next strike. We have to figure out where the next strike will be." They stood in front of a large wall map of Manhattan and surrounding Burroughs. There were two red flag pins inserted on the map, one at the Port Authority Bus Terminal and the other ten miles from Penn Station.

"Obviously," Mac said. "If it really is Abd Al Jabbar, you can be sure he'll strike again. He's having fun. But the one thing we know about him that could trap him is his obsessive-compulsive personality. He has to tie up his packages in a neat, orderly fashion. So, just knowing his personality, I would say the most likely places he'll strike would be Madison Square Garden, the Kryler Building, Grand Central Terminal, the American Post Federal Building and the Empire State Building." MacKenzie inserted yellow flag pins in the first four areas and examined the map. He picked up a black flag pin. "These targets will be practice." He inserted the black flag into the location of the Empire State Building. "This is the real target. The one selected to demoralize, to terrify."

"What makes you think that?" Randy Perry asked.

"Jabbar's weakness is circular." Mac saw the confused expression on Randy's face. "According to Jabbar, the most perfect thing in the world is a circle. It has no beginning and no end. In his mind, it's impenetrable. He pointed to the red and yellow flags. Look, the Port Authority Bus Terminal, Penn. Station, Kryler Building, the American Post Federal Building, Madison Square Garden, and Grand Central Terminal all form a circle. Inside of that circle is the Empire State Building."

The buzzer on the intercom sounded and Mac picked up the phone. "What is it, Joan?" His eyebrows came together in a frown. "Send him in."

The door opened and a tall man with thinning blond hair limped to the desk.

"Peter Aziz, Randy Perry, meet Jim O'Brien." The men shook hands.

O'Brien opened the folder he carried and put it on the desk. Inside was a photograph of a dead body that was found floating in the East River. Mac looked at the photo and waited for an explanation.

O'Brien apologized to the newcomers. "Ordinarily we don't get involved with this sort of thing. However, this particular victim might have a connection with the bombings. I got a call from the medical examiner and he asked me to come over because they fished this man out of the East River. He was shot three times. Ballistics identified the shells as 9 mm and sent them to our lab. We identified the weapon as a Marakov PM. Of course it could be coincidental that a favorite weapon of Middle East terrorists was used to murder a cab driver in New York." He shrugged. "It wasn't something we could just pass over in light of the two bombings. The peculiar part is that this guy's cab is still missing. His wife reported him missing when he didn't come home after he completed his shift a week ago. You know how the police treat missing persons, particularly men that suddenly disappear. The first conclusion is that he skipped out on his wife and kids and ran off with a younger woman. When his body was discovered, his wife came down and made a positive ID. She said he didn't have an enemy in the world. Obviously she was wrong."

CHAPTER 10

Moose Morrison, alias Kaliq Fatin, carried out his assignment and was walking toward the revolving door when he heard a familiar voice. "Hey, Moose."

A short stocky man was hurrying toward him. He thought, *Damn. Alan Chambers, what the hell does he want?* He looked at his watch impatiently.

"Hey, Alan. What are you doing here; I thought you were working at the zoo."

"Yeah, I am, Gladys works here. She left home this morning without her glasses so I dropped them off to her. What are you doing here?"

"Delivering office supplies, stationery, that sort of thing. Look, I'll see you around. I have nine other stops to make before noon. Take care."

Both men left through the revolving doors.

* * *

Manhattan
F.B.I. Building

Duncan MacKenzie picked up the phone on the first ring and

glanced up at the clock. It was ten-thirty-eight. He held up his hand, requesting the three men to wait. Mac hung up the phone, and cleared his throat.

"There's been an explosion at the Kryler Building. Jim, cover from this end. Peter and Randy come with me."

As they were passing through the secretary's office, she called to him.

"Mr. MacKenzie, there's been an explosion."

"I know, Joan, we're on our way to the Kryler Building."

"No, sir. Another explosion. This one's at The American Post Federal Building."

The men stared at the phone she held in her hand.

"Jim, get Ellis and Lowery over to the Federal Building." He turned back to the CIA men. "Welcome to New York's Desert Storm."

* * *

Washington, D.C.
May 16

Atsu Jabari, alias Bengal, stood in front of the wall of the Vietnam War Veterans Memorial, reading the names and occasionally touching the smooth wall. He watched as the three Arab terrorists and Omar Tarafah, whose real name was Willie Jones, followed suit. Willie Jones placed a metal vase with six long stem roses in front of the Memorial. Bengal nodded and thought, *A clever touch, I should have thought of it myself. But then, he's an American and I'm an Egyptian. My people didn't fight in Vietnam. But if he genuinely feels empathy for the veterans of that war, why the hell is he getting involved with these terrorists? It's impossible to figure some people.* He walked away from the wall and the others joined him. They talked in subdued tones.

"Everything is set for Friday night. I'll be making the explosive charges the day before and the timing mechanism will be set for 9:30. Together, we'll go to the Lincoln Memorial and I'll indicate to you where the charges will be set. Tonight we'll meet at my motel, the Paradise, and we'll go over everything, step by step, until you feel comfortable with the project."

Five CIA agents were posing as tourists, taking pictures of the wall and of the five men meeting to discuss the intended sabotage. Each agent was assigned to follow one of the terrorists. The agent taking the pictures finished the roll of film and removed it from the camera, putting in a new roll of film. He put the exposed film in his jacket pocket; it was skillfully removed by another agent.

* * *

Templeton Osbourne opened the door. A courier held out a large manila envelope and a pad for his signature. He signed for the envelope and handed the courier a dollar. He studied the envelope for a moment, noting that it was for Mike Redmond. He walked out to the patio where they were having breakfast and handed the envelope to Mike.

Without looking up, Mike tore open the flap and pulled out the contents. He looked at Glenn without raising his head and handed her the pictures. She scanned the photographs of Bengal and four other men, which in and of themselves were meant to identify the four men assigned to assist Bengal at the time of the explosion. The real focus was to point out two men in the background.

The photo had been enlarged to concentrate on these men, Paul Qadir and Karim Russal. It was obvious that the tall, thin, bearded man with the evil eyes who orchestrated the plot was being his usual suspicious, stealthy, cunning self. Since it was impossible for him to trust anyone, his checks and counterchecks were neatly in place.

Mike picked up the coffee pot and refilled their cups. "I would have bet my life that it wasn't Karim. This is going to devastate Gabriella."

Templeton hurried through the patio entrance carrying a small radio. He turned up the volume. The announcer said, "Casualties could be in the hundreds." Mike hurried into the library and switched on the television. Glenn and Templeton followed. The Kryler Building loomed like an uncompromising specter of doom. Fire rescue and policemen moved quickly in and out of what had once been the entrance but was now a large gaping hole spewing smoke. Emergency medical technicians carried stretchers with victims. The area above the tenth floor showed billowing smoke and large areas that had once been offices. The same scene was repeated outside the American Post Federal Building.

Medical teams from local hospitals had set up triage areas and were assessing injuries to establish priorities for treatment. Ambulances were loaded as quickly as they arrived on the scene. The somber voice of the commentator droned on. "The bombs are thought to be the work of terrorists but this has not been confirmed by the FBI."

The phone rang and Templeton answered, "It's for you, Miss Glenn."

"This is Glenn Alexander." She listened. "Yes, sir, I'll put him on an extension phone." She motioned to Mike to pick up the other phone at the opposite side of the room. To say that Clifford Ardell was upset would have been a gross understatement.

"That won't be necessary, Cliff, I've had a tail on Karim Russal and Paul Qadir. After our meeting with Bengal we alerted the bomb squad and gave them all the information. We're covered, at least as far as the Lincoln Memorial is concerned. I don't think any other attractions have been targeted in the Washington area. They want all the attention to be focused on New York, so that when the big hit comes, no one will suspect the prime target is in Washington. The man in the photograph standing next to Bengal is an American, named Willie Jones. We've had him under surveillance for quite a while. We knew about his fascination with terrorist groups for at least the past year. We just couldn't pin anything on him, until now. Have you heard anything from Peter? Keep us posted." He was about to hang up when Ardell dropped a bomb of his own. "Come back on that one, Cliff?" Mike's brow creased into a frown. "Damn it, that's all we need. Okay, we'll get right on it."

He stared at Glenn across the room. "Do you believe this guy? People on three continents are trying to save his ass, but does he give a shit? Where the hell was our Mr. Breckenridge the day they gave out brains?"

"He thought they said trains, and he missed his. What's wrong?" Glenn asked.

"Damn." He swung at an imaginary figure. He promised to tell us when he was going someplace that wasn't on his schedule. Now, there he is, out in the open, playing golf, for chrissake. Come on, let's go play golf. It's a good thing Cliff put two extra undercover men on him. He may be our President but he's got about as much sense as an idiot. What the hell happens to these guys when they get to the White House? The crazy Arabs damn near succeeded in blowing him away last year. What the hell makes him think they won't keep trying? I mean no disrespect but he's acting like a jackass."

"No he's not, Mike. He's showing his enemies he's not afraid of them or their terrorist tactics. He's no coward and he's no fool either. He's talking to them in the only language they understand and respect. He's not afraid. He'll go nose-to-nose and toe-to-toe with them. He's going to be in full view if it kills him."

"Bullshit. He's going to be in full view if it kills…us."

* * *

New York City

Duncan MacKenzie stood at the counter in the FBI laboratory and picked up a sealed plastic bag that contained bits of metal. "Not much to go on, is it?"

Peter Aziz was reading the laboratory analysis. "Apparently, there was enough of the blasting cap left to identify that it came from Palestine and the technique has all the earmarks of Abd al Jabbar. Now all we have to do is find him."

The door opened and a petite secretary with a turned-up nose stood there and smiled at Peter. She reminded him of Laura Madison and he felt an ache somewhere in the vicinity of his left rib cage. "Mr. MacKenzie, there's a call for you. You can take it on line three."

"Who is it Ginny?" he asked.

"He said his name is Alan Chambers, something to do with the bombing of the Kryler Building."

Mac hurried to the phone and picked it up.

"This is Duncan MacKenzie."

"Yes…eh, my name is Alan Chambers. I…ah…I'm not sure but I think I know who put the bomb in the Kryler Building." It was apparent that the caller was nervous. "Eh, I can't be a hundred percent sure…It's just a suspicion. Eh…look, maybe I should just forget it."

"No, wait! Look, Mr. Chambers, a lot of people were killed today and a lot of people were killed in two other explosions three days ago. I don't care how far fetched you think your hunch is, it could throw some light on the terrorists who are holding this city hostage. Where are you now, Mr. Chambers?"

"Ah…I'm at home. But…but I don't want you to come here. If I'm wrong, I don't want a lot of people calling me a whistle blower. I'll," he hesitated, "come to your office. I have to be at work by four o'clock so I'll be at your office at one-thirty. You gotta promise you'll let me go so that I'll be at work on time. I got a wife and four kids. My wife works at the Kryler Building. She could have been killed today but by the grace of God she's alive. So I feel like I got an obligation to say thanks for her life. But if I'm wrong, I don't want to crucify an innocent man."

"I understand, Mr. Chambers. No one will be arrested until we're certain we've got the right men and your name will be kept out of it for now."

"Well…okay. I…I'll see you later, Mr. MacKenzie."

Mac looked up when the door opened and a technician said, "We got the number. He was calling from the Bronx."

"Good. If Mr. Chambers doesn't show up this afternoon, we'll pay him a visit."

At one-twenty-five the door to MacKenzie's office opened and Joan announced that Mr. Chambers was in the outer office.

"Show him in please, Joan." Mac walked around his desk and extended his hand to the man. "Thank you for coming, Mr. Chambers."

"Hello, Mr. MacKenzie. I don't know how good my information is but I felt I had to do something. Gladys, that's my wife, agrees." He looked around the office. He was uncomfortable. He kept pulling at the knot of his tie. "Gladys left her glasses at home this morning and called me to bring them to her before I left for the Bronx Zoo. That's where I work, I feed the animals." He took out a handkerchief and wiped his sweaty palms. "I was leaving the Kryler Building when I saw this guy I grew up with. He was going out the door so I yells, 'Hey, Moose, wait up.' You know, I figured we could talk for a few minutes." Alan Chambers kept licking his lips.

"Would you like a cup of coffee, Mr. Chambers?"

"Thanks. I take it black."

MacKenzie prodded, "Before today, when was the last time you saw your friend Moose?"

"About a year ago. I heard he joined some far out group but I didn't think nothin' about it at the time." He took a sip of coffee and looked down at the cup in his hand.

Mac sat on the edge of the desk. "What was he doing at the Kryler Building, did he say?"

"He said he was delivering supplies. You know, typing paper, stuff like that. He looked edgy…you know, like he couldn't wait to get out of there. He didn't tell me to say hi to Gladys for him. He always said hi to Gladys. We was like the three musketeers when we was kids." Alan Chambers frowned. "He said he couldn't talk to me because he was late…he had other deliveries. When I left, I saw him hop into a van. I couldn't see through the tinted window but when he opened the door, there was another guy inside. I guess he was the driver."

"Could you describe the other man, Mr. Chambers?"

"Well, to tell the truth, I didn't pay much attention. He was dark like a Mexican or an Arab. It didn't bother me until I got home when I heard about the explosion on the radio. I called Gladys at the office but couldn't reach her. I tried to get back to the building but there were cops and paramedics and firemen all over the place and they wouldn't let me go in. They wouldn't let me go in, even after I told them my wife worked there." His hand shook when he put the empty cup on the desk. "I just wanted to see if she was okay. That's the only reason I went back. I guess they did what they had to do."

Alan Chambers began pulling on his tie again. "So I went back home and waited for Gladys to call me. I'm tellin' you, Mr. MacKenzie, I thought I would go nuts. When she finally got through on her cell phone and I told her about seein' Moose. Gladys and me, we talked about whether or not I should call you. We agreed I had to tell you what I know." He looked nervously around the room again, seeing his reflection in the two-way mirror. "It was me, Mr. MacKenzie; I was the one who wasn't sure I should make the call. Moose and Gladys and me went to school together. When Gladys and me got married, Moose was our best man. We don't see much of Moose no more. I can't believe he would do something like that. Maybe he changed jobs and really was making a delivery to the Kryler Building. You know what I mean?"

"Yes, I know what you mean. We're not going to go over there and arrest him without sufficient cause. We need to have a lot more than that to go on. We'll see if we have anything on him in our files and do a background check. If he's involved, Mr. Chambers, you will have done a great service to your city and your country." He waited until his last remark registered.

Mac said, "You called him Moose. What's his real name?"

"Eddie. Eddie Morrison. He got the nickname Moose when we was kids."

"Do you know where he lives?"

Alan Chambers looked uncomfortable again. "He lives in the Bronx, in the Mott Haven district, 142nd Street near Willis Avenue. You promised you wouldn't tell him I blew the whistle."

"We'll keep your name out of it. By any chance, did you notice the color of the van?"

"Yeah. It was light tan."

"Were there any markings on it? You know, like the name of the stationery store on the side or on the door?"

Alan thought for a minute and shook his head. "No. The paint was rough looking, like it had been repainted. Not a professional job, not done with a spray gun, kinda loused up, like it was done with a brush. You know, there were brush marks all over the van."

Mac stood up. "We're grateful that you took the time to come here."

Chambers stood up and said, "I hope I did the right thing."

The door closed behind him. Peter Aziz emerged from the anteroom behind the two-way mirror.

"What do you think, Mac?"

"I think he was scared. Scared and concerned that maybe he was fingering the wrong man." He pulled the button down on the intercom. "Jim, see if we have anything on Edward or Eddie Morrison, also known as Moose. He lives in the Mott Haven district of the Bronx. Check the motor vehicle bureau to see how many vans were stolen within the past month.

* * *

Washington, D.C.

Mike went to the second floor of the clubhouse and looked out at the golf course. "Where the hell are the Secret Service men?"

Glenn stood next to him. "Probably where they're supposed to be…with Mr. Breckenridge. Relax. Do you know the man walking toward us?"

"Come on." He took the stairs two steps at a time. He breathed a sigh of relief. "That's Darby. He has been with Mr. Breckenridge since he took office. The men shook hands and Mike introduced Glenn.

"Who's out there, Darby?"

"The Pres and his wife, and Senator and Mrs. Cameron are in the first foursome. Mr. and Mrs. Russal, Anita Gregory and Paul Qadir make up the second foursome. After they teed off the manager closed off the course." He didn't miss the look that passed between Mike and Glenn.

"What do you know that I don't know?"

Mike said, "Karim Russal and Paul Qadir are under suspicion. We've had our men following them."

"I thought I saw two men in the rough," Darby said, "dodging between the trees. Do you have two other men at the other end of the course?"

"The Bossman requested extras. What the hell precipitated this surprise golf game?"

"I think Mr. Breckenridge just got restless. He was never happy about having bodyguards. When the call came in from the senator, he said yes. I'm sure he never considered the possible consequences of his decision. He doesn't like being hemmed in by a threat of assassination."

"Where do the Russals fit into the picture?"

"I'm not sure, Mike. I know nothing was said about them in the telephone conversation. Coincidence?"

The first foursome came into view and Mike put on his sunglasses. "I don't think so. Mr. and Mrs. Russal plan every move they make down to the last detail. I won't believe this was a coincidence. Where was the golf pro when you got here?"

"In the Pro Shop. He gushed over the Breckenridges like most people who meet the President."

Mike's attention was diverted by the approach of another man. He saw Darby reach behind him. "It's okay, Darby, it's Pat McMurtry from National Security Agency."

"Hello, Mike…Glenn." He sized up Darby and looked at Mike for reassurance.

"Pat, this is Darby. He's with Secret Service."

Pat nodded in Darby's direction. "That information you wanted on George Davet? His real name is Griad Basq. He has been in the States for three years and was, as far as we know, an active member of the fat, bald headed man's organization. Do you want him picked up?"

"No. I have a tail on him. It's the senator I'm concerned about. He lets his wife, Blanche, call the shots. She can be dangerous. She'll push the senator until he becomes what she wants. I'm curious as to how she got to know the Russals."

The second foursome, with the Russals came into view. "Glenn and I will be in the cocktail lounge when they finish this hole. Pat, Darby, thanks."

Glenn leaned close to Mike and whispered, "How could you possibly have known about George Davet? He doesn't even have an accent."

"He probably got his schooling in this country then went back to Iraq when his student visa expired. They hate the U.S. but they love the education their men get over here."

They stood as the Breckenridges entered the cocktail lounge. Secret Service men were all around the room. When he saw Glenn, Alden Breckenridge smiled and came to their table.

"Glenn, you must be doing something right, you look radiant." His eyes studied the man at her side. "I've seen you before, haven't I?"

"Yes, sir. Mike Redmond, CIA."

"Of course." He smiled and the devil seemed to dance in his eyes.

"Glenn, I thought you chose your friends more carefully." He laughed, shook hands with Mike and put an arm around Glenn. "Join us for lunch."

Marcia Breckenridge embraced Glenn and smiled her approval of Mike Redmond. When the other foursome came into the dining room, they were ushered into the private dining room, reserved for Washington notables. Marcia Breckenridge put her arm through Glenn's. "Did Alden tell you we were with Clayton at your place in the Adirondacks?"

"No. As a matter of fact, I was talking to Dad Thursday. He never mentioned it."

"We didn't get there until Friday and we stayed until last night then came on to Washington. We'll be here until Saturday. Alden is addressing the midshipmen at Annapolis, in honor of Armed Forces Day. Then we're going up to Maine for a few weeks, why don't you and Mike join us for a weekend?"

"That's sweet of you, Marcia, but I'm a working woman. We'll try. If I can coordinate my schedule with Mike's, either way, I'll call you."

Gabriella and Karim entered the private dining room. Mike looked for Paul and Anita, but they weren't with the Russals. Gabriella's musical laughter interrupted the conversation. "Glenn, darling. I didn't know you had a time slot to tee off."

"We didn't. We were on our way back from Baltimore and decided to stop off for a cocktail and some lunch. What a happy surprise to see you and Karim."

Gabriella smiled at Marcia Breckenridge, the only reason I'm so delighted to see Glenn is that I get the chance to hug this beautiful hunk of a man. Mike, are you sure you don't want to switch partners?"

Marcia Breckenridge looked around and realized Paul and Anita were not with them.

"Gabriella, what happened to your friends?"

"Anita's agent is meeting them for lunch at La Bergerie."

"Perhaps we'll have the pleasure of their company at another time."

Blanche Cameron gushed. "You simply must try the Canard a l'Orange Cremaillere, it's so delightful and if accompanied by aubergines farcies aux champignons, is to kill for."

Mike thought, *Not a good choice of words.*

Marcia Breckenridge gave the senator's wife a tolerant smile. "Thank you, Blanche, but I couldn't possibly eat that much for lunch." To the waiter, she said, "Salade d'Endives et de Pamplemousse…with a lemon dressing, please."

George Davet, alias Griad Basq, and an athletic-looking redhead were sitting at a table close to where the president's party sat. His back was to their table. The redhead was an animated talker. Glenn got the impression George wasn't listening to her, instead he seemed to be more interested in the conversation at the Breckenridge table, although occasionally he would smile at his companion and nod appreciatively. Blanche Cameron noticed the couple and commented to no one in particular, "I think it's a very poor policy to allow the help to eat in the dining room with patrons of the club, don't you?"

Gabriella looked in the direction of the other table. "Darling, a golf pro is hardly considered as the club's help. He's a professional."

"But, Gabriella, you pay for his services, therefore, he is part of the help of the country club."

"Blanche, you pay for the professional services of a physician, or an attorney. Should they be barred from the club?"

Before the word exchange could continue, Marcia Breckenridge entered the conversation. "She's absolutely right, Blanche. If they started barring professionals, soon it would extend to senators and their wives."

Blanche took the rebuff well, especially since she had no choice. Glenn noticed the expression on Blanche's face; it was one of raw hate. She tolerated the First Lady because socially, she was very much in demand. She breathed a resigned sigh and focused her attention on the duck l'orange the waiter put in front of her.

Mr. Breckenridge spoke to Mike "What do you think about the terrorist attacks in New York? Is any progress being made in finding the perpetrators?"

Mike saw George Davet lean back in his chair, cocktail in hand, smiling at the redhead across from him.

Mike looked around at the others at the table and thought, *Damn, what's he trying to do? Blow my cover? How the hell do I handle this situation?* He said, "Like any other citizen, Mr. President, I resent my country being held hostage by a few madmen. I would venture a guess that the Immigration people have a profile on all aliens and it's only a matter of time until the criminals are brought to justice."

Mr. Breckenridge realized his blunder. "I'm sure you're right. I often wonder how the ordinary citizen regards such things. I must say you seem to be very calm about it."

"That's because I'm a chemical engineer, so I leave the spy work to the counter-espionage men. Now if you have a problem regarding chemicals, I'm your man."

"Good, now what are you doing about all the chemicals they're spraying over our crops?"

Everyone at the table laughed. The tension eased and the conversation turned to less inflammatory subjects.

CHAPTER 11

New York
May 16

Sean Cleary downed his beer and asked the bartender for another. His attention was riveted on the television. The scenes from the Federal and Kryler disaster areas brought an unnatural silence to the customers of the Lion's Claw. The door opened and five men and a woman entered and sat at a table near the bar. He recognized the journalists from the *Times* and the *Journal*. They came for one of the Lion's Claw's famous corn beef sandwiches and beer. Their conversation was loud and confusing, with all of them talking at the same time. A waitress put a couple of pitchers of beer on the table, a standard order for the group. The door opened again and a thin, bearded, scar-faced man slithered onto a bar stool and ordered a brew.

Tom Finch, a political journalist, took a long swallow of his draught and said, "I can't believe that nobody saw the guys responsible for the bombings. They're not ghosts, for chrissake, they're men. You can't go anywhere in New York without being seen. So how come nobody saw anything? How come, all of a sudden, New Yorkers are like the three monkeys? Nobody sees or hears anything, and they sure as hell aren't talking about it."

Sean Cleary looked down at the other end of the bar and saw the same strange man he had seen after the first double bombing. The man was making circles on the bar with the moisture at the bottom of his glass. He didn't look as threatening as he did when Sean saw him the first time.

Sean thought, *So I was wrong about the guy. He's probably a hard working bastard like me. These reporters have the life. They expect the public to come forward and hand them the scoop of the century. What the hell are they doing in here? Why aren't they out interviewing people? Somebody had to have seen something. But they sit here, armchair quarterbacks, criticizing the FBI for not being more alert.*

Sean Cleary picked up his glass and moved to the other end of the bar and sat beside the scar-faced man. "Hey, buy you a beer?"

Abu Ammar's eyes raked over him. "No." Then as an afterthought. "Thank you."

Sean's pale blue eyes met the icy, steel gray eyes of Ammar. He felt a shiver course through his blood. *Boy,* he thought, *wouldn't it be a kick in the head if this guy is one of the terrorists?* He looked at Ammar's hand when he lifted the glass to his lips, and marveled at the soft, manicured condition of his hands. *Shit, those aren't the hands of a laborer.* While Sean was thinking about pursuing a dialog with the man, Ammar drained his glass, dropped some money on the bar and left. Sean watched as the man walked in the opposite direction from the route he had taken the night Sean followed him.

Sean turned his attention to the somber face of the TV news anchorman. His expression gave credence to the number of deaths and injured in the blasts. He was saying, "No terrorist group is claiming credit for the bombings. Authorities are saying that there is a strong suspicion that the bombings could be linked to terrorist groups in the Middle East."

Sean Cleary had an uncomfortable feeling, one of having been violated. He looked out the window of the bar, to the park across the street. It had been a dark night when he first saw the scar-faced man. He had not gotten a good look at the men who followed the man. When he thought back on that night, it was peculiar that the men didn't stop to talk at all. He couldn't be sure but they didn't even walk side by side. They walked behind him in a line, like the kid's game of follow the leader. When he picked up Ellen, he told her everything that happened. She told him to stop playing detective and forget it. He could still hear her words "Don't get involved."

* * *

Manhattan FBI Office

Duncan MacKenzie passed the file to Peter Aziz. Peter stared at the face in the photo. The olive skinned, pox scarred face was topped by unruly black curly hair. The clear blue eyes had a faraway look. Under the photo was the name Edward (Moose) Morrison, alias Kaliq Fatin, age 44. Home address 142nd Street, Bronx, New York, formerly a member of the Communist People's Party. Currently involved with a branch of the Arab Nationalist Movement. Bases of operation are Lebanon, Kuwait and South Yemen. Ideology is Palestinian Nationalist, Marxist. Although little is known about their operations, most of its members also belong to radical terrorist groups, like the Democratic Front for the Liberation of Palestine, the Lebanese Armed Military Faction and the Popular Front for the Liberation of Palestine. Most terrorist organizations have the same ideology, with a firm Marxist base.

MacKenzie said, "He spent six months in the Middle East, in 1989. He has an arrest record of aggravated assault. He spent time in jail on four different occasions. He was married to Eileen Crosby in 1978, and divorced in 1984. Extreme cruelty was the reason given for the grounds of divorce. There were no children. Eileen Crosby Morrison resumed her maiden name after the divorce and in 1990 married Mario Triani, a cop with the NYPD."

Peter looked up. "Mmmm, impressive. He's a third rate hoodlum, who sees himself as a hero. According to his arrest record, he couldn't have had anything to do with the World Trade Center catastrophe. He didn't get out of jail until September 14, 2001. When he was picked up at his apartment the last time, the police found an AK 47 with a folding stock in his living room. He works for the Bronx Tool and Die Manufacturing Company. His hours are three to eleven. It doesn't say anything about working for a stationery company. That's what he told Alan Chambers, isn't it?"

"That's what Chambers said. I guess we should go over to talk to Mr. Morrison, or Mr. Fatin, or whatever he's calling himself these days."

The street was alive with activity. Some boys were playing stickball, there were street vendors with carts and a man with a contraption strapped on, which consisted of a base drum, cymbals, a horn mounted on top of the base drum, a kazoo and extra cymbals strapped to the inside of each knee. He made enough noise for a full band.

All of the apartment buildings looked alike. The buildings on one side of the street were six stories high, while the ones on the opposite side were eight stories high.

* * *

Mac checked the address and they mounted the brownstone steps. At the top of the landing, two boys were playing in the vestibule. One sat with his back against the open door. Peter scanned the mailboxes and found the name E. Morrison. He was on the top floor, apartment 604. The elevator creaked and labored its way past the other floors and the doors scraped and stuttered as they gradually opened. Mac stopped at E. Morrison's apartment and knocked. They heard the sound of a chair scraping on a bare wood floor and a voice called out, "Yeah—who is it?"

"FBI, Mr. Morrison, we'd like to talk to you."

Silence. Then, "Wait a minute till I put some clothes on."

Peter and Mac drew their guns and stood on either side of the door and waited. Then they heard the sound of glass breaking and a heavy thud.

"Mr. Morrison?" There was no answer.

Mac pushed Peter out of the way and fired at the dead bolt. The door opened slowly, silently. Sun flooded the room and the glare made it difficult to see.

Peter saw him first. A lifeless figure sprawled on the floor in front of the window leading to the fire escape. The figure lay face up, with a perfect hole between his eyes but the back of his head was missing. There was an assault rifle on the table in the room but it hadn't been fired. Mac and Peter stood on either side of the window, looking at the apartment building across the street. There was no one in sight.

Peter felt for the carotid pulse and shook his head. "He's gone. Poor bastard never knew what hit him."

Mac was on the phone. "Get forensics over here," he said in a soft voice. He gave them the address.

"Let's check out that building across the street," Mac said. They hurried to the apartment building across the street. On the sidewalk Mac stopped and looked at the range. The front door was propped open with a brick wedged between the door and the jamb. Mac's voice was almost a whisper. "The roof first." The elevator was out of order and they climbed the stairs to the top of the eight-story building. The roof was deserted. At the parapet they found a single shell casing. Peter scooped it into a plastic bag. Below, the one-man band continued with his cacophonous playing.

Mac looked at the casing. "What do you want to bet this was fired from the same gun that killed that cab driver…eh, what's his name?"

"Briggs. Raymond Briggs. I think you're right. Jabbar has been a busy man. How could he have found out we were on to the Morrison guy?"

"He probably didn't know. I think this was his way of tidying up the loose ends. He knew all along Morrison's pay would be a bullet between the eyes. If there are any other U.S. based terrorists involved in these explosions, we'll probably find them dead too. You can't question a dead man."

Peter Aziz shook his head. When they reached the street, the forensics van was in front of the building where Moose Morrison was sprawled on the floor in apartment 604. They walked into the apartment, now crowded with technicians, laboratory personnel and the medical examiner. They stood aside until Doctor Levick finished his cursory examination and motioned for the technicians to remove the body.

"What do you think, Doc?"

Doctor Levick looked over top of his granny glasses and smiled at Mac. "Death never takes a holiday, does it? I would say he was shot from the roof across the street. The bullet came through the window, entered just above the bridge of his nose and took a downward path, thus blowing out the back of the head below the crown, closer to the base of the skull, a perfect shot. Death was instantaneous. He was shot here at the window. There's a spatter of blood on the sill and the floor. The force of the bullet propelled him back about five feet. I'm afraid, that's all I can give you for now. I'll be doing the post in the morning." He took off his rubber gloves, bagged them and dropped them under the sheet covering the body of Moose Morrison. "Incidentally, Mac, thank you for arranging this death at a convenient hour. Usually the calls I get from your department come at three a.m."

"That's okay, Doc, I'll try to arrange future deaths to coincide with your normal working schedule."

The doctor patted Mac's shoulder as he passed him on the way out. "You're a good man, MacKenzie."

Outside, the one-man band had disappeared, the street vendors were gone and the boys who had been playing stickball were busy looking at the body being loaded into the ambulance.

Mac looked around. Sitting on the steps of the building next door was a well-dressed young man, about sixteen years old. Peter and Mac walked over to him. "Hi," Peter said. "We'd like to ask you a few questions. A pair of trim legs appeared on the step above where the boy was sitting. Mac looked up into soft blue eyes. He took out his leather folder with his identification and flashed it at her. "We're with the FBI."

"I don't give a damn if you're with God; you're not going to question and upset my brother."

"It's not our intention to upset him. All we want to know is whether or not he saw anyone enter the building across the street with a large package, or perhaps an attaché case."

"He wouldn't know an attaché case if he fell over one. He's severely retarded. I doubt if he knows what you're talking about." She scrutinized the two men. "What's this all about, anyway?"

Mac decided it was better to level with her. "We're not sure but we think the murdered man had something to do with the bombings at the Kryler Building and the American Post Federal Building."

"Who was he?"

"His name was Eddie Morrison."

She gasped and her face registered the confusion she was feeling. "Moose?"

"Did you know him?"

"Well…sure. Everybody knew him. He was odd but I don't think he was dangerous."

The boy sitting on the step looked up at his sister and began hyperventilating. She sat next to him and put her arms around him. "It's okay, Matthew, it's okay." She stroked his hair and spoke reassuringly until his breathing returned to normal. She made him stand up. "Go inside, honey, I'll be right in."

He held on to her arm and shook his head, pulling his hair with his other hand. She held him by the shoulders and forced him to look into her eyes. She smiled. "Would you like to have an ice cream bar?"

At first he shook his head but she kept repeating the words ice cream bar, until she interrupted the train of thought that was frightening him. "Ice cream bar?" Finally, he smiled.

"Go get one out of the freezer." She held up one finger. He matched her one finger with his. "Yes, Matthew, one."

The boy turned and went into the apartment building. She turned to face the two men. "He was hit in the head with a stray bullet when he was five years old. When he came out of the hospital, he was the way you see him now. He got upset because Moose was his friend. He's not sure what happened to him but he knows it's not good. Good things never happen around here."

Mac was impressed by her protectiveness. "Does he talk at all?"

"A word here and there but nothing that makes any sense. He can't help you and all you can do for him is upset him. Please leave us alone. He can't take any more trauma in his life."

Mac studied the pretty face. "Do you work?"

"Yes. I work for the telephone company."

"What happens to Matthew while you're at work?"

"He's in a special school for the mentally handicapped. I pick him up after work and drop him off in the morning."

"How come you're home today?"

"I took a personal holiday because I have to take Matthew for special testing today over at University Hospital. Thanks to you, we're going to be late."

"Get Matthew. We'll drop you off on our way uptown."

She blinked then raised her eyebrows. "Really?"

"Honest injun."

"We'll be right back." She raced into the building to collect Matthew and her purse. When she returned with Matthew, she had applied a light coat of lipstick to her sensuous mouth.

Mac held the car door open and she looked down as she passed him. He got behind the wheel and adjusted the rearview mirror so that he could observe her in the back seat. He said, "What's your name?"

"Sam Boyer."

"Sam?"

"Short for Samantha."

"Are you married?"

"No."

"How old are you, Sam?"

"Twenty-six. Are all these questions necessary?"

Mac blushed. "Not really. I just feel a need to occupy space with words or sounds."

Her eyes met his in the rearview mirror. "Are you that insecure?"

Peter almost choked on his silent laughter.

Mac looked straight ahead at the traffic. "Okay, for the record then, what do you do at the telephone company?"

"I'm a programmer in data processing."

Mac pulled up outside the front entrance to the University Hospital, got out and walked around to the other side and opened the door. Matthew got out first, then Samantha.

Mac said, "Talk to your brother. See if he saw anyone on the roof of the apartment building across the street from you. Obviously, you can communicate with him quite well. I'll get back to you in a day or so."

She nodded and followed Matthew into the hospital.

Mac slid behind the wheel of the car.

"Nice legs." Peter said as his eyes followed Samantha's progress toward the entrance.

"Nice ass." Mac smiled. "Tits aren't bad either."

* * * *

The barricades and hardhats were stenciled, *Property City of New York.* The manhole cover had been removed. A shadow fell across the sewer opening. Khalil Najjar didn't have to lift his head. He knew the long, fateful shadow belonged to his nemesis.

Ammar asked, "What have you been doing?"

Abdul Shakir handed Ammar a hardhat, and answered, "What many municipal workers do…manage to look busy while doing nothing."

Ammar stared into Shakir's face until the other man looked away. He said, "Perhaps if you were busy instead of trying to look busy, you wouldn't have so much time to make bad jokes." He turned and disappeared into the twisting sewer system. He made his way to the target area and sketched a diagram of the tunnel openings. Satisfied that he found the inlet to the Empire State Building, he pried the grate open that led into the sub-basement crypt of machinery and aluminum duct work, pulled himself up into the air conditioning system and slithered along on his belly, pulling himself up as the ducts rose in a gradual incline. Carefully, he passed screened, louvered, openings into the office complexes, and established the location where he would tie in the explosive charges that would bring the proud landmark down in a twisted heap of concrete and steel.

He thought the wives of many men would be lost, just as his own wife was lost to him. *Let these American infidels feel the agony I suffered. Let them see what it was like to be alone, completely alone.*

Ammar studied the structure for a long time, estimating how large a charge would be necessary for the devastation he planned.

When the plan crystallized in his mind, he knew Khalil Najjar's fate. The excitement he felt at coming to grips with the two driving forces in his life was as satisfying as sexual release. His mission would be accomplished and the death of his old army comrade would be at his hands. The picture took form in his mind. Najjar would go into the system ahead of him. Ammar would pass the charges forward and Najjar would secure them at given points. When the last of the explosives was ready to be placed, he would carefully remove a hypodermic syringe which he would tape to the last charge. After it was secured, he would inject the unrepentant viper with curare. It would not be the slow death he had planned but he could watch the agony of the traitor.

The paralysis that would start with his eyelids and facial muscles would terrify him. The fear on his face when he could no longer swallow or lift his head would panic him, then the final insult when his lungs refused him air. Then he would know Jabbar's revenge was complete. "Yes," he said aloud, "that's the way it must be. I'll leave his body in the air conditioning duct. Once the explosion takes place, there will be nothing left to identify."

Flushed and exhilarated, he nodded his approval of the plan. "When this is over," he said, "I can allow the healing of my soul to begin."

He knew that his ability and reputation for instilling mass fear equaled that of Osama Bin Laden. He was a force to be reckoned with and when he returned home, he would be a hero.

He made his way back through the sewer to Madison Avenue and stood in front of his intended victim. He put one hand on Najjar's shoulder. "You'll be the one to assist me. There'll be more explosives than one man can carry and it has to be done in one trip. I found the perfect spot."

"I'm honored. Would you allow me to assist you in assembling the bomb? I've never done it before. When the explosion happens, I would be proud, knowing I had a hand in it."

Ammar studied the man who had been his friend until that fateful day. He thought, *It's a strange justice that allows Najjar to help build the bomb that will destroy his miserable body*. He smiled to himself. *In the end, Najjar will see the beauty in such a plan, because he's a true Arab.* Aloud, he said, "Yes, Khalil, it'll be good for you to learn something about explosives. You never know when you'll need to make one of your own."

He lifted himself out of the manhole and looked around. No one had disturbed the "MEN AT WORK" signs or the sawhorses that blocked the work area.

Ammar said, "The garage we're using to store the van is the ideal place to assemble the toy...for our little game. We'll assemble it Wednesday morning." He spoke to Najjar. "Be at the garage at ten o'clock. We'll put it in place on Thursday afternoon and watch as New York falls to its knees on Friday." He turned to the others. "Shakir, assemble the others here on Thursday morning so that Najjar and I have sufficient time to put it in place for the grand finale." He checked the street, pointed to the sawhorses and signs, and said, "We're finished here for now. Get these things back to the garage. We don't want anyone to become suspicious at this late date."

Shakir watched the retreating back of the bomb expert. The others loaded the equipment into the van, painted to look like a city work vehicle. Shakir drove the van and Khalil sat next to him staring out through the windshield, at nothing.

"Why did you volunteer to help Ammar assemble the bomb?"

Najjar studied Shakir's profile. "Why not? He selected me to help him put the bomb in place. It's a trip from which I'll not return. He'll leave me with the bomb, helpless, with no choice but to watch my life tick away. I should know what goes into making such a bomb, especially if I have to reset the timing mechanism. It'll give me time to escape and at the same time, it will be the supreme insult to Ammar if the bomb doesn't go off as scheduled."

Shakir looked at his friend and nodded his approval. "I'm glad to see you're fighting back."

"At the last minute, I may revert back to the coward I have always been but for now, it seems a little brighter than it has been."

Abdul smiled. "You're right. The only way to get to Ammar is to destroy his pride."

To himself, Khalil said, *I can't believe that Allah wants me to die at the hands of a madman. I don't believe that Allah wants innocent people to die. We're not at war. Rosha and Alula were killed in an air attack, during war. Such is the fate of people in time of war. But to kill women and children deliberately, is not the will of Allah. It's a sick revenge of the warped mind of Jabbar. Between now and Thursday, I'll have to come to some kind of decision. Until then, let him think I'm taking part in my own execution.* Aloud, he said, "For the first time since the assignment began, I can breathe freely, not breath that's drenched in fear.

CHAPTER 12

Washington, D.C.
May 16, 5:45 p.m.

Glenn sat on a stool in the Pro Shop examining the wedge George Davet handed her. "They did a good job on this grip. It's good and tight, almost like new."

"I'm glad you're pleased. I'm using a new service, Brown and Crosse. So far, they're reliable. They've come out with a new set of clubs. Nicely balanced. If you're interested, I'll have them in the shop next Monday."

"I'd like to see them." She looked at her watch. "I've got to make a phone call."

"Use my phone. I'll leave and give you some privacy."

"Thank you. I don't need privacy; it's just a call to my father."

Davet handed her the phone. "How is Mr. Alexander?"

"Handsome and sassy," she said as she dialed his number. "Hello? Nicholas, this is Glenn. Is Dad there?" She frowned. "No, nothing important. Just thought I'd say hi. When do you expect him? Look, tell him I'll call him tomorrow. Thanks."

In the cocktail lounge, Gabriella reached across the table and touched Mike's hand. "Hello…? Where are you?"

He came out of his reverie and smiled at her. "Just reminiscing, sorry, I didn't mean to be a bore."

"You're very sexy when you reminisce. It's like sneaking into your bedroom while you are making love." She squeezed his hand and shook her head. "What a waste, thinking about the past when the present is so inviting."

He laughed and withdrew his hand. He leaned over and in a stage whisper, said, "Lady, that's the nicest proposition I've had in the last half-hour."

Gabriella laughed with him; her red tinged full lips were a startling contrast to her white, even teeth. The dimple in her cheek gave her a coquettish look.

He said, "You're a very sensuous woman, Gabi. Karim is a lucky man."

Gabriella was pleased with his assessment.

Glenn approached the table. "Don't believe a word he says, Gabi."

Gabriella wrinkled her nose. "But I want to believe him. I enjoy thinking I'm sensuous. Anyway," she said, changing the subject. "How's Clayton?"

"He wasn't home. Nicholas said he was over at Marie Talbot's."

"Oh dear, I hope he doesn't get involved with her. She's such a leech." Gabi looked at Mike. "Have you met Clayton Alexander?"

"No. I haven't had the pleasure." He covered Glenn's hand with his. "But we're planning a trip to New York for the Memorial Day weekend." He looked around. "What happened to Karim?"

"He promised Paul he would show him how to handle the yacht. Paul is planning a very small party on the yacht. So small, in fact, that the guest list contains only one name. I think he and Anita have gotten quite serious about each other. Of course, he's no Ali Khan but then again she's no Rita Hayworth. I tell him to amuse himself but not to get involved." She winked at Glenn. "But you know men, they never listen. They're complete slaves to their libidos and I guess she's a great lay."

"GA—BI!" It was apparent Glenn was uncomfortable with the conversation.

"Don't be embarrassed, darling," Mike said, as he kissed her cheek, "I think you're a better lay than she is...not that I've tried her but I can tell from looking."

She smiled sweetly. "Well, darling, if you haven't tried her, she's probably the only one on the East Coast."

"Ouch!"

Gabi's laughter floated through the small cocktail lounge. "I have to go too. I'm getting a little thick through the hips, so I had better start jogging again." She picked up her purse. "Are you going to the fundraiser at the Algonquin Club on Friday?"

"Yes," Glenn answered. "You didn't tell me you were going too."

"Darling, I'm a very heavy contributor to both parties. I get invited to every function and I mean every function. I'm one of the few people who can cross party lines with impunity. Money does such marvelous things...especially in Washington."

Glenn said, "From what I hear, there's going to be a large turnout. How are they going to fit everybody in the club?"

"It's going to be outside on the back terrace, Chinese lanterns, soft music, the works. I'm on the planning committee. Hopefully, the weather will cooperate but if it doesn't, we'll have large tents in place. I'm glad you and Mike will be there."

Mike watched her walk away. "I wonder whose idea it was to put her on the planning committee. Karim's, I'll bet."

Glenn laughed. "How could she be the modern-day Pearl Mesta, without getting herself appointed to lots of social committees? When we were in college she was always serving on some committee. She was president of our class and head of our sorority. She was a trailblazer. If you wanted something done, you asked Gabi."

Mike wasn't listening. "If we go out to the yacht basin I have a sneaky suspicion we won't find Karim or Paul."

Mike picked up the cellular phone in his car and called the CIA office. Sally Vance answered the phone.

"Hi, gorgeous. What are you doing still hanging around there? Does the Bossman handcuff you to the desk?" He smiled into the phone. "Call Brock Douglas, and have him contact me on the cell phone. Thanks, Sally."

Within minutes, the phone rang.

"Helix." He listened. "Where are you, Brock?" He chewed on his bottom lip. "Have Russal and Qadir been to the yacht basin? Okay, give me what you have." He listened, the expression on his face never changed. "If anything develops, get in touch with me right away. You have the numbers? Good." He turned the phone off and looked at Glenn. "As I thought, they never went to the basin. They spent two hours at a porno movie. No one tried to contact them while they were there. Then they went back to Karim's house in Chevy Chase. There were only three calls that came in all day. One was for Qadir, from Anita Gregory and she left a message to call her back. That call came in at two p.m. The second was from Gabriella's hairdresser confirming her appointment for Friday morning at seven-thirty. That call came in at two-forty-five. The last call was for Gabriella, from a man named Joe Dimitrius, concerning the number of tables to be placed on the terrace of the Algonquin Club on Friday. He said he had to have a definite number before the end of the day and the number of tents that would be needed because they had to be ordered from the warehouse. He left a telephone number where he could be reached. Our boys checked the number. There is no such number and that was confirmed by the telephone company. That call came in at five-ten. Gabriella called in from Washington and got her messages at five-forty-five. Since then, there has been no activity."

Mike drove off the interstate, turned the car around and entered the interstate going in the opposite direction.

"Where are we going?"

"To the Algonquin Club."

"Why?"

"I'm anxious to see the man who is going to deliver the tables for Friday's dinner."

Mike parked the car off the road behind the Algonquin Club and walked through the woods to the back of the club's property. They watched from a distance.

Glenn whispered, "Look, that's Gabi over there."

Mike nodded. "Well, she was true to her word; she's wearing a jogging outfit." The man with her had his back to them. She was talking and he was making notes on a pad held in his hand. He closed his notepad and walked to a car parked on the other side of the building. It was impossible to identify the man and by the time they got close enough, the car and driver were both gone. Still hidden by the trees, they observed Gabriella, sketching the table placement. She studied the seating from every possible angle. When she was satisfied, she put her sketches in her car and began jogging uphill, her red-gold hair bouncing on her back. Her slim hips blended into firm thighs and nicely rounded calves, making her look much taller than her five-foot-two height.

Glenn watched Mike as his eyes followed Gabi up the hill. "She is beautiful, isn't she?"

"She is that," he said. "She seems to have been schooled in what makes men happy. She must have been the top student. That's a well-disciplined body and mind, in spite of the fact that she tries to give the impression of being flighty. She has a mind like a steel trap. If she hadn't gone to college with you, I would have sworn she got her education at the police academy. She's like a fine racehorse. Every fiber of her being is alert and aware of what's happening around her."

They watched as she disappeared over the hill. Mike opened Gabriella's car door and picked up the sketches she had made. Instinct, more than anything made Mike take pictures of each of the ten sketches she had done. He replaced the sketches exactly as he found them, closed the car door and they disappeared into the protection of the trees. They watched for a half-hour until Gabriella returned, her skin glistening with perspiration and her mane of red-gold dripping. She opened the trunk of her car and toweled off before getting behind the wheel. She gunned the motor and sped away in the direction of Chevy Chase.

Glenn smiled. "She hasn't changed. She's still a whirlwind. In some ways, I envy her. I've never known anyone so completely satisfied with what and who she is. While I was trying to find myself in college, she already knew where she was going. She idolized only one person. There were no schoolgirl crushes for her. I think she was in love with him but would never talk about it. That was Tory, the boy I told you about. He was killed in an accident in Rome, some kind of explosion. I couldn't get any details. That was the only time I ever saw her depressed. She took a quick trip back to Rome and when she came back, she was changed. Oh, she still knew who she was and what she wanted but she was more pensive, more subdued…the light had gone out of her eyes. When she thought no one was watching, she buried her face in her pillow and cried. I didn't think she would ever get close to anyone again. But I guess time heals all wounds…even the deepest ones."

Mike looked in the direction of the speeding car that was quickly becoming a dot in the distance. "I wonder…"

He picked up the cellular phone and punched in some numbers. The voice at the other end answered, "Unicorn."

"Helix, here. I need some information as quickly as you can get it to me. Gabriella Cammeo Russal. All information on her ties in Rome. Her grandmother's name and where she lives. I want to know about the grandmother's hospitalizations, the diagnoses and prognoses, also all information on her brother, Salvatore Cammeo. I want to know why brother and sister no longer talk to each other. See if you can uncover any information on a former boyfriend, first name Tory. Last name is not known. He was killed in some sort of explosion in 1986 or possibly 1985. I want to know how many trips Gabriella Cammeo Russal has taken to Rome since she graduated from college in 1986. Give me her family background, social and political contacts abroad. I asked for information on her a few days ago, just to satisfy a gnawing curiosity, now it's imperative and I don't have to remind you that time is running out."

Unicorn handed a piece of paper to Sally Vance. "Get somebody on this, now." Then he spoke into the telephone. "Our man in Rome has been busy on this since you requested the information. Something should be coming in soon, but I'll light a fire under him anyway. Do you have something concrete to go on?"

"Just a gut feeling that I can't shake."

"Keep in touch." Clifford Ardell hung up the phone.

Glenn Alexander's look was incredulous. "You actually suspect Gabriella? Of what? Because she cares about her grandmother? Is she suspect because she and her brother don't get along? What do you think she did?"

"I'm not sure. Something isn't sitting right. Something is out of kilter. If she checks out all right, she'll be dropped from the list of suspects and she'll never know we investigated." He watched Glenn closely out of the corner of his eye.

"I'm sorry you're on this assignment. It must be difficult when people you love become suspects in a plot like this."

"It's all part of the job, isn't it? I think you're wrong about Gabi and I think you're wrong about Karim. Maybe Paul Qadir is involved but I don't think he has the brains to carry out an assignment like this one. I think George Davet fits into this scheme somewhere and perhaps Blanche Cameron."

"Why would you suspect Mrs. Cameron?"

"There are too many coincidences when she's around. She wants you to think her slips of the lip are unintentional blunders but her look of absolute hate when Marcia Breckenridge put her in her place in the country club dining room spoke volumes."

* * *

Gabriella parked her car in the turning circle in Chevy Chase and walked into the foyer. She crossed the marble floor, walked into the library and poured herself a cognac. The door opened and a short, dark skinned man stood there smiling at her. "Good day, misses."

Gabriella smiled back at the old man who had elected to stay with her and Karim when given the choice to stay in Arabia or go with them to the States.

"Lufti. Where is everyone? I thought Karim and Paul would be home long before now."

"Sahib Karim is in the bedroom. Mr. Paul had an engagement with Miss Gregory. Is there anything I can get for you?"

"No, thank you, Lufti, I got what I wanted." She held up the snifter. "I'm expecting a parcel to arrive any day. It's a gift for Karim. When it's delivered, will you hide it for me? Don't let Karim see it, or it will spoil his birthday surprise."

"Of course, misses."

Gabriella downed the cognac and headed for the stairs.

"Hello, my love." Karim took her into his arms. She lifted her face and his lips took possession of hers.

"This is the best part of each day, my darling, when I'm with you. I was afraid you wouldn't be home yet. Did Paul set up the boat for his tryst?"

"He changed his mind about the yacht, so instead of going to the marina, we went to a porno movie."

Her eyebrows arched in surprise. "A porno movie? You and Paul?"

He nodded. "I think it was his first porno movie."

"Darling, you're leading him astray." She reached for the zipper on his trousers. "Paul is strictly a vanilla sex man. What did he think of all the kinky sex in the movie?" She had removed his shirt and his pants were down around his ankles. That he was a man, there was no doubt. She stood back to admire his erection and saluted.

"All I can say is when we got back here; he called Anita and within minutes was on his way to her hotel." He was delightfully surprised to find that under the jogging outfit she wore nothing but her beautiful flesh.

CHAPTER 13

New York City
May 16

Peter Aziz leaned back in his chair and stretched.

"You know, this is damned frustrating. There are what, a few thousand people from the Middle East living in the metropolitan area? How many do you think are still living at the addresses shown on these files?"

MacKenzie put down the file he was reading and took a sip of cold coffee. "I have a feeling New Yorkers are getting really angry. We lost the Twin Towers and now, four bombings in as many days…it's a bit much."

"Alan Chambers came forward. Maybe there'll be others."

"Don't hold your breath," Mac said, sifting through files on Middle East immigrants.

The intercom buzzed and Mac depressed the key.

"Yes, Joan?"

"Jim O'Brien is here, he said he needs to see you."

"Send him in."

O'Brien nodded to Peter. "Mac, I think we have a lead." He didn't wait for a response. "I had men working on cabbies to see if anyone saw Raymond Briggs the day he was murdered. Today I talked with Joe Murphy. His cab was sitting behind Briggs' cab outside Figaro's Cafe around Bleeker Street and Sixth Avenue. They were standing along the curb, talking, when a man got into Briggs's cab. That was the last anyone saw of Briggs until his body washed up in the East River. When I questioned Murphy, he remembered the man who got into Briggs' cab. I showed him the sketch of Jabbar. He made a positive I.D. There's probably a good chance Jabbar is living in the Village. The cab was found at noon today across town. It was clean. No prints, no butts, nothing…except…"

"Except?"

"Hair…probably human hair. We should know something soon. Incidentally, the cab was rigged to ignite. We got our hair samples but that was all. It went up in flames twenty minutes after we got there."

Joan opened the door. "Mr. MacKenzie, there's a woman to see you."

Mac was annoyed. "Damn it, Joan, who is it?"

"She said her name is Sam. Sam Boyer?"

Mac looked stunned. "Put her in the conference room, I'll be there in a few minutes." His face was flushed. He looked questioningly at Peter. Together they walked into the conference room.

"Miss Boyer, it's nice to see you again. How's Matthew?" Mac said as his eyes appraised her.

"Hello, Mr. MacKenzie." She nodded to Peter. "Matthew is fine, thank you. I came to tell you that one of Matthew's friends was sitting with him on the stoop the day Moose was shot. He saw a man with a long scar on his face. He said the man stopped for a minute to watch John Pitt."

Mac held up his hand. "Who's John Pitt?"

"I guess you can call him a one-man band."

"Okay, I remember seeing him. I'm sorry. Please go on."

"Then the man with the scar hurried across the street and went into the building across from where Moose lived. Franny remembered that the man carried a long wooden box, like a toolbox. He said the man wasn't in there very long. When he came out, he walked across the street where John Pitt was still playing and dropped some money in the cup. That was about the time you came out of the building and went across the street."

"Did this kid notice where the man went?"

"He said he headed toward the subway at Christopher Street and Sheridan Square."

"Very observant. Who is this kid?"

"Franny Renzo. He lives in the building across the street."

"The same building where the gunman went?"

"Yes."

"Did he see the gunman go up to the roof?"

"No. He told me everything he saw. He has no idea the man was carrying a rifle in that box. He thinks Moose accidentally shot himself while he was cleaning his gun."

"How old is Franny Renzo?"

"Ten—maybe eleven."

"If we showed him a picture of the suspect, would he be able to identify him?"

"I don't know. Please don't make any problems for Franny and his family."

"I promise the Renzo family will have no problem with us. I would appreciate it if you would have Franny Renzo meet with us in your apartment. We need to have a positive identification of the man he saw going into the building. Are you friends with the Renzo family."

"Yes, we've been neighbors for years." She hesitated. "What if the man finds out that Franny identified him?"

"He won't. If it's the man we think it is, he's responsible for more than Moose's death. I'll have one of my men drive you home. Mr. Aziz and I will be at your apartment tomorrow morning, at eight."

"Thank you, Mr. MacKenzie." Two pairs of eyes followed her out the door.

"Great legs," said Peter.

"Nice ass." Mac smiled. "Tits aren't bad either."

Mac called Jim O'Brien into the conference room.

"The day we went to Eddie Morrison's apartment, there was a one-man band in the street. His name is John Pitt. Our suspect is believed to have dropped some money into his cup. Find him. See if he can identify Jabbar."

CHAPTER 14

Najjar looked out the window of his small, but comfortable apartment. He liked living in Brooklyn. He liked living in the United States where he had grown accustomed to freedom. Abdul Shakir had been his friend for many years. He didn't trust the other two terrorists who were to work with them. They were too eager for notoriety but he had only known them two years when they came to the States together. Najjar thought, *These are religious fanatics. Abd al Jabbar will have us believe this is Jihad, a religious war on behalf of Islam. But I know it isn't. This mission is not the Sahri'a. It is not the straight "pathway" which Allah revealed to regulate human behavior. No, this is Jabbar's serpentine, warped pathway, outlined by his blind hatred. Those other poor bastards see themselves as martyrs. To Jabbar there is no God but Jabbar and we, poor fools, are appointed as his messengers. If it is the will of Allah that innocent women and children be sacrificed to appease the wrath of Jabbar, I am willing to bow my head and beat my breast and cry, Insha'allah, God willing, but in my heart I know Allah frowns on such senseless sacrifices. Jabbar professes to praise Allah but his praise is given only if he can manipulate things to accomplish his own depraved objectives.*

Najjar prayed, "Allah, show me the correct path that will please you and give glory to you. Perhaps I must pay for deserting Jabbar and his family in their time of need. But that debt is mine and I alone can satisfy it. There have been too many deaths and injuries in the last four days, harm to people who have been good to us. For many years, I deprived myself of the love of a woman, of the pleasures of marriage, of any form of entertainment. I did all this because I was convinced that I should carry out the will of Allah. Now I'm in the twilight of that goal and it feels…wrong. My heart doesn't rejoice and my soul cries out in despair. Hear this unworthy servant, glorious Allah and guide my actions." He took a pad of paper from a drawer in the small kitchen table and began to write.

* * *

It was exactly ten paces from the front wall to the back wall of his room, and Ammar paced like a man stepping in someone else's footprints in the snow. The right side of his neck ached, where the scar widened and disappeared beneath his shirt. The pain made it difficult for him to calculate the amount of explosives he would need to complete his assignment. He was suddenly aware that someone was at his door. He sensed rather than heard the light step. Slowly he walked to the bed and reached under his pillow. He felt the cool grip of the Soviet Marakov PM pistol and released the safety. He tiptoed to the wall beside the door and waited. There was a light tapping sound on the unpainted, grease stained door. He thought, *This can't be happening to me. How could anyone know where I live? I'm too close now to give it up.* Again, he heard the tapping on the door. He walked to the window and looked out. There were no cars on the street and everything seemed normal. He crept along the wall to the door.

"What do you want?" he asked. His soft voice barely penetrated the barrier between him and the person on the other side of the door.

"Please, mister, would you like to order Christmas wrap and ribbons?"

He tucked the pistol in the back of his trousers and opened the door. Only his face showed. To his surprise the little girl didn't pull away in horror at the sight of him. She held out a pamphlet showing the types of wrappings and ribbons. The child captivated him with her dark somber eyes and curly black hair that framed her cherub-like face.

He took the pamphlet and pretended to look it over but he was studying the child. She looked to be around nine or ten but seemed to be unusually small for her age. She reminded him of his own daughter, Alula. She looked amazingly like his child and he felt empty inside. When she smiled, the cleft in her chin seemed to deepen. Her teeth were small, white and even. She carried a small paper bag, where she kept her money for the orders she took. He handed her the pamphlet and reached into his pocket and pulled out a five-dollar bill. He pointed to his selection. "This paper and this ribbon."

She smiled and wrote in a shaky hand the catalog numbers. "Will you spell your name for me, mister?"

"S-A-K-H-I-M."

She calculated the amount he spent and counted out fifty-two cents change. He held out his hand and her fingers touched his hand. He felt the bittersweet pain of memory as his fingers closed over her tiny hand. He turned her hand over so that the change was in her palm.

"Keep the change. Buy yourself a piece of candy."

She smiled at him again. "Thank you, mister," she looked at the spelling of his name, "mister Sak-him. I'll deliver this order to you at the beginning of November. She looked up at his door and wrote his room number on the order sheet. "Thanks for the tip."

"What is your name?"

"Marisa Chevez." She pointed to the floor. "I live downstairs in the room below yours. I live with Grandma."

He watched her walk down the hall before he closed the door. He put his gun back under the pillow and sat on the edge of the bed. He thought, *My Alula would have been beautiful, like the child from downstairs*. He stared into space and once again, he was back in his garden in Baghdad. Alula was riding on his back, her arms wrapped tightly around his neck. Her laughter and squeals of delight brought tears to his eyes. "More, Papa, more," she cried, as her thick black hair bounced on her back. He saw Rosha coming toward him in the shade of the date palms, smiling, touching him, loving him. This was his beautiful Rosha with whom Allah had mated him for all eternity. For him, there would never be, could never be any other. His heart cried out for her, his body ached for her and his accursed mind would not let him rest. He covered his face with his hands and realized there were tears on his cheeks. Tears he had been unable to shed, tears for his lost family, for his lost life…for his lost soul. In despair, he fell back onto the pillow and allowed the tears to flow freely. They flowed over his temples, into his thick, jet-black hair. He was brought back to reality by the sound of sobbing. It was only when he sat up that he realized the sobs were coming from him. He vowed that if the sight of Marisa Chevez could cause this reaction, he had to get as far away from her as possible. He stood in front of the cracked mirror and studied his face. He took a razor and shaved off his beard and mustache. From a small hand case, he took out a jar of flesh tone, plasticized makeup, covered the scar on his face and neck. There wasn't much he could do about the eye that was pulled down, except to cover it with tinted glasses. He took out a new identification card from his suitcase and studied the photograph. Carefully, he bleached his hair to a sandy color and put in blue tinted contact lenses. He pulled on a turtleneck shirt to cover the scar on his neck and stared at himself in the mirror. He packed his meager belongings into the one piece of luggage he owned and left the room.

On the stairs, he hesitated at the landing below and looked into the empty hallway. He whispered, "Goodbye, little Marisa, may Allah be good to you."

He found an efficiency apartment on Sixty-Sixth Avenue, just off of York in the Upper East Side of Yorkville, an area settled mainly by German and Austrian immigrants. Across from his apartment was St. Catherine's Park, a small square of grass and trees. When he inquired about lodging, the manager eyed him suspiciously.

"The rent is seven hundred dollars a month. In addition to the current month's rent, I have to have two months rent in advance, in case you decide to…leave, unexpectedly, of course. The advance rent money will be kept in escrow. If there are no major repairs to be made, you'll get your money back when you move."

His eyes widened when he saw the stack of bills Ammar pulled out of his wallet. He counted out five five-hundred dollar bills, and put them on the counter. The manager pushed over a registration form and Ammar filled it out, using a name he had not used for years, Chisisi Badru. Under citizenship, he wrote U.S. pending, currently a citizen of Egypt. Under occupation, he wrote engineer. He returned the registration form to the manager, Kurt Herrick. Herrick went into a back room and opened a metal box and took out four one-hundred dollar bills, went out to the desk and gave Mr. Badru his change. Herrick asked to see some identification. Ammar took out his wallet and extracted a card that matched the information on the registration, which identified him as Chisisi Badru, an engineer, employed by one of the major oil companies. Hesitant, but satisfied he would not be stuck for the rent, he showed Badru the apartment, which overlooked the small, quiet park. The furnished apartment on the fourth floor had been freshly painted and was bright and attractive. There was a modern elevator, in good repair down the hall and to the left. He nodded his approval and accepted the key and closed the door. He unpacked his suitcase and put it on the upper shelf of the closet. The suitcase had a false bottom, where he kept his guns. He walked through the neighborhood to familiarize himself with the area. There were restaurants and delicatessens, pastry shops and specialty stores. He went into the small restaurant down the street and ordered schnitzel and red cabbage. He ate slowly, familiarizing himself with the attitudes of the people in the neighborhood. It was less impersonal than the last neighborhood. Patrons of the restaurant were mostly regulars and called the waiters by their first names. When he finished, he paid his check and returned to his new home. He stood in front of the mirror looking at his reflection. He shook his head realizing that no matter how many times he moved, he could not leave his memories and the pain behind.

CHAPTER 15

New York

Sean Cleary put down the newspaper, walked to the refrigerator and took out a can of Coors beer and held it up. "You want one, hon?"

Ellen Cleary looked up from her ironing and shook her head. She was concentrating on television coverage of the police and emergency units digging through the rubble at The American Post Federal Building and the Kryler Building, looking for bodies buried under concrete and steel.

"Why would anybody do these things, first the World Trade Center, now again we seem to be under attack? Do you think it's terrorists like they say on the news?"

"And if it is? What would you be doin' about it? When I saw that strange man, I wanted to call the FBI but you insisted I stay out of it. Now what is it you're sayin', woman?" His brogue was still pronounced after twenty-five years in the States.

"I still think we shouldn't get involved. Just because that man had a bad scar on his face doesn't make him a terrorist. Besides, I hear terrorists look like us, like ordinary people, not like comic book characters." She stood the iron on its end. "If he is a terrorist and you blow the whistle, the next thing you know he'll be coming after us. Do you think the FBI is going to protect us? In a pig's eye they will." She picked up the iron, shook her head and put the iron down again. "Sean...do you really think that man could have been involved?"

"I think there's a good chance, love. He looked like he was enjoyin' the fear that was bein' generated." He shook his head. "And make no mistake, these hucksters of terror, know how to instill fear. That's their stock in trade. How long do you think it'll be before you're afraid to go out in the streets of a city you've lived in all your life? I'm sure you know that one of the major aims of terrorists is to intimidate people by makin' them aware of their own defenselessness. But once you give into it, sure it's like hangin' by a thread for the rests of your life...and anybody can come along and cut the thread. It messes with your mind, sweetheart, and destroys whatever peace lies within."

Sean took a few swallows of beer and wiped his mouth on the back of his hand. "Of course, the media coverage doesn't help much, now does it? I don't pretend to know a lot about terrorists and how they operate but I do know that they're using psychology on us by messin' with things we feel most comfortable with. Just like what you said. What if they come after us next? They've already succeeded in what they wanted to do. They set up fear in your mind, so that you see danger lurkin' behind every door. Pretty soon, love, you'll be afraid to go to work. After that, you'll be afraid to go outside of your own home. Can't you see what it is they're doin'? Is that the way you want to spend the rest of your life? I remember reading about the Genevese murder, when all those people stood around and watched while that loony killed that poor woman. They didn't want to get involved either but what if she had been married to one of the men in the crowd. Do you think the outcome would have been different?"

Ellen disconnected the iron and sat at the kitchen table studying her husband. "Of course you're right, Sean. The picture you paint isn't very pretty. What if they had hit one of the colleges?" She shivered. "What if our Kate or Breen had been victims?" She stared at Sean. "I don't even want to think about that possibility. I wonder how many young college graduates were among the victims. Think about their parents who sacrificed to send their kids to college, only to have them blown to pieces in the work place." Tears of frustration rolled down Ellen's cheeks. "You've got to go to the FBI and tell them what you suspect. Maybe the information you give them will help stop these senseless killings…this…" she spread her hands in a gesture of helplessness, "this…madness."

His put his arms around her and kissed the tip of her turned-up nose. "It's in love with you, that I am, woman." He walked to the closet, took out a lightweight sweater and put it on.

"Sean?"

"Yes?"

"I'm proud of you, Sean Anthony Cleary." She came to him and kissed him on the mouth. "Now don't let them push you around. You say what you have to say and get out of there."

"When you have a fightin'-mad Cleary, nobody wants to mess with him."

* * *

Peter Aziz looked over the list of possible suspects, a list that was based on place of origin, with possible ties to terrorist groups. His eyes rested on two names in particular, Khalil Najjar and Abdul Shakir. Both men came from Iraq, seeking political asylum and lived in the city. Both applied for citizenship. Neither man was married; and according to their answers on the application for citizenship, neither had a family in Iraq. He went into Mac's outer office to ask Joan to pull the files on both men. She wasn't in the office. He was about to write a note when the outer door opened and a goliath of a man filled the doorway.

He closed the door quietly and said, "Good day to you, sir." The Irish brogue was as natural as the man's smile. Sean extended his hand. "The name is Sean Cleary."

The man's grip was firm and friendly. "I'm Peter Aziz. What can we do for you, Mr. Cleary?"

Sean's eyes scanned the office. "I guess you could be offerin' my family some protection if the information I have has anything to do with the bombings."

"Mr. Cleary, please have a seat, and I'll see if Mr. MacKenzie is free." He hurried into Mac's office and stood against the closed door. "There is a Mr. Cleary in the outer office; he thinks he may have some information about the bombings."

Without lifting his head, Mac looked up from the papers he was scrutinizing. He closed the folder in front of him and nodded to Peter. Mac's six-foot frame was dwarfed by the size of the man who entered his office. He judged the man to be about six feet six or seven, with massive shoulders and a contagious Irish grin. "Mr. Cleary. I understand you may have some information for us."

"I can't be sure about that. What I have is a suspicion. I'll tell you what I think I have and you can determine if it's worth followin' up." He related the story of the man at the bar. Peter and Mac listened attentively.

Mac offered Sean a cup of coffee. "Can you describe the man for us?"

"Thank you," Sean said as he accepted the coffee. "His face was pretty well beat up, you know. He had a scar that went from his temple, to the other side of his face and down his neck." He traced an imaginary scar on his own face to indicate the trail of the scar he had seen.

Peter Aziz pulled out his sketch of Abu Ammar and set it in front of him. "Is this the man you saw?"

"Looks like him, except that he had a beard and mustache."

"When did you see him?"

"Actually, I saw him twice. The first time was after the bombings at the bus terminal and the one that caused the wreck just outside of New York. Then I saw him again at the same bar, the day of the bombings at the Kryler Building and the Federal

Building. I got the feelin' that he was enjoyin' the whole spectacle. When he left, I watched him go into Christopher Park. He met two other men there. But they didn't seem to talk, you know? The man with the scar started walkin' and they followed him."

"Did you notice the direction they took?"

Sean Cleary seemed embarrassed. "As a matter of fact, I did. I followed them."

An undisguised excitement showed in Mac's eyes. "You followed them?"

"Yes, sir. They went to a roomin' house…kind of. It was like they were playin' follow the leader. Nobody talked. I waited across the street for a while, maybe ten minutes. When they came out, they went in different directions." Sean asked for a piece of paper and drew a map showing the route they took from the park to the rooming house. "I've no idea what room they went to after they got inside. When they came out, I went to pick up my wife at work. That was on May thirteenth." He sipped the hot coffee and put the styrofoam cup on the desk. "Then I saw him again today, at the same bar. It may be only a coincidence that I saw him on the two days of the explosions."

"Did you happen to get a look at the other two men?"

He thought for a moment, searching his memory. "I'm not sure I'd be able to identify them. I saw the man with the scar, up close. I got a look at the others when they came out of the roomin' house but it was a quick look, not a studyin' kind of look, you see."

"Tell me what you saw, Mr. Cleary."

"The man with the scar and one of the other two were dark skinned, like foreigners. The third man wasn't as dark. To tell the truth, he looked like a black Irishman." He grinned. "Pardon the expression but that's what we call an Irishman with an olive complexion and black hair. That's about all I can tell you about them."

Peter picked up the folder with Edward Morrison's name on it, took the picture out and showed it to Sean.

"Could this be one of the men you saw?"

He studied the picture. "Could be. I couldn't say for sure. Hell, I don't want to get an innocent guy in trouble."

"No danger of that, Mr. Cleary. This man was shot in the head this morning."

Sean Cleary blinked hard. "Holy Mother of God."

"Not to worry, Mr. Cleary. No one will know you gave us this information and we'll check it out carefully. If you think there's a chance you were followed, we'll be glad to provide protection for you and your family."

"Saints preserve us. No, I don't think I was followed and I certainly don't need protection. I can take care of my family without outside help. No offense intended."

Mac smiled. "None taken."

The big Irishman turned when he reached the door. "I hope you get the bastards."

Mac stared at the closed door and said, "Thank God for the Sean Clearys of this world."

Peter said, "Amen to that."

* * *

The black Buick pulled into an empty parking space across the street from the rooming house. Peter Aziz looked in the rearview mirror and saw a second car double park behind them. It was their backup. A foul smelling drunk staggered up to the car, took a swig from the bottle concealed in a brown paper bag and leaned against the car as if he was going to vomit in the gutter. His eyes met those of MacKenzie and in a low voice, he said, "His room number is 213, second floor, back. He hasn't been in or out since I've been here."

Mac checked the area first and spoke into a microphone. "Okay, let's go." He and Peter used the front entrance. Two of the men from the second car went around back, while the third man stood outside the car and covered the basement entrance. Peter checked the mailboxes in the entry hall. Most of the boxes had room numbers as identification. There was no mail in the box for Room 213.

Peter and Mac, with guns drawn, approached the room cautiously. Mac knocked on the door and stepped aside against the wall. There were no sounds from within. Peter reached over and turned the knob. It turned easily and he pushed the door open. Again, they waited but there was no sign of life inside the room. Mac took out a small mirror and tilted it so he could see into the room. It was empty. Quietly, they entered. All their attention was drawn to the closet door. Stepping out of the way, Mac took out his handkerchief and opened the closet door, inside, it was dusty and empty except for the top shelf which was the only place without dust. Something had occupied that particular space. He pulled open the drawers of the bureau with the chipped green paint and looked at the undisturbed dust.

Peter shook his head and said, "What a dump."

Mac stepped out into the hall and motioned to one of the backup men. "Check for prints and anything else you can find." He replaced his gun in the shoulder holster. "Check the other tenants in the building. Maybe we'll get lucky and find somebody who saw him."

In the Chevez efficiency apartment, they asked the usual questions and received negative answers until Marisa, realizing they were asking about the man upstairs said, "Are you talking about Mr. Sakhim?"

Peter smiled at the child and stooped down to talk to her. "Do you know Mr. Sakhim?"

"I saw him today. He bought some Christmas paper and ribbon from me. He even told me to keep the fifty-two cents change."

"Wow," Peter said. "What are you going to do with all that money?"

She giggled. "It won't buy very much, maybe some candy for Grandma and me."

"Can you tell me what Mr. Sakhim looks like, Marisa?"

"Well..." She hesitated.

"It's okay, Marisa," Peter assured her. "We just want to talk to him."

"He has a really nasty scar on his face. He has black hair. I don't know what color his eyes are. I was standing in the hall and it's always dark in the hall. He was a very nice man and he paid me with a five-dollar bill and I told him the order would be here in November. That's all I can remember."

Peter smiled and patted her cheek. "That's a lot for a little girl to remember." He showed her the sketch of Abu Ammar. "Is this the man?"

She glanced at the sketch and without hesitation, answered, "Yes, that's Mr. Sakhim."

On the ride back to the office, Mac banged the steering wheel with his fist. "Damn. Damn it, he's an elusive sonofabitch."

"There's a silver lining around that black cloud," Peter said. "At least now we have a positive identification."

Mac picked up his car phone and punched in some numbers.

"Joan...put me through to Jim O'Brien, please." He waited. "Jim, it looks like we have another positive I.D. Get his picture in all the papers. Tell them to get out an extra if they have to. Notify every precinct in the city. Let's nail this bastard."

* * *

Washington, D.C.

Mike Redmond drove to the office and stopped the car. He turned to Glenn. "I'll stay with the car. You go in and see if the film I dropped off earlier is processed."

Glenn took the elevator to the top floor and walked quickly down the hall. In minutes she was back in the car. Mike said,

"Open the envelope." When she took the pictures out, he asked, "What do you see?"

"The sketches that Gabi did at the Algonquin."

"Describe them to me."

She studied each of the photos. "The sketches have the same pivotal point, the dais. Tables are arranged in groups of five and they form a semicircle around the front of the dais. Wait a minute," she shuffled through the pages, "there's a single table to the left of the dais. That table is in the same position on each sketch."

"Okay, that's the table where the speakers will be sitting, prior to the speeches."

She flipped through the pictures. "Other than that, the sketches are just rearrangements of the tables."

Templeton Osbourne opened the front door as they approached. He smiled. "Good evening, Miss Glenn." He nodded to Mike.

They went into the library and Mike studied the sketches.

Glenn leaned over him. "Well, do you see something I missed?"

"I'm not sure. He laid out the ten pictures on the desk and tapped his fingers against the side of the desk. He pulled one photograph out of the group. "This is what I was looking for." He passed the photo to her.

She looked it over, shrugged and handed it back to him. "It's like the other nine, a different arrangement perhaps, but I don't see why you selected this one over the others."

His index finger traced a path on either side of the table arrangements in the other pictures. "There's no path in this one." He saw the confused expression on her face. "You don't see the significance?"

"Not really."

"When you go to a movie, the exits are clearly marked, right?" She nodded. "Exits or pathways are incorporated into buildings, to get people out, to get them moving in a single direction in the event of an emergency, fire, tornado, earthquake or whatever. There is always a path for people to take which allows them to escape without trampling others to death. It's a designated point of departure for people at a gathering." He held up the last picture. "When you remove that designated departure route and something threatening happens, people panic. Do you know a better way for an assassin to escape than to create chaos, thus diverting attention from himself? It's a perfect setup. If such a thing happened, the Secret Service men would have no way to protect the President. People would be running hither and yon trying to get away from an assassin's bullets, or trying to get away from the source of an explosion. There would be a stampede." He tapped the photo. "For Alim, organized chaos."

Glenn was awestruck. Her mouth formed a perfect "O." She saw the look of amusement pass over his face and regained her composure. "I knew that," she said.

The sound of his laughter reverberated through the large room and Glenn was certain the sound would hide behind the books and come out at some distant time to haunt her.

"What if Gabi doesn't use that particular setup?"

"Then obviously, I've misjudged her. I wish we had gotten a glimpse of the man she met there."

"You mean the one who contacted her about the seating arrangements?"

Mike nodded. "He may have been the hit man."

"You're pulling that one from left field. You don't have one shred of evidence to link Gabriella with the plot to assassinate Mr. Breckenridge."

"You're right, I don't."

"You make her sound like Mata Hari."

"On the contrary...Mata Hari was a klutz. Gabriella is very polished, very shrewd, very cautious. She's resourceful, charming, witty, interesting, beautiful, rich and a hell of a lot smarter than anyone can guess. If Mata Hari had Gabriella's qualities, Germany would have won the First World War. Her execution by the French was more to vindicate the Germans than to put an end to her life. She never gave German Intelligence anything of real value."

"Then you think Gabi knows who the assassin is?"

"I didn't say that. I just think it's prudent to watch her. We know for sure that Paul Qadir is involved and there's a good possibility that Karim is too. The three of them are as thick as thieves, Birds of a feather…and all that nonsense."

"She stands to lose everything. Surely, she would hedge her bets. I can't picture Gabi putting everything at risk for the sake of a thrill. She's smarter than that."

"Maybe it's not for the thrill. Maybe it's fanaticism, or dedication to a cause."

"Gabi?" Glenn shook her head. "Get real." But even as she spoke, an ominous shiver passed through her. The only other time she felt like that was the night before her mother was found dead in her hotel room in Budapest. Linda Pietra Alexander had just finished a concert tour and was scheduled to return to Washington the following morning. That night, Glenn was awakened by the sound of her mother's voice, calling her. She sat upright in her bed and listened. Softly she called out, "Mama…Mama?" But there was only silence. She pulled the covers up under her chin and the same death chilling dread seized her. There was an immediate rise in her heart rate and she had difficulty breathing. The next morning, there was a knock at her bedroom door. She pulled the door open and there stood Clayton Alexander. She knew without being told.

"It's Mother, isn't it?"

He could only nod before the sobs punctuated his words. She held her father in her arms, rocking him, softly whispering words of comfort. The only thing missing from the picture were tears, her tears. She told herself it was because she was in shock. The tears would come later. But they didn't.

Mother and daughter were little more than strangers and you

don't cry for strangers. Expressions of sympathy poured in from all over the world. So why couldn't she cry? Everybody else was crying.

At Edelweiss Cemetery, Linda Pietra Alexander was laid to rest in the family mausoleum. Through it all, Templeton had been very protective. Ariette was there for her as she had always been.

Glenn thought, *Why am I not grieving? What's wrong with me? Look at Dad, he's devastated and I have no tears to shed for her.* She loved her father and knew he loved her. She had never been sure about her mother. The memory faded when she heard Mike repeating her name.

Mike had a strange look on his face. "Well?"

"I...I'm sorry, Mike, I didn't hear the question."

"I know. You were light years away. I asked if you would like a cognac."

"Yes, thank you. I'll call Templeton."

"I think I'm capable of pouring drinks without assistance." He went behind the bar, picked up a bottle of Remy XO and two brandy snifters and carried them to the sofa. He looked concerned. "Did I say something that upset you?"

"You said, maybe it wasn't for the thrill, maybe it was dedication. My blood ran cold. I experienced that feeling only once before. The night before my mother was found dead. I guess I was remembering."

"Premonition?" He poured two generous belts of cognac and handed one to Glenn. "I don't believe in premonitions and neither should you." He sat beside her and put his hand on hers. "What kind of memory did it trigger?" His eyes held hers. She felt herself swimming in a sea of blue. She never thought eyes could have such depth.

She told him about the night her mother died, omitting nothing. Her raw feelings were part of the story. When she finished, she realized the tears she couldn't shed then...she was shedding now.

Suddenly, she was in his arms, sobbing out all the grief she had been denying for so long. Just as she had held and crooned to her father the day of her mother's death, Mike was holding and crooning to her now, letting her know she didn't have to face it alone.

"I f…f…feel like such a f…f…fool."

"You jumped over a skyscraper tonight, a giant step in your life." His hand slid under her chin and lifted her face to his. Her tears continued to track their way down her face. Gently, he kissed her cheeks, then her eyes and finally her mouth. A faint moan escaped from her lips and his arms tightened around her. The tip of his tongue caressed the delicate softness of her lips, probing. Her lips parted, answering his passion with her own. He drew her to him until the full length of her body was pressed against him. Her fingers worked deftly, unbuttoning his shirt, while his hands explored her smooth, soft flesh. Their kisses became more passionate as they unfastened and pulled the clothes from their bodies. Mike knelt over her, touching, kissing, exploring. The mystery of her unbridled desires was detonated by his touch. Her arms and legs gathered him to her, pressing, teasing, compelling him to scale the heights of his own desires. The currents of yearning escalated with each new catalyst of wonder. Their bodies merged, parted and merged again. He whispered, "Damn you, Glenn."

He delighted in the response of her body to the demands made by his.

Her back arched higher and he could feel a spasmodic gripping, as her muscles pulled him deeper inside of her. Time was suspended. Her breathing seemed to halt momentarily and she sighed his name, "Michael…oh, Michael."

He knew it was okay to let go. His gave a final thrust, his eyes closed involuntarily and his body convulsed in a pleasure that emptied, yet regenerated him. He found a bliss he had experienced with only one other person…Caitlin O'Hara.

Afterward, he had a vague recollection of staggering up the stairs to their rooms. He kissed her again before she opened her door. "I take back every negative thing I ever thought about you."

She answered his kiss with one of her own. "Me too."

The early morning sun slashed through the curtains of Glenn's window and danced on her pillow. She stretched, luxuriating in the feel of the silk sheets against her naked body. She turned and looked at the clock beside her bed. It was 7:30. She got up and turned on the shower. When she went down for breakfast she dreaded having to face Mike but the internal happiness outweighed any possible regrets she might dream up later. Mike hadn't come down yet.

Templeton smiled his usual greeting. "You look radiant today, Missy."

"Thank you, Templeton. Mr. Redmond hasn't come down yet?"

Before he could answer, the phone rang and he hurried to answer it. He turned to her. "Miss Glenn, it's for you."

"This is Glenn Alexander." She listened. "Yes, sir. We'll be watching for him." She hung up.

"Did you say Mr. Redmond is still in his room?"

"I presume so, Missy. I haven't seen him. Would you like me to call him for you?"

"Just get me a cup of coffee for him…black. I'll take it to him myself." She hesitated at his door before knocking.

Mike opened the door, shined and polished. He smiled when he saw her standing there. "This is a great hotel. The maids get more beautiful every day." He took the cup she held out for him and stepped aside to allow her to enter. He closed the door and when he turned he was facing her. His eyes searched her face for any sign of hostility and finding none he put his arm around her and pulled her to him. His kiss was once again, gentle.

"Top of the morning to you. You're beautiful."

"And the balance of the day to you. Thank you, I feel beautiful." She took a deep breath. "I hate to change the subject but the Bossman just called. He's sending over an information packet."

Mike gulped down his coffee. "It's a shame we can't just take the day off."

They went in to breakfast together and the buffet was laden with eggs, bacon, sausage, fresh melon, Danish pastry, and lots of fresh, hot, black coffee. They helped themselves and sat at the round table on the patio. The front door chimes sounded and Templeton walked silently in that direction. He escorted a young man to the patio. Mike looked up and smiled. "Randy Perry. I thought you were in New York with Peter."

"I was for every bit of five hours, until the Bossman called me and sent me to Rome. My flight landed at the Washington-Baltimore Airport at seven this morning. I went right to the office. I swear, Mike, Unicorn never sleeps."

Mike said, "Glenn, this is Randy Perry, one of our newest operatives."

"You must be famished. There's a buffet inside, help yourself and join us out here. It's a glorious day."

He handed a sealed envelope to Mike and went inside to get some food.

Mike tore the flap open and pulled out the contents. He glanced at Glenn. "It's a dossier on Gabi." His eyes scanned the pages. He frowned. "Didn't Gabi tell us she hadn't seen her brother Salvatore for a couple of years? Didn't she say when she goes to Rome, it's to see her grandmother?"

"Yes, that's what she said."

"It says here, that her brother Salvatore Cammeo died in 1985. Didn't you tell me she went home briefly because her boyfriend Tory was killed in an explosion?"

She nodded. "Yes, that was the year before we graduated from college and that would have been 1985."

"Salvatore wasn't her biological brother, but an orphan her parents took in and adopted before Gabriella was born. If you take the last four letters of his first name, SalvaTORE, you come up with the nickname of Tore, or Tory as you understood it. He worked with a terrorist organization in Italy called the Red Brigade and he may have been involved in the Aldo Morro assassination but nobody actually fingered him. However, the proof is conclusive that he was involved in the bombing of the Jordanian Embassy in Rome in April 1985. Either he was on his way to deliver a bomb or somebody planted a bomb in his car. Anyway, the result was the same. There wasn't enough left for his family to identify. It seems the reason Gabi was sent to school in France was because she and Tore were having an affair. Her father sent her away hoping things would cool down. Before that could happen, he had to call her home for Salvatore's funeral." His eyes traveled down the page and came to rest near the bottom of the page. "Her grandmother is Concetta Renaldi. She had a brain stem stroke in July 1986, and died August 29, of the same year. Gabi and her father moved to the United States in September. She met and married Karim Russal in September 1987. From 1987 to the present time, she made twenty trips to Rome. Of those twenty trips, eight of them have been continuation trips from Rome to Iraq and back to Rome before returning to the United States. Obviously she used a different passport to go from Rome to Iraq, because those forays into Iraq don't show up on her U.S. passport. However, she called Karim from Iraq and all those phone calls went on her Rome telephone bills. She still maintains a villa on the Via Vittorio and keeps a staff of servants there." He looked at her over the top of the pages. "Guess who she went to see in Iraq?"

Glenn shrugged. "Karim's family?"

He shook his head. "Griad Basq…alias George Davet. Davet had been linked to Abu Nidal's organization, until Saddam Hussein made him an offer he couldn't refuse."

Glenn's face paled.

"I'm sorry, Glenn," Mike said. "Right now, it looks like Griad Basq could be the assassin, but it doesn't look good for Gabi. She could be the one supplying him with information. How would you like to bet the guy at the Algonquin Club, the one we couldn't see...was Basq. We'll make sure he is kept under lock and key until after the nineteenth."

"With Salvatore Cammeo dead and her grandmother Renaldi dead, the nagging question, is...why did Gabi make all those trips to Rome?"

CHAPTER 16

New York City
May 17

Khalil Najjar spread the morning paper on the kitchen table as he sipped his coffee. His eyes were drawn to the picture on the front page. He read the caption under the picture of Abd al Jabbar, alias Lamen Abd Sakhim, *Terrorist wanted by FBI in connection with recent bombings and the possible murders of cab driver, Raymond Briggs, and Edward (Moose) Morrison.* Najjar sucked in a mouthful of coffee, swished it through his teeth before gulping it. He stared, unbelievingly at the likeness of Abu Ammar. As Najjar read the account, he thought, *How could the Bureau have found out about Abu Ammar?* "My God," he said aloud, "they even know his real name is Abd al Jabbar. If they know about him, they must know about me and Shakir. Do they know the site of the next bombing? Will they be waiting for us when we come out of the sewer?" He went into the living room and cautiously parted the curtain to see if there was anything suspicious or different on the street below. There wasn't. He chewed on the corner of his fingernail and began pacing. "We took so many precautions, how could they have known? It's like Allah is taking control, to show Ammar that he does not approve of his methods or his vengeance." He was startled out of his trance by the shrill ringing of the telephone. He reached for it but then withdrew his hand. *What if it's the FBI?* Then reason took over. "If it was the FBI they wouldn't be giving me a telephone warning," he consoled himself, "they would have broken down this door and taken me into custody." On the fourth ring, he picked up the phone.

"Hello." His voice sounded dead, even to him.

"Khalil? Is that you?"

He recognized the voice of Shakir. "I was almost afraid to pick up the phone. Have you seen the morning papers?"

"That's why I'm calling. They know about Ammar. Do you think they're looking for us too?"

"I don't know, Abdul. I don't like it."

"Did you have time to read the entire article?"

"No. I read the caption under the picture when the phone rang. Why?"

"He's suspected of shooting Edward Morrison. Morrison's Islamic name is Kaliq Fatin. The newspaper said he was seen at the Kryler Building just before the explosion. When the FBI went to question him, he was on the floor of his apartment with a bullet between his eyes. Is this the way we are to be rewarded? I told you I thought Ammar was an evil man, now I'm certain of it. How can he go outside now? His face is on the front page of every newspaper in the country. They'll surely catch him and he'll involve all of us."

Najjar said, "I agree, he is an evil man but I don't think they'll catch him until his work is done. He is a man of many disguises."

"It would be impossible to disguise that scar on his face."

"Ammar is familiar with the properties of plastics. He could cover that scar so that you would never know it was there. Believe me, my friend, they will not catch him. You and I have been very cautious but he has been ten times more cautious. We made sure there were no fingerprints or any way of connecting us with the theft of the vans or with the bombings on Friday. He has eluded capture as Abd al Jabbar, despite a worldwide manhunt. He will be sure to carry out his mission, even if he has to kill each one of us to do it. He attaches no value to human life, except his own. He is not even human anymore. He's an automaton, a machine that is programmed to kill." He took a deep breath and let it out slowly, in a long sigh. "Perhaps he is that way because of me. Things might have been different if I had the courage to help him when Baghdad was bombed. I was afraid and bombs were falling. I had one thought and that was to get out of there. I ran away, convinced he would die. Part of his face had been torn away. His neck and chest were a mass of gaping wounds. I can still see the bloody hand he extended to me, pleading for help. Not for himself but for his wife and child. Instead of trying to help him or them, I ran away." He glanced at the face in the newspaper, staring back at him. He continued, "A lesser man could not have survived that attack." Najjar paused. When he continued, his voice was raspy. "We heard the cries of Rosha and Alula, trapped inside their house. By the time I had gone twenty meters, their cries for help had stopped and the house was consumed by fire. So, he has good reason to hate me."

"That's nonsense, Khalil, and you know it. In times of war, people die, cities are destroyed, there's no way to prevent it. You were a soldier and so was he. Why didn't he go after Saddam Hussein? He started the war."

"You don't chop off the hand that feeds you." Najjar looked at his watch. "I have to meet Ammar at the garage."

"He won't show up. He'd be recognized the minute he steps foot out of the place where he's hiding."

"He's driven. I have never seen such single-mindedness. He will be there.

* * *

Duncan MacKenzie pulled up in front of the Markham Hotel. The doorman leaned down and spoke to Mac. "You can't park here."

"I was to meet Mr. Aziz."

"Are you Mr. MacKenzie?"

Mac nodded.

"Mr. Aziz called down and asked that you wait a few minutes." He motioned to his right. "Park on the other side of the hotel canopy."

Five minutes later Peter hurried out of the hotel and got in beside Mac.

"Anything wrong, Peter?"

"I got a call from the Bossman. He wants me back in Washington tonight."

"Do you have time to go to Sam Boyer's apartment with me?"

"You bet. My plane doesn't leave until late this afternoon. Are you sure you want me tagging along?"

Mac blushed. "She's a hell of an attractive woman."

Peter laughed. "Great legs."

"Great ass. Tits aren't bad either." They laughed. "No wonder women accuse us of sexual harassment. Long before we ever notice the color of their eyes or their hair, we study the wrapper. If she's got great legs, tits and ass, then we're interested. I wouldn't want to be a woman in today's world."

He turned into 142nd Street and found a parking space. Matthew Boyer was sitting on the stoop, like a sentinel guarding the fort.

"Hello, Matthew." Mac put his hand on the boy's shoulder. "Are you all right?"

The boy nodded.

"Is Sam inside?"

Matthew nodded again.

Peter knocked on the door of the first floor apartment that Matthew shared with his sister. The door opened and Samantha stood there smiling at them.

"Good morning. Please come in." The small apartment was clean and nicely furnished. "I have coffee on, would you like a cup?"

"I'd love it," said Peter. "How about you, Mac?"

"If that coffee tastes as good as it smells how could I resist?"

Sam disappeared into the kitchen and returned carrying a tray with coffee, mugs, milk, sugar, and cookies that were obviously home made. "Help yourselves to cookies. Franny Renzo will stop on his way to school."

Peter glanced at his watch. It was 8:32. Mac took a cookie and popped it into his mouth.

Matthew came into the room, followed by Franny Renzo. Sam put a protective arm around the boy. "Franny, this is Mr. MacKenzie, and that man, is Mr. Aziz. They want to ask you a few questions about the man you saw going into your apartment building, yesterday."

Mac shook hands with the youngster. "Where do you go to school, Franny?"

"St. Dominick's. I'm in fourth grade."

"Do you like school?"

"Sometime. I'll be glad when June gets here and we have the summer off. Then I'll have time to play with Matthew."

"How old are you, Franny?"

"Nine. I'll be ten in August."

"How come you were home yesterday? Wasn't it a school day?"

"It was teachers' conference day."

"Tell me about the man you saw going into the building across the street."

Franny looked at Peter Aziz.

"He was about as tall as Mr. Aziz. His skin was a little darker, like he had been at the beach and got a good tan. He was carrying a box like the one I carry my clarinet in…maybe a little bigger and it was made of wood. He waited outside until somebody from the building came out, then he went in before the outside door closed and locked him out again. At first, I thought he lived there and maybe forgot his key. Anyway, Matthew and me were watching the man with the drum and cymbals. He was pretty good."

Mac knew Franny was scared. "Have you ever seen the man with the drum and cymbals before?"

"Oh, sure, everybody knows John Pitt. He comes every week…almost."

"How long would you say the man was in the building across the street?"

"I don't know. It wasn't very long. When he came out, he crossed to this side of the street and put some money in the tin can John Pitt had strapped to his belt. Then he walked in front of John Pitt, up the street. A little while later, you came out of this building and went across the street."

"If I showed you a picture of the man, do you think you could identify him?"

"I don't know. I think so."

"Good." He took the picture out of his jacket pocket and handed it to Franny.

"Yes, sir, that's him."

Mac nodded to Peter Aziz. "Thank you, Franny, you've been a big help."

"Mr. MacKenzie? Do you think that man shot Moose?"

"There's a good possibility that he did. Do you want us to drive you to school?"

"Yes, sir, maybe you can tell Sister Agatha it's not my fault that I'm late."

Peter stood up. "I'll do it, and then I'll drop by and pick you up. Come on, Matthew, you can come along for the ride."

Matthew turned to his sister.

"It's okay, Matthew, you can go. Mr. Aziz will bring you back after he takes Franny to school."

Matthew grinned and took Peter's hand. When the door closed behind them, an awkward silence made Mac uneasy.

"Would you like another cup of coffee?"

He held out his cup.

"How long have you been with the FBI, Mr. MacKenzie?"

"Call me Mac. I joined the Bureau in 1988."

"Do you like what you do?"

Strange, he thought, *No one ever asked me that before.* "Yes, most of the time, sometime, I even get to meet a pretty woman, like you." He smiled when she blushed.

"You're not wearing a ring," he said, looking at her left hand. "Are you married?"

She looked at her unadorned fingers and reached for the coffeepot. "No. I was engaged a couple of years ago but Jack said if I wanted to marry him I would have to put Matthew in a home for retarded children. I couldn't do that. So we broke up." She studied his profile. "Does your wife object to your work?"

"My wife died when my son, Todd, was born. He's ten years old. My mother lives with me, so she's there for him. God knows I rarely am."

"How sad for you…how sad for both of you." She refilled his cup, sat back and crossed her legs. He leaned forward and put his cup on the floor. He thought, *Peter was right, she has great legs.*

"Where's Matthew when you go to work?"

"The Harlan School for Handicapped Children, they pick him up in a van at eight o'clock and drop him off around four-thirty. Mrs. Pierce, from upstairs, keeps him with her until I come home at six."

"That doesn't give you much time to socialize, does it?"

"I don't mind."

"How about if I pick you and Matthew up on Sunday afternoon and take you both for a picnic?"

She lowered her head. "That would be lovely, Mac, thank you."

They heard running footsteps in the hall outside the apartment. The door was flung open and a laughing Matthew ran in, followed by Peter. Mac stood up and handed her his empty cup. He smiled and said, "I'll see you Sunday afternoon."

* * *

Khalil Najjar approached the garage with caution. He walked around the block, until he was sure no one was watching the place. When he felt it was safe, he opened the door. The small panes of glass had been coated with black paint and it kept everything in darkness. He heard the bolt on the door slip into place before he saw the lone figure of a man beside him.

"Abu Ammar?"

"Walk straight ahead," Ammar said in a soft, almost gentle voice.

When they reached the other end, Ammar turned on the single light bulb over a makeshift workbench and faced Najjar.

Najjar stared at him. "I would never have known you. You look so…different."

Ammar's upper lip curled back in disdain. He stood at the workbench with Najjar beside him. On the shelf over the workbench, were containers with labels written in Arabic.

Ammar began his tutorial. "We're using Triton, which is TNT, a secondary explosive. This is used as a component of the bursting charge in the bomb. We use the primary charge, ammonium nitrate, as a base charge and add a slurry blasting agent." He started mixing and talked as he did so. "This is an aqueous oxidizing solution, I'll thicken it with guar gum, which I have gelled with some borax and it's sensitized with ethylene glycol. This acts as the dispersing agent for the main component of ammonium nitrate." He worked quickly, occasionally glancing at Najjar. "We now have a binary cast explosive. We mold this with wax. Now we make the blasting charger using cyclonite. Because cyclonite is too sensitive in pure form to be used as an explosive, it can only be used as the base for the detonating mechanism. When this baby goes off, it'll have a brisance that has only been seen on a battlefield."

Najjar's voice shook when he spoke. "What is brisance? What does it do?"

Ammar's thin lips stretched into a smile. He picked up an empty jar and slammed it hard onto the ground. It shattered into tiny pieces. His eyes met those of Najjar. "That is brisance…the crushing or shattering effect of an explosive. Like that jar shattered, that's the way the explosive will shatter anything around the blast. It may not bring down the whole building but it will kill everyone within a wide range. To be certain, we'll give it a booster charge."

A mixture of awe and fear flooded Najjar's facial expression, lots of fear.

Ammar was pleased with the effect the demonstration had on Najjar. He said, "Meet me here Thursday afternoon and we will carry this to its final resting place." To himself, he added, *It will also be your final resting place, Khalil. Then, on Saturday, I can begin putting my life back together. I can return to Baghdad, a hero. Rosha would have been proud of me.* Aloud, he said, "Check outside before you leave."

On the way home, Khalil tried to remember everything Ammar told him about the bomb. He stopped at Shakir's apartment and told him how the bomb was assembled. "There is no doubt he knows everything about explosives but he knows nothing about mercy. Thursday, when we put the bomb in place Ammar will come out alone. I know he is planning to leave me inside with the bomb."

"What are you talking about? He can't just leave you there. Aren't you going to fight him? Don't you care about your life?"

"Of course I care about my life. It's…kismet. I can't fight my karma."

"Fate has nothing to do with it. This is Ammar's doing. He has terrified you and that is his stock in trade. Now, he sits back and enjoys your pain. This is how he gets his revenge. Look at you. Fear oozes from you like sap from a tree. We talked about this before." He turned his friend around to face him. "Khalil, when are you going to fight back? Can't you see he enjoys the destruction and the killings? Do you need Allah to stop him?" Abdul paused to allow his words to register. "Sometime Allah waits for us to do something for ourselves. Do you think Allah wants to see all those people killed? Do you believe it will bring glory to his name? Remember what happened to Kaliq Fatin? If he was doing the will of Allah, why would Allah want him killed? We are not at war." He stood toe-to-toe with Khalil and shouted, "We-are-not-at-war."

Najjar shook his head in despair. "We can do…nothing. Even if we tell what we know to the police, we'll be arrested and executed because of our part in the first two bombings."

"You're right. He has entangled us in his web and now we have no choice but to do what he orders. What happens to the rests of us? Do we get paid with a bullet as Fatin did?"

"Of course not," Khalil said. "He has no reason to kill you."

"He had no reason to kill Kaliq Fatin either. But Fatin…is…dead."

"He's dead because Ammar believes that if you turn on your own people, you can't be trusted. Sooner or later, you'll turn on the country you embraced after you betrayed your own nation."

"We're all doomed to suffer the same fate. Wake up, Khalil; don't you see what he's doing? He can't afford to leave witnesses. Especially not one who knew him before he became Abu Ammar. Until this morning, when the newspaper printed his picture, the world thought Abd al Jabbar was dead, now…"

"Jabbar is dead, truly dead. The man known to us as Ammar is not the man I knew and served with in the army. That man died in Baghdad with his wife and child. From the ashes of that incinerated soul was born this monster who calls himself Abu Ammar."

CHAPTER 17

Washington, D.C.
May 17

Clifford Ardell opened the door to his outer office; weariness was reflected in the set of his shoulders. Randy Perry sat at the secretary's desk, haltingly pecking at her typewriter. He looked up when the Bossman closed the door.

"Sally not in yet?" He glanced at his watch.

"Cliff, it's only a quarter till eight. She's not supposed to be here until nine."

Ardell sank into a chair that squeaked its protest at his two-hundred-twenty-pound form. "Who's available for surveillance?"

Perry turned on the computer and pulled up a list of available agents.

"We have Conway, Belson, Ordway and me."

"Okay, Randy, I guess you're it. I want you on George Davet's tail like a troublesome wart."

"You want Davet brought in?"

"Not yet. I want to know where he goes, whom he sees and talks to on the phone. I'll tell you when I want Davet brought in. When that happens we'll send backup. Griad is high on the madman's preferred list. He's alert and cautious. He could slit a guy's throat and the poor bastard wouldn't know it until his head fell off. Randy, I want you to call in…often." He stretched his long legs in front of him. "You did a good job on the report on Gabriella Russal."

Perry looked up from the computer screen. "Puzzling, wasn't it?"

Ardell nodded. "Very. However, going back to Italy is hardly a crime. What bothers me is why? To visit the graves of her lover and her grandmother? She never stayed very long. Why did she go to Iraq to see Griad Basq? We know it wasn't for golf lessons. Could she have had an affair with him?"

He shook his head. "I doubt it. Could he have been her mentor in terrorism?"

He frowned. "Possible and makes more sense but it poses more questions." Ardell took out a pack of cigarettes, offered Perry one and lit one for himself. He said, "Why would a macho organization use a woman to carry out what they believe is a man's job? According to the Arab mentality, she's not of their faith; therefore she's an infidel. Why would you teach an infidel terrorist tactics that she could use against you? Maybe she was being taught to observe. In that capacity, she could be invaluable to them. She knows the English language and has lots of friends in the U.S. She's free to go anywhere without arousing suspicion. When she wants to pass on information, all she has to do is go to the country club where Davet is the pro."

Perry said, "Maybe she's passing the information on to her husband. What do we know about Karim Russal?"

He opened the thin folder in front of him. "Not much. We know he was militaristic and belonged to a dissident group while he was in college. After graduation, he became a dutiful son and moved in the opposite direction, politically. There's no proof that he belongs to a terrorist organization now but many of his friends do, including Boulus Qadir." He pulled a professional photograph of Anita Gregory out of Qadir's file. "He's dating Anita Gregory. She doesn't seem to have an affiliation with a terrorist or dissident group. I think we can eliminate her from suspicion. She has no important Washington connections. If she's with important political figures, it's simply as an attractive ornament on the arm of Qadir, a very convenient guest, at a very convenient time. The puzzling part of Qadir's presence, other than being at the Vietnam Veteran's Memorial when the Washington terrorist contingency met, is that he hasn't made an attempt to see any of the other terrorists. He doesn't accompany Gabriella when she goes out, he stays with Karim and he hasn't made any suspicious moves. So…we're back at square one."

The door opened again and Mike and Glenn walked in.

Ardell said, "Come in, come in. I'm assigning Randy to tail George Davet. But first, I think we can use a brainstorming session. We have more questions than we have answers. That's not acceptable." The Bossman led the way into the conference room, where the automatic recording device turned itself on at the sound of the door closing. They sat at one end of the large table.

Ardell addressed Randy Perry. "You spent a couple of days in Rome, other than the report, what did you come up with?"

"Nothing concrete."

"It doesn't have to be concrete. What have you got?"

"What are you after, specifically?"

"Why would Mrs. Russal make so many trips to Rome when she has no family there? Why does she still maintain a home and keep servants?"

"I'm not sure but as I watched the villa, I saw Filomena Lucca, who was Gabriella Cammeo's governess when she was a child, leave the house on the Piazza Vittorio, with a package under her arm. I followed her. She went to a convent school, Madonna Del Fiore, on the outskirts of Rome. When she came out, a girl of perhaps eighteen, with reddish blond hair, accompanied her. I was curious, so I began snooping. The child was born at the Ospedale Santo Cristoforo, to Maria Renaldi, in 1984. The age of the infant's mother was eighteen. Filomena Lucca, who is about sixty years old, has no children. Maria Renaldi is the maiden name of Gabriella Cammeo's mother, who, incidentally, died in 1974. The certificate of birth does not contain the name of the father. Soon after the birth of the child, named Violetta Renaldi, Gabriella was sent to France to school. It's my belief that she goes back to Rome to visit the child. I think that Mr. Russal has no knowledge about the existence of Violetta Renaldi. Senora Lucca took the child to the house on the Piazza Vittorio, where she appeared to be very much at home. Violetta Renaldi has red-gold hair and looks like a younger version of Gabriella Cammeo."

"There was no indication as to the name of the child's father?"

"Not on the official records. I think the father was Salvatore Cammeo, Gabriella's adopted brother. The birth of the child was probably the deciding factor in sending her to school in France. She was still able to see the child on holidays and vacations. I don't think the girl knows her true relationship to Gabriella Cammeo."

Clifford Ardell took a cigarette out of his pocket and toyed with it before snapping it in half. "Got to kick this filthy habit." He looked at the others present. "Any questions?"

Glenn put down the copy of the dossier on Gabriella Russal. "What do we know about the trips she took to Iraq? Did she go alone? Do we know for certain that she went to see Griad Basq?"

Ardell cleared his throat. "I'm afraid we don't know very much about those trips. We know that on one occasion, while she was in Iraq, she saw Griad Basq. The meeting could have been coincidental. We know that on several of those trips to Iraq, she was accompanied by a female child, probably Violetta Renaldi. Other times, she took the trip alone. There's no evidence that she stayed in Iraq, she could very easily have gone to Arabia or Kuwait, and returned to Iraq for the flight back to the States. Glenn, you roomed with Gabriella Russal at college, how well did you know her?"

"Apparently, not well enough. I had no idea she led a double life. She never talked about herself or her family. Once, after a party at which we both had too much to drink, she said, "Someday, when I marry my Tory, we will live on top of a mountain and make love all day and all night."

Glenn frowned remembering the scene. "When I asked her who Tory was, she seemed to sober up fast. She didn't want to talk about him. I didn't know she had a child. When she first came to the university, she had a few extra pounds, but I never thought anything about it. She exercised religiously and lost the extra weight. She was constantly studying her figure in the mirror, obviously pleased with what she saw. She swore she would never have a child and ruin her figure." Glenn rubbed the back of her neck "And all the time, she already had a child in Italy. She seems to have so much…and yet, she has nothing."

The meeting ended at noon. Randy Perry took up surveillance of Griad Basq, alias George Davet. Mike and Glenn went to the country club for lunch.

They were seated at a table overlooking the lake. Mike reached across the table and covered her hand with his. "Smile, sweetheart, we're on."

She pursed her lips and blew him a kiss across the table. "Who's watching us, darling?"

"Blanche Cameron and Gabriella. They're sitting on the other side of the room. I don't see Karim or the senator. That's an odd liaison. What could those two women possibly have in common?"

"Golf?"

"Golf could be an excellent reason to pump information out of someone. Especially someone who loves to show off that she's the wife of an important senator, therefore, part of the inner circle of Washington society."

Glenn laughed, as though Mike had told her a funny story. "Gabi is heading in our direction. You take the lead in the conversation."

He stood up and smiled as Gabi neared their table. "Gabi, you always manage to look like you just stepped out of a fashion magazine."

"Darling," she said as she kissed the air on either side of his cheeks, "you have a way of making a woman feel beautiful." She turned her attention to Glenn. "Chere, where have you been? I've been calling you all morning."

Glenn smiled at Mike. He took the lead.

"We were at my apartment making love. I didn't want Templeton walking in on us."

Gabriella suppressed a giggle. "Last week, I wouldn't have believed you. Today, I look at Glenn's face and I know you're telling me the truth. Look, she's blushing, not from embarrassment but from the memory of what happened between you." Her laughter bubbled out. "You poor darling, you never could keep a secret. I approve. You look absolutely radiant. Whatever you're doing, Michael, darling, don't stop. Our Glennie looks better than she has in years." Gabriella looked toward the door of the dining room and a frown creased her forehead. "Oh dear, it looks like Blanche is giving poor George a hard time because her new putter didn't come in. Honestly, that woman can be so obnoxious at times; you would think she had been born with a silver spoon in her mouth instead of beside the railroad tracks...and the wrong side of the tracks at that. I'd better rescue him before she tar and feather's him. Let's have dinner tonight at Donatello's. Okay?"

Mike had to laugh the way she went from one subject to another without taking a breath in between. "Okay, Gabi. What time would you like to meet us there?"

"Wonderful. Seven-thirty, darlings."

They watched her walk away. She was a whirlwind with her quick light step, so full of energy and joie de vivre.

It became evident that Blanche Cameron was more than a little angry with George Davet.

"She's wearing the same expression on her face that I saw when Marcia Breckenridge had lunch with us, a look of unbridled hate. What can make this woman hate like that?"

Mike said, "Offhand, I would say her anger has nothing to do with her putter. There's another reason, a more serious one."

Anger was reflected on George Davet's face and although they couldn't hear the words, it was clear he wasn't going to stand there and be abused by her. They were almost nose-to-nose when Gabriella came between them. There was a smile on Gabriella's face but it was evident she was talking through clenched teeth. They separated and Gabriella put her arm around Blanche Cameron and they walked toward the parking area.

Glenn swallowed. "That was a close one. I wonder what that was about. I've known George for a few years and I've never seen him lose his cool. I think Blanche can make God lose his temper."

"Maybe we can get Gabi to tell us what it was all about at dinner tonight." Mike opened the menu and scanned its contents.

* * *

New York City

"Mr. MacKenzie, John Pitt is here. Do you want to see him in your office?"

"Yes, hold calls while I talk to him, please, Joan."

"Yes, sir."

When the door opened again, Mac could see John Pitt's bass drum with its attachments standing beside Joan's desk. He walked around the desk, extending his hand to John Pitt. "Mr. Pitt, I'm Duncan MacKenzie. Thank you for coming down here on such short notice."

He accepted the extended hand. "Is something wrong?"

"No, Mr. Pitt. We called you here because we believe you can help us catch the terrorist who is responsible for all the bombings."

"I don't see how I can help you, Mr. MacKenzie, I don't know any terrorists."

"No, but you may have come in contact with one without being aware that he was a terrorist. Yesterday, on 142nd Street, about the time Moose Morrison was murdered, you were performing on that street, playing your multitude of instruments; your one-man band, as the neighbors referred to you."

"Yes, sir, that's right. But I didn't know a murder was happening."

"I know you didn't. A man came from the opposite side of the street from where you were and put some money in your tin can. Do you remember that?"

"Oh, sure, you always remember when somebody puts in more than a quarter. That guy put a dollar bill and a couple of quarters in the can."

"Can you describe the man for us?"

John Pitt shrugged his shoulders. "He was dark, medium height, skinny, like he needed a few good meals under his belt. He had a mustache and beard." He thought for a moment. "Oh, yeah, he had a bad scar on his face."

"You play your instruments in that neighborhood often, don't you?"

"Sure, it's part of my circuit. I cover a wide area, got to, if I want to earn a living. Nickels and dimes don't go far these days. I can't hit the same neighborhood too often. About once every two weeks."

"Have you seen this man anywhere else?"

John Pitt thought for a time before answering. "I'm sure I did, but I can't remember where. That's a face you're not likely to forget. Something inside me says Christopher Park but I couldn't swear to it. Hell, I cover parts of Brooklyn, the Bronx, and the Village. You name it, I cover it."

"Thank you for coming in, Mr. Pitt. We'll be in touch."

Mac thought, *Christopher Park. That confirms what Sean Cleary said. But where did he go from there? Who could have tipped him off? He has a thing about circles, everything has to be neat, tied up and finished before he can walk away from it. Could he also have a thing about parks? Small parks where he could go to be alone? Stranger things have happened. Where could he have gone? Is the big hit going to be the Empire State Building? Did the other terrorists see his picture in the papers? Do they know he killed Moose Morrison? Did they rationalize, that murder is the pay they could get for being part of his conspiracy?*

He went through the files of Middle Eastern aliens with green card status and those that were pending. He pulled one hundred files from the New York City area. Of these, twenty were from Iraq. The others were from the Emirates of Bahrain, Qatar, and Kuwait. He sat at his desk, studying the faces of the aliens and their reasons for coming to the U.S. He pulled the files of single men, without families, which narrowed the field to ten files. Among the ten files were the names of Khalil Najjar, Abdul Shakir, Sami Aban and Hamid Marid. Mac picked up his phone and dialed a number. "Peter. I think I might be on to something. Can you come to the office? I have some files I'd like you to look at. Good, I'll see you in an hour."

Peter opened each of the ten files, reading the information and studying the photographs. When he came to the file on Khalil Najjar, he stared at the picture.

"This one looks familiar. He came here seeking political asylum and strangely enough, just after the Persian Gulf War. He served in the Iraqi army and was fleeing persecution from Saddam Hussein's purge." He looked through the other files and pulled the one for Abdul Shakir. "Here's another one." He closed his eyes, trying to remember the circumstances that brought the two men to his attention. He said, "The dhows."

"The what?"

Peter realized he has spoken aloud. "The dhows, small boats used by fishermen in the Persian Gulf. During the war, someone sabotaged the docks and many of the dhows were destroyed. I had a profitable business on the waterfront, my presence on the docks went unnoticed but I was able to observe many things without arousing suspicion. These two men were on the waterfront many times before the explosions that rocked the area. I think the one known as Abdul Shakir was connected with the Black September Organization. This one, Khalil Najjar, was with the Iraqi army."

"Would they have been experts in explosives?"

"I doubt it. They were probably given the task of carrying and planting the bombs. The explosives were definitely the work of Abd al Jabbar." Peter pulled two other files from the group. "Shakir and Najjar are both stevedores. So are Aban and Marid. They came to the U.S. within one month of each other."

"Do you know Aban and Marid?"

"No. I've never seen them before. It bothers me that these men weren't Kurds, fleeing persecution by Saddam. They were Iraqis claiming asylum to escape political reprisal, reprisal for what? Why is it so simple to get into the U.S.? It's amazing these terrorist attacks haven't happened before."

"When will you be leaving New York?"

"My plane leaves at two o'clock. I should be in the Washington office by three-thirty."

The men shook hands. "Give 'em hell, Peter." Mac knew about Laura Madison and he smiled. "What's the first thing you're going to do when you arrive in Washington?"

Peter smiled. "The second thing I'm going to do is put down my suitcase."

* * *

Baltimore, Maryland

The hall on the eighteenth floor was dimly lit. Apartment 1802, at the far end, was in darkness except for a quiet glow that filtered under the door. The door buzzer sounded and from inside came the sound of soft music. Slowly, the door opened and the safety chain was visible from the hall.

"If you don't open this door in the next five seconds, I'll break it down."

There was a muffled cry and the door slammed shut. The safety chain dangled from the doorjamb as the door sprung open again.

Laura Madison's arms locked around Peter Aziz's neck and her lips explored every centimeter of his face.

"You didn't tell me you were coming back today. I would have met you at the airport."

"I couldn't have controlled myself at the airport. It was less embarrassing if I came here." He picked her up and kicked the door shut and his mouth hungrily sought hers.

Later as she lay next to him, one arm flung across his chest, her head in the hollow of his shoulder, he felt her hot tears as they fell on his chest.

"Laura." He pulled her on top of him. "Don't, sweetheart, please don't."

She sobbed out her frustration. "You were in New York and all those bombs were going off and I didn't know if you were alive or dead. I had no way to contact you. I was frantic, I didn't know where to turn, I..." Her voice trailed off.

"I know. I couldn't call you. Calling you could have put you in danger and that," he kissed the tip of her nose, "I would never do. I couldn't live without you. I realized it more and more while I was away from you. We can't live like this." He tilted her chin so he could see her face. "I love you, Laura. I want to marry you."

Her sobs subsided, and she sniffed, "Really?"

"Really, when this assignment is over, I'm quitting. It's about time I started thinking about children instead of intrigue. Is that okay with you?"

Her eyes searched his face. "How about a football team?"

He smiled. "How about a basketball team to start?"

"Sounds good to me, when can we start?"

"If things go well, this assignment should be concluded by Saturday."

"Then we can start on a family right away. That's wonderful." She hesitated, "Especially...especially since I forgot to take my birth control pill this morning."

* * *

Washington, D.C.

Mike studied the abstract designs in the stained-glass wall insets. He smiled at Glenn. "Very nice."

Gabriella's eyebrows arched. "Don't tell me you've never been here before."

"I told you, I don't do the Washington scene."

Karim devoured his wife with his eyes. "I love everything about Washington. Gabriella is truly in her element here. Look at her she is positively and sinfully radiant."

The waiter took their order and sent the wine steward to their table. Karim ordered the appropriate wines with each course. Gabriella reached for his hand.

"Darling, are you trying to get me drunk so you can take advantage of me?"

"Of course I am, amatissimo, why else would I order wine? You know I don't particularly like it. But it does make you very passionate."

The maître d' approached the table. "Please forgive the interruption but Mr. Redmond has an urgent telephone call. You may take it in the office. Please follow me."

Gabriella frowned. "How did anyone know he was here?"

Glenn said, "I'm afraid that's my fault. I haven't been able to reach Dad for a couple of days, so I told Templeton where I could be reached if Dad called. I think all of Washington knows Mike's staying at my house, so it's not difficult to track him down."

Gabriella patted her hand. "Don't be embarrassed, there are a lot of women who would love to be in your shoes. Mike is a very sexy man."

Glenn laughed. "Tell me about it."

"Here comes the dear boy. Confidentially, he doesn't look very happy."

Mike sat down. "I have to beg off. That call was from the police. My office was vandalized. They need me to tell them if anything is missing. If you want to stay, sweetheart, it's perfectly alright." He touched Glenn's cheek.

"I wouldn't think of staying. Gabi and Karim understand."

Gabi asked, "Would you like us to go with you?"

"Thank you, Gabi," said Mike, "that won't be necessary. No sense in ruining everybody's evening. Enjoy your dinner. We'll make it for one night next week." He kissed Gabriella on the cheek and shook hands with Karim.

He let the clutch out slowly and glided into traffic.

"Tomorrow's paper will mention that my office was vandalized but that nothing of value was taken."

Glenn looked troubled. "What's wrong?"

"That was the Bossman on the phone. They just fished two bodies out of the Potomac, in the Georgetown channel. One of the bodies was Randy Perry. The other was George Davet. Both were shot in the back of the head, execution style."

"Oh, God."

"Yeah, and at this point, he's the only one who knows anything. That means Davet can't be Abd al Alim. Where was Boulus Qadir today?" He picked up the phone. "Helix, here, let me talk to Unicorn." He waited.

"We're coming in. Is Blue back yet?" He listened. "Good. We'll see you in a few minutes."

Ardell was pacing the floor when they arrived and Peter Aziz stared out the window. Both turned around when the door opened.

"Cliff, what the hell happened?" Mike asked.

"I'll tell you what happened," Peter sat on the edge of Ardell's desk. Randy Perry took a bullet intended for me. He shouldn't have been tailing Davet. He was still a neophyte. I should have been on that surveillance."

"Bullshit," Ardell said. "He had to start somewhere. He did a great job in Rome. He got us a hell of a lot of information based on his hunches. His former training as an investigative reporter paid off for us. I think he was right on the mark. Somebody knew he was there, asking questions and that's why he bought it. He was following Davet but somebody else was following Randy. That person killed both of them."

Mike put his hand on Peter's shoulder. "He's right, you know."

Glenn asked, "Were both bodies found in the same place?"

"Yes, near the Key Bridge. We have the weapon."

Mike blinked hard. "What?"

Peter nodded. "Abd al Alim is playing games with us. I'm sure there won't be any prints on the weapon. But, there's no way the triggerman could avoid getting splattered with blood, since both men were shot at close range.

Mike asked, "What make gun?"

Ardell said, "Browning, hi-power 9 mm parabellum."

Glenn mused aloud, "The Browning…isn't that the model made by Beretta in Italy?"

Mike smiled, impressed, "Right on the button. The question is who was carrying the gun? Was it Davet's? Did Randy pick it up when he was in Rome? Or, does it belong to Alim?"

Peter said, "Randy told me he wouldn't carry anything but a .44 Magnum. It couldn't be his revolver."

Ardell said, "Here's what we're going to do. The news media is having a field day. The police will inform them about the body of Davet and they'll tell the media identification of the second man was impossible because of the extent of the wounds."

"But what about Randy's wife?"

Mike thought, *Boy, leave it to a woman to bring up a touchy subject. I still say women shouldn't be in this business. They just don't have the stomach for it.* Aloud, he said, "Ex-wife. She lives in California. They were divorced last year. She remarried a couple of months ago. He has no other family. He was brought up by an aunt, but she died two years ago." Mike lit a cigarette. "Do we know when it happened?"

Ardell stopped pacing and planted his feet in a determined stance before answering. "The medical examiner is doing the post now. The last time Randy checked in was four o'clock. He was supposed to check back at six, but didn't."

"While you have men out, you might question Blanche Cameron?" Mike studied the lit end of his cigarette.

Ardell resumed his pacing. "The senator's wife?"

"Unless you know another Blanche Cameron."

"What the hell does she have to do with it?"

"Glenn and I were having lunch at the country club and Mrs. Cameron and George Davet were having a very nasty, very loud argument just outside the French doors to the dining room. I don't think it's a secret that there was no love lost between them. We were hoping to talk to Gabriella Russal at dinner tonight, to find out what the argument was about but your phone call got to us before we could get to her."

"Interesting, didn't you say Mrs. Cameron announced that the Breckenridges would be at the Algonquin Club on the 19th? And now this? Is she just a blundering idiot or do you think there was a method to her madness?"

"I think she would love to see the President dead, for several reasons." Mike ticked off the reasons on his fingers. "She blames him for the failure of her husband to advance higher in the Senate pecking order. She'd be nasty enough to enjoy Mrs. Breckenridge's grief if her husband was assassinated. I don't think she's Abd al Alim, but if she knew who was, she wouldn't hesitate to feed him information. That woman is spitefully dangerous."

"Then," Ardell said, "I guess we had better find out what the argument with George Davet was about. We'll have the police pay her a visit. They can also question Mrs. Russal. We'll stay in the wings. Let the local police do their thing. Only let's request that both women be questioned separately but at the same time, so that there will be no phone calls to set up alibis. Mike, find out from our men who were tailing the Middle East contingency, where each guy was while the murders were taking place. I want to know where Qadir and the Russals were and I want to know where the three terrorists, who came over the Mexican border, were. I want to know where that bastard turncoat, Willie Jones was today. We need somebody who can do a positive I.D. on Atsu Jabari."

Mike and Glenn looked at each other.

Ardell continued, "For all we know, the real Jabari could be dead and this guy could be using the name of Bengal. I'm putting in a call to SIS. I think we need Tony Emerson here to verify the identity of this agent," he said. "Let's play the what-if game. What if…the information he gave us is wrong? What if…the real target is Union Station instead of the Lincoln Memorial? Nine-thirty on the 19th would be a little late to find we made a mistake."

CHAPTER 18

New York City

Jim O'Brien picked up four files from the batch he was scanning. The additional information requested had just come in on the fax machine.

"Mac, take a look at this." He put the fax copies on top of each of the four folders.

Mac scanned the copies and raised one eyebrow. "So! How come stevedores make so much money?"

"Only those four stevedores make that kind of money."

"I think we should put on our Immigration hats and go see these high priced stevedores."

* * *

Khalil Najjar sat at the kitchen table writing everything he could remember about the construction of the bomb, the bomb that would take his life. The only thing Ammar did not tell him was how the timing mechanism worked. He banged his fist on the table. "How can I delay the explosion if I don't know about the timer? I know he uses clocks but he didn't show me how he wires it. Knowing Ammar, he will have the bomb booby-trapped so that it will be difficult to disarm." His thoughts raced back to conversations. Was Shakir's feeling that Ammar would kill all of them nervousness, or did he too have a premonition? They all knew of Ammar's compulsion to tie up loose ends. Did this compulsion include elimination of his associates who could possibly finger him? None of them could get help. Where could they go? They were trapped. Each man had become a terrorist. They couldn't go to the FBI or anyone else. They were exactly where Ammar wanted them…at his mercy.

In his frustration, Najjar pounded his forehead with his fists. "But there is no mercy in this man. There is no feeling except hate but most of all, there is no forgiveness in his heart." Najjar was brought back to reality by the sound of the chimes at the door to his apartment. Once again fear gripped him, a fear different from his dread of Ammar but just as real and just as immediate. He moved away from the table, silently moving into the bedroom. The perspiration dripped from his forehead into his eyes, burning and blurring his vision. The chimes sounded again. He was sure the beating of his heart could be heard through the walls of the apartment. He tried to slow his rapid breathing and slid down the wall onto the floor. The chimes sounded more insistent this time.

He heard the voice of the building superintendent. "Here, whata you guys want?"

"We're looking for Khalil Najjar. Who are you?"

"I'm Benot, the super. Whata ya want with him?"

"We need to talk to him."

"Yeah, well, you'll have to come back when he comes home from work."

"He's not at work. We checked there first."

"Well, he ain't here either. You cops?"

"Immigration and Naturalization Service."

"He still ain't here. Come back tonight."

"My name's Paul McKenna. I'll leave this card under his door. Tell him we'll be back." Duncan MacKenzie pushed the super out of his way. "Don't you ever take a bath?"

The super showed yellowed teeth in what could pass for a smile. "It ain't Saturday night yet."

Mac and Jim moved toward the front door. Jim stopped, pulled a cigarette out of his pocket and lit it. When he turned back to Mac, he winked. "The card you put under the door disappeared. Najjar's in the apartment."

Mac nodded. "Let's see if we can get to Abdul Shakir. He lives down the street."

They hurried to Shakir's apartment building. They walked behind a short, thin man, carrying a bag of groceries up the steps to the front door.

O'Brien caught up to the man. "Mr. Shakir?"

The man looked at him suspiciously. "What do you want?"

"Are you Mr. Shakir?"

"Yes."

O'Brien pulled his INS identification out of his pocket. "I'm Brian Kelly, with Immigration, this is Paul McKenna. We'd like to ask you some questions."

Shakir's eyes narrowed. "Why? What have I done?"

"Well, for one thing, you moved out of your last residence without notifying the department."

"I moved here because it was closer to where I work. I told that to the lady in your office when I called."

"That's the other thing we wanted to talk to you about. We know what your earnings are as a stevedore but your bank account shows a balance of over $200,000. Where did you get all that money?"

"Where did you say you were from?" He didn't hear the answer. His thoughts raced back to the time when he and Najjar applied for citizenship papers. *One of the reasons they didn't question our applications for citizen status was because we had money in the bank and were employed and they knew we would not go on welfare and become wards of the state. Something's wrong, these men are not from Immigration or they would have this information in that folder the big man is carrying*. Aloud, he said, "I won't answer any more questions. My attorney is Karif Tamir. You can reach him at his office in SoHo."

Mac remembered that after urban renewal, SoHo, once a commercial slum area, south of Houston Street had become the art deco district, bordered by West Broadway, West Houston Street, Broadway and Broome Street where high priced professionals now lived. "We'll have to ask you to come with us, sir. You may call your attorney from our offices."

Shakir's annoyance showed. "May I put my groceries in my apartment?"

"Of course."

Shakir took out his key and slid it into the lock. With a quick burst of energy, he was in the apartment, slammed and bolted the apartment door behind him and quickly made his way to the back entrance. For once he was happy to have a first floor apartment. He was quick and agile and was gone before the two investigators could find their way to the back of the building.

"Damn it," Mac said and motioned for O'Brien to go around to the rear of the building on the outside. He raced to the end of the long hall to the red exit sign. There were trashcans stacked in front of the door leading to the outside. Mac gave vent to his frustration by kicking the cans and sending the contents spilling on the vinyl covered hall floor. When he made his way outside, there was no sign of Abdul Shakir. He met O'Brien coming around back.

"Let's pick up Sami Aban. We'll use our own identification. Assuming these four men know each other and I think that's a fair assumption, we've got to get to Aban before Najjar or Shakir have time to contact him."

* * *

It was a mild spring day and people were sitting on the front stoop. Jim O'Brien pulled into a vacant spot halfway up the block from Aban's apartment. MacKenzie checked the photograph before they got out of the car.

"We're in luck. That's him sitting on the front steps." Aban sat watching two children riding their tricycles on the sidewalk. O'Brien unbuttoned his jacket to give him easy access to the gun in his shoulder harness. Mac took out his shield and showed it to Aban.

"FBI. We'd like to ask you some questions."

Aban looked at the shield and the identification.

"What have I done?"

"We want to talk to you about the recent bombings."

Sami Aban looked sick.

"Come with us, please."

"Is it alright if I lock the door to my apartment first?"

"Give your key to Mr. O'Brien. He'll lock it for you."

Aban took the key from his pocket and handed it to O'Brien. My apartment is on the second floor, number four." He looked at Mac. "May I call my attorney?"

"You can do that from downtown. Who is your attorney?"

"Karif Tamir, his office is..."

Mac finished the sentence for him. "In the SoHo district."

Aban was amazed. "Do you know him?"

"No, but his client list is very interesting." At the car, Mac told him to spread his feet apart and lean on the car. Once he was sure Aban had no weapons, he put the Iraqi in the back seat. He stood beside the open door and waited until O'Brien came back and got in the back seat beside Aban. Mac drove to the street where Hamid Marid lived. O'Brien saw the concerned expression on Aban's face when Mac climbed the steps to Marid's apartment. When Mac returned, Hamid Marid walked beside him. Mac put him in the back seat with O'Brien and said, "At least we're batting 500. He's clean."

As the car pulled away, Hamid Marid spoke in Arabic to his friend. "Do you think they know what we did?"

"No. I think they're questioning everybody from the Middle East. They know nothing. How could they? Remember how many suspects they took in after the first episode at the World Trade Center? Just keep your wits about you. Everything will work out. Karif Tamir will get us released. Tell the infidels nothing and above all, never mention the names of our friends."

The two men were put in separate interrogation rooms and Mac barked some orders into a telephone.

"Mr. MacKenzie, Alan Chambers called while you were out. He left a number for you. He said something about the van that Edward Morrison was in at the Kryler Building. He thinks it's abandoned under the Verrazano Narrows Bridge, on the Staten Island side."

He smiled at his secretary. "You know, Joan, some days you even earn your salary."

She smiled back. "And a happy Wednesday to you too."

"Ask Sanders to come in." He picked up a slip of paper from his desk. "Is this Alan Chamber's number?"

"No, sir. That's Miss Boyer's phone number. You wrote it down then left it on your desk." She handed him the message from Chambers.

Mac felt his ears get red. "Aren't you glad you have such an efficient, mentally stable boss with a memory like a steel trap? Get Chambers on the phone for me."

Her laughter drifted back as she closed the door. He turned to Jim O'Brien. "Maybe this is the lead we've been waiting for."

The door opened and Alberto Sanders filled the open space.

"You wanted me, Chief?"

"The two men we just brought in, I want them put on ice until we get back. One of their friends may have contacted their attorney, a man named Karif Tamir. I don't want them talking to him or anyone else. Most of all, I don't want them talking to each other. Put them in the observation rooms, I want all of their actions on videotape. Get them some food and coffee but no visitors. Question them. Their files are on my desk. Get out an all points bulletin on Khalil Najjar and Abdul Shakir. Their files are on my desk too."

Alberto Sanders' white teeth gleamed against the ebony skin of his handsome face. "You got it."

The buzzer sounded and he saw the light on his telephone flashing. He picked it up. "This is MacKenzie."

"Mr. MacKenzie, this is Alan Chambers. I was driving back to Brooklyn from Staten Island when I spotted the van under the approach to the Verrazano Narrows Bridge. The one Moose Morrison was in when the Kryler building went kaboom. At least it looked like the same van. Did you get to talk to Moose? Did he tell you he saw me?"

"Moose Morrison was dead when we got to him. He had been shot."

"Oh, my God. You don't think it's because I told you about him?"

"No, Mr. Chambers, he got shot because somebody didn't want him talking. I think it was all planned that way before he ever accepted the dirty job. Tell me exactly where you saw the van." Mac listened. "Thank you, Mr. Chambers; this may be the lead we were looking for." He hung up the phone. "Okay, Jim, let's go."

* * *

Najjar picked up the phone on the first ring. "Abdul, where have you been? I've been calling you for the past two hours. There was no answer at your apartment."

"I am not at my apartment. I went down to the old shack on the waterfront. I had a visit from two men who said they were with the Immigration Service. But I don't think so. I think they were with the FBI. They were going to take me into custody but I escaped and came here. Every time I tried calling, your line was busy."

"That's because I was trying to reach you at your apartment. The men from Immigration were here too and the super told them I was not at home."

"Khalil, get out of there before they come back for you. I've been calling Aban and Marid. There is no answer at either place.

They may already be in custody. They know about our bank accounts; that was one of the questions they asked me."

"What did you tell them?"

"Nothing. I told them nothing. I said I would not talk to them without Karif Tamir being there too. After that I escaped. Why are we talking on the phone, you should be getting out of there before they come back for you."

"I'll leave now."

Shakir stretched out on the floor of the shack, listening for any sounds out of the ordinary. He heard footsteps on the gravel approaching the shack. He crawled to the wall beside the door, so that when the door swung open, he would be behind it. Slowly the door opened and a shaft of sunlight cut a path across the littered floor.

"Abdul. Abdul."

"I'm here, Khalil. Come in and close the door."

"What's going on? Why is Immigration looking for us?"

"Khalil, I think they were from the FBI."

"What makes you think so?"

"What does Immigration care about how much money we have? All they care about is that we do not become dependent on the government. If they were truly INS men, they would have known how much money we had when we came to the United States. They would also have a record that we notified them when we moved to our new addresses. They're on a fishing expedition and they're baiting us. It's up to us, whether or not we take the bait. They have nothing to connect us with the explosions at the bus terminal or the one on the train. There's nothing in the vans to link us to the other bombings. If the men from Iraq were careless, that's their problem. The FBI will try to intimidate us. Their methods are not much different from those used by the KGB or any other police state. We've been tested by the best. Our training in the desert camp was far superior to anything the Americans can come up with. If they torture us, we will prevail.

They can't do anything worse than what we endured at Abd Al Bari Camp. Now we know why the camp leaders were so savage in their treatment of us. If we are captured, our leaders must know we would never involve them in the plan. It must always look like we did the planning and execution of all attacks."

"Abdul, we're expendable. You said so, yourself. You said none of us would be permitted to live after the project was done. I know Ammar has definite plans for me but what about you and the others? If the plan fails, you could never go home but neither can Ammar. If you must stay here, you will always be looking over your shoulder because one of those times, when you turn around, Abu Ammar will be there…waiting. He would never consider the failure to be his but yours and he would be your executioner, just like he was Edward Morrison's executioner."

"How do you know that? We never saw this Morrison person, what makes you so sure he was part of Ammar's plan?"

Khalil shook his head. "Now, who is it with his head buried in the sand like an ostrich? You saw the newspapers with Ammar's picture on the front page. They wouldn't publish his picture unless they were positive. In addition to the explosions, he's wanted for the murder of Morrison. He's wanted for the murder of a man named Raymond Briggs, a cab driver. They say Ammar killed the man and took his cab and used it in the last two hits. The more I thought about it, the more convinced I was that you were correct in your assumption. We all know too much. Our lives aren't worth two fils, because we're part of the New York project. Ammar's fiendish plan is to eliminate everyone connected with the attacks. Dead men cannot testify, my friend. The only reason the FBI hasn't picked him up yet is because he no longer looks like Abu Ammar. I have known this man since we were boys and even I would not have recognized him, except for his voice. He has even changed the color of his eyes and hair. He covered up the scar on his face, like I told you he would and it's impossible to detect that it is only makeup. If he was not demonic, how could he have known when to assume his new identity? When to leave the place where he had been living? It is said the devil protects his own."

Abdul shook a cigarette out of the pack. "We have so many choices, don't we? You know as well as I, that there are no options open to us. We have never had options. If we do not perform as he thinks we should, we'll die. If we do perform as he thinks we should, we'll die. You can change the scenario but the outcome is always the same."

"Abdul, have you thought about how the plan is to be carried out? If Hamid and Sami have been taken into custody, how can we set things up at the sewer and get away with looking like city workers. If there are only three of us, that will attract attention. It takes only one suspicious person to put all of us in danger."

Abdul shook his head and said, "Either we live inside the American prisons or we die by Ammar's hand. Those are the choices. We have nothing to show for our lives. We have no wives, no families, and no friends, other than those who are part of the operation. There will be no one to mourn for us when we are gone and no one to hold fond memories. How sad to realize that we will have passed through this life without a sign that we were ever here. I don't want to be remembered by the number of people whose lives we stole."

Najjar was resigned. "Perhaps that's the way it should be. If we had wives and families, it would be too painful to leave it behind."

* * *

Washington, D.C.

Rain whipped against the broad windows of the airport, obscuring their view of the L-1011 at the overseas terminal. Glenn and Mike watched as the passengers deplaned, until the familiar face of Antony Emerson emerged from the crowd. Glenn waved to attract his attention. His smile brightened and his eyes caressed her. For a brief moment, Mike found himself resenting the suave Englishman. The resentment deepened when Tony took Glenn in his arms and kissed her. The warmth of his handshake was genuine, however, and Mike realized suddenly that his resentment stemmed from a feeling of jealousy, an unfamiliar emotion to him. That in itself was a blow to his mighty ego. Ostensibly, Tony came to Washington for the annual board meeting of The Alexander Hotels International. Glenn's limousine was waiting when they braved the gusty winds and rain. Templeton Osbourne walked to meet them with two extra umbrellas dangling from his arm. He quickly covered Glenn with the open umbrella and handed one to each of the men.

"Good to see you again, Templeton." Tony shook hands with the tall, proud guardian.

"Good to see you too, sir. I trust you had a pleasant flight?"

"Yes, thank you."

Mike Redmond watched the two Englishmen with amusement. *Damn it,* Mike thought, *these Limeys have to do all the fancy footwork before you know where they stand. What the hell does Templeton care about how his flight was? He's here, isn't he?* He found himself studying Glenn and Tony together. He wondered if Tony had taken her to bed. *They've known each other since they were kids. She was with him in Kuwait, last week. Damn, she's got a great body and knows how to use it.* He felt a strong surge of desire. *Stop it, Redmond, she's not your girl. Pretty bad when you begin to believe your own press. If you know what's good for you, you'll stay out of her bed and remember she's your partner on this project. When this is over, you'll see her at meetings and maybe some social affairs. Wait a minute, Redmond, what the hell are you talking about, social affairs? You don't go to those things. You're doing it now, because your job requires it. Right?*

When they reached the car, Glenn got in back, followed by Tony. Mike walked around the car and sat on the other side of Glenn. Templeton got in the driver's seat and closed the window between the front and back seats.

Tony asked Mike, "Is there a problem about Bengal?"

"Some weird things have been happening and we have to make sure that Bengal is who he says he is and that the opposition didn't take out the real Bengal and send in a ringer. You're the only one who knows what he looks like. We're close enough that if we got the wrong information, it could mean the lives of a lot of agents, to say nothing of the Washingtonians. One of our agents got taken out along with one of theirs. Both were shot in the back of the head. If Bengal is who he says he is, then we have no problem. If not, then conceivably, he's Abd al Alim or knows who is."

"Who was the Arab agent killed with your agent?"

"His name was George Davet."

The name meant nothing to Emerson.

Mike continued, "He worked as a golf pro at the country club. Had lots of contacts, and nobody suspected him until we came up with his real identity. Griad Basq."

Tony's eyebrows arched and he whistled through his teeth. "Basq. He had to have trusted the person he was with. He would never have turned his back on anyone he wasn't certain about. He was Iraq's super agent. If he wasn't Abd al Alim, the person who is has to be sharper, faster, smarter, more polished, and ten times deadlier. He must have resented having to answer to someone he felt was beneath him. It was probably his conceit and arrogance that got him killed."

"Do you think there's a chance Bengal is a double agent?"

Antony Emerson studied his well manicured fingernails. "There's always that possibility with any agent, you know that. Bengal is a good agent and it took a long time before we could infiltrate any terrorist organization. We tried it once before. The agent went to the desert camp for training and was never seen again. Poor chap. Bengal is as trusted as anyone can be. He didn't start in Nidal's group. He began with Munathamat Khamista'shar Mayo. Then for two years, he was part of Al-Jibha al-Sha'biya before he joined Abu Nidal's organization. You can't get more specialized than that. There are perhaps thirty members of that group. Very elite. Bengal was handpicked by their leader. The group was formed from the remnants of Wadi Haddad's special operations command, after he was killed in 1978. The new group had links to Iraq and Libya. Bengal was recruited by the Iraqi Madman himself. When this band of terrorists was organized, it was given the name of Husam al Din, which roughly translated means the determined sword of faith. Since it was formed for the purpose of this one particular target, in all probability, it will be disbanded once the target has been obliterated. Bengal was specifically requested by Bin Laden because of his reputation in the Arab world. He may not trust Bengal but he recognizes talent."

"Then how come he wasn't picked to be Abd al Alim?"

"I doubt if we'll ever know the answer to that question. I think it was because the choice for Abd al Alim rested with the man with the money. The guy who pays the tab names the assassin. Saddam chose Alim and Bin Laden chose Bengal. *Ne plus ultra,* the highest level of perfection."

"Glenn, did Bengal mention where he would be staying?" Mike asked.

Before she could answer, Tony said, "He's staying at the Midway Motel, just outside of Washington."

"We'll take Glenn's car and drive over. It's less conspicuous than my red Ferrari."

"What do you want me to do when we get there?"

"Sit in the car until he comes out. All I want is for you to tell me that the Bengal you see is the real Bengal."

* * *

New York

Duncan MacKenzie walked cautiously around the van, examining the doors and windows. Jim O'Brien crouched beside the left rear tire and focused a mirror to see the underside of the van. Both men moved away from the vehicle back to the car. Mac wiped his hands on a handkerchief, picked up the phone and called his office.

"Joan, we're on the Staten Island side of the Verrazano Narrows Bridge. Send out the bomb squad. We've got a live one." He listened; then smiled. "Where are they now? Tell Alberto Sanders to make them comfortable. I'll be back as soon as we're finished here. Oh, and send out the lab guys. Once the van is disarmed, we'll need them to go over it very carefully."

Jim unwrapped a stick of gum and folded it into his mouth. "Did I detect a glimmer of hope in your voice? What did Joan have for you?"

"Three Arabs were picked up at the overseas terminal. They came in a few days ago from Kuwait and were making plans to get on the first available flight out. Alberto will keep them on tap until we get back."

O'Brien watched the approach of the armored van used by the bomb squad. "Here come the crazies. Don't they have any fear at all?"

"Sure they do. How do you think they stay alive? You wouldn't want to do it and certainly I wouldn't, but thank God, somebody has the guts to disarm bombs or there wouldn't be much left of our civilization." They got out of the car as the van pulled to a stop beside them. Mac walked over and shook hands with the four-member squad. He pointed to the abandoned van. "It looks like it's wired from all directions."

Jerry Mears nodded and walked around the van, scratching a diagram on a pad and putting check marks where wire connections were made. He said, "She's wired tight, that's for sure. It's well placed. If it goes, the whole goddamn bridge goes with it and last night's rain left a lot of mud. Not good."

Mac said, "I can't be certain yet but it looks like the van that was used to pull off the bombing of the Kryler Building."

Jerry Mears whistled softly, "Well, I guess if you want to destroy evidence, this is as good a way as any. We'll do whatever we can but we need equipment and fast. We've got to stabilize the van, there's a gradual lateral slide."

"I'll see to it. Anything else you need?"

"Yeah. Get the goddamn traffic off the bridge. Close it down."

"I'll do that right now and I'll send out the equipment. If you need anything, Jim O'Brien will be here. When you say it's safe, our lab boys will go in to see what they can find. Good luck."

Jerry Mears had already forgotten MacKenzie existed. His only concern was the safety of his men and disarming the bomb. When Mac put his car in gear, Jerry Mears was squatting on the ground, the front bumper of the van just above his shoulders.

Mac slid into the traffic on the bridge and drove to the tollgate. He flashed his I.D. and gave the order to clear the bridge until the bomb squad gave the okay. Then he pushed a button on the phone and waited.

"Joan, the boom-boom boys need some heavy equipment at the bridge. They need it now. The van's unstable in all that mud. Jim will be out there until the lab finishes their work. Send a car out to him, so he can keep in touch by phone. I should be at the office in thirty minutes…give or take a few."

* * *

Chisisi Badru pushed the button for the elevator and placed the box he was carrying on the floor. The doors opened and Kurt Herrick, the building superintendent, stepped out.

"Mr. Badru. Do you need help with the box?"

Ammar's hostile eyes studied the manager. "No, thank you. I can manage."

Kurt Herrick shrugged his shoulders and walked into his office on the first floor. Ammar picked up the box and pushed the button for the fourth floor. He took the television from the box and plugged it in. He turned to the news channel and saw his face on the screen. His face as it had been before the makeover. He said, "Three days. Then I can leave this accursed country and go home." His eyes opened wide when he saw the faces of Sami Aban and Hamid Marid on the twenty-inch screen. He turned up the volume.

"...have been taken into custody. They are suspected of taking part in the bombings that have rocked New York. Three other suspects were picked up at John F. Kennedy Airport early this morning. Authorities have not revealed their identities." The voice of the commentator droned on.

Ammar stared unbelievingly at the screen. "This can't be happening. Everything was perfect. It was foolproof." He slammed his fist on the arm of the overstuffed chair. "It can't fall apart now...I planned it." Droplets of perspiration beaded his forehead. "What about Najjar? Has he been taken into custody too?" He began pacing the length of the room. "His picture wasn't shown with the others." He took some coins out of his pocket, went into the hall to the public phone, inserted his coin and punched in Khalil's number. There was no answer. He called Shakir. No answer. Ammar checked his makeup in the mirror, then walked to St. Catherine's park. He needed to think. He needed to be outside. He was too restless to sit. Walk, he had to keep walking. He began to piece together probabilities. *If Najjar and Shakir were not picked up, where would they have gone? Neither could go back to his apartment. New Yorkers were angry, calling for action. No Arab was above suspicion. It'll be impossible for them to rent a room without the FBI being notified. Mr. Herrick is suspicious of my activities but money impresses him and I have lots of it. I feel reasonably sure Herrick won't report me. The fate of Shakir doesn't mean that much to me, except that I will need help setting the bomb in place. Najjar must forfeit his life. The score must be tallied and offset with a long delayed punishment.* He wiped the perspiration from his forehead with the back of his hand. *Think, Ammar, think. There is no way for Najjar and Shakir to contact me, so it's up to me to find them. The waterfront! Of course, they must be at the shack where we met that first time. That's the logical place to go. Fools, idiots. Don't they know the FBI would scour the waterfront? Both of them work on the docks. It's just a matter of time before they're picked up. That could mean, one, or both of them could talk and all my plans will be ruined. I have to find them. I can't allow anything or anyone to interfere with the success of my plan.*

He checked to make sure his wallet was in his pocket before he left the park and took the subway to Lexington Avenue and Sixty-Eighth Street. He remembered seeing a Salvation Army Thrift Shop near the zoo, when he met the three men from Kuwait.

The packages from the Thrift Shop were neatly tied in one large bundle. When he got to the waterfront shack, he waited. No one was there on stakeout. There was no hint of movement anywhere around the shack. His approach was slow and cautious. He pushed the door open and quickly stepped inside, closing the door behind him.

"Najjar," he called. "Shakir." He waited. He saw a slight movement coming from the far corner. He called out again.

Najjar lit the lantern. Ammar walked forward.

"The FBI has Marid and Aban. I'm glad to see they didn't get you. This is the next place they'll look. We've got to get out of here."

"How? Our pictures are in the papers. We'll be recognized before we've gone a hundred meters."

Ammar put the package on the floor, took out his pocketknife and cut the twine. There were two battered old hats, a wooden cane and a pair of crutches. He dug into his coat pocket, produced a key, and handed it to Najjar. "This is the key to the garage where we made the bomb. You can sleep in the van until Friday. Get out of here as quickly as you can. It won't be long before the FBI looks here. There's a newspaper for each of you in the package. Take the subway. Keep your faces hidden by reading the paper on the train. Khalil, you know the way to the garage. Do you have the exact change for the subway?"

Khalil checked his pockets. "Yes we have enough. What'll we do about food?"

"There is a sandwich shop down the street from the garage. Get enough food to last today and tonight. Stay out of sight. Whatever happens, don't go back to your apartment. I'll meet you at the garage tomorrow."

Shakir looked at the closed door and shook his head. "So. The project goes ahead as planned. Business as usual."

"Everything's ready. It's only a matter of putting the bombs in place and setting the timing device." He looked at his watch. "We have to get out of here. I wonder if I should take the chance and go back to my apartment for a few things."

"This is the only time I agree with Ammar. It would be foolhardy to go back there. You narrowly escaped the last time. Why would you even consider going back now? Khalil, has your brain turned to mush?"

"We have no guns. Nothing with which to defend ourselves."

Shakir took a switchblade out of his pocket, and pressed the release. The deadly blade seemed to have a glow all its own. "Where is your knife?"

Najjar felt in his pocket and produced a clone of the one held by Abdul. "Well, at least it's something."

Najjar practiced walking with the crutches. *Keep one knee bent,* he told himself, and swinging through onto the other foot. "I used these things once for about two months, when my leg was broken. At least I didn't forget how to use them."

Shakir was practicing with the cane.

"Abdul, I believe that if you have injured the left leg you should hold the cane in your right hand." He took a large, red bandanna out of his pocket, lifted Abdul's trouser leg and tied the bandanna at the knee. "That will remind you to keep that knee stiff and to keep the cane in the opposite hand." He tried on one of the hats and fixed the brim so that it shadowed his face.

Abdul pulled the brim of his hat down to the bridge of his nose and turned the collar of his jacket up. "How's that?"

Khalil nodded his approval. At the subway, they separated. Abdul got into the first car and Khalil sat in the back of the last car. The subway stops registered in Khalil's mind like the countdown of a moon shot. Careful not to make eye contact, the newspaper was a perfect shield for his face. They breathed a sigh of relief when they got off the train and headed for the garage. Khalil went first, unlocked the garage door and waited for Abdul.

Najjar said, "Did you notice the supermarket two blocks away?"

"I was too busy concentrating on which leg was supposed to be injured. Why?"

"I think we can be spotted in a small sandwich shop. It's always the same person who takes care of you. If I go to the supermarket, I pick up what I want, then I go to one of many cashiers. I'll try to pick a cashier who is more interested in going home than in the customers."

Abdul nodded. "That makes sense."

"I'm taking the key with me, so don't open the door to anyone. The light is over the workbench in the corner. There's no switch, you have to pull the chain on the bulb."

Abdul said, "Get some bottled water while you're at the market."

Najjar shed his crutches, but kept the hat on.

* * *

Office of the FBI

Jim O'Brien limped into the office and slid into the first chair near the door. "I wouldn't be on the bomb squad for love or money. No, sir. Those guys got balls of steel." He pulled his handkerchief out of his back pocket and mopped at his face. "Look at this." He held the wet handkerchief out in front of him. "I'm still sweating bullets. What a cool cat Jerry Mears is. I'm almost shittin' my pants and he's there, calmly talking the other guys through the steps he wants them to take. When it's all over, he takes off his spacesuit and sticks a lollypop in his mouth. A lollypop, for chrissake, Kojak of the boom-boom boys."

Mac laughed. "He probably feels the same about your job. Maybe he prefers to take his chances with explosives rather than look down the barrel of a gun and not know how nuts the guy is on the trigger end."

"Shit, if he makes one wrong snip—goodbye, Jerry Mears."

Mac laughed. "It's all relative. An elephant will face the wildest jungle animal but go crazy over a mouse."

"That's a myth."

"It gets the point across. Did the lab crew find anything?"

"They lifted some prints and got lots of samples of hair. Looks like human hair. They're working late to give you something to dig your teeth into. They figured if somebody was anxious enough to destroy the van, there must be something worth finding. There was an incendiary device set to go off at eight o'clock tonight, in case the bomb didn't go off. Even Jerry Mears was surprised to see that. He doesn't look like the type of guy to be surprised by much of anything."

The intercom buzzed. Mac answered, "What is it, Joan?"

"Beth just called in from the information desk. There's an attorney out there making quite a ruckus. His name is Karif Tamir. He claims to represent Hamid Marid and Sami Aban. I understand he's causing quite a scene."

Mac smiled. "Really, how interesting. I wonder if he's also representing Abu Dawud, Saqr Kharouf and Asfour Riyad. Just tell him the bosses are out on assignments. Tell him anything but the truth. Where is Alberto Sanders?"

"He's holed up in one of the observation rooms. Seven, I think. Anyway, he's back and forth between seven and two. Do you want me to find him for you?"

"No thanks. I'll find him. Get Dave Brodski at INS for me. When I find Alberto, I'll let you know which room I'm in."

Mac opened the door and saw the gargantuan form of Sanders sitting in a chair, with his long legs outstretched, watching the slightly built man on the other side of a two-way mirror. Potted plants were arranged in such a way as not to impede the vision of the observer.

"What's happening, Al?"

"This one is Sami Aban. He's beginning to sweat. The other one, Hamid Marid is like iron. I think we got the right men but I don't think either one is the kingpin."

"I don't think so either. The kingpin called their attorney and he's in the reception area making a fuss."

"So, Mr. Kingpin is worried?"

"Appears that way, did we get fingerprints on these two?"

"On these two and the other three. We faxed their photos to Aziz in Washington and this is what we got back." He handed the papers on the table in front of him to MacKenzie, but his eyes followed Sami Aban. Aban's nervousness was becoming more apparent as he walked to the corner table and poured himself a cup of coffee. His hands shook and the coffee spilled over his fingers.

Mac studied the papers, pursed his lips and let out a low whistle.

"Damn, I wish Peter Aziz was still here. The one called Abu Dawud is really Gadi Qasim, one of Iraq's top henchmen. This sonofabitch was involved in a skyjacking in 1989. An American, Philip Meyer, was shot in the head and tossed out onto the tarmac. Gadi Qasim was identified as the triggerman." Mac passed the photo to Sanders. "Peter says Philip Meyer was married to CIA Agent, Glenn Alexander." Mac looked out the window and took a deep breath. "Damn, I hate to be the one to drag the past back in focus. Keep this bastard on ice. We've got enough now to hang him." He studied the other sheets of paper. "Saqr Kharouf is one of Abu Nidal's top officers. He was second in charge of the interrogation compound at the training camp. It seems he enjoys torturing people. Peter said he has known

Asfour Riyad since they were boys. He didn't know that Riyad joined the terrorist camp. Riyad has a sister living in New York but Peter can't remember her married name." A red light flashed over the mirror, indicating one of them was wanted on the phone. Mac stood up. "I'll take it in the corridor." He picked up the phone. "What have you got, Joan?"

"There's a man here by the name of Aldo Benot. INS sent him over. He wanted to talk to an INS agent named Paul McKenna. Do you know anything about McKenna?"

"Put him in my office. Were you able to reach Dave Brodski at INS?"

"Yes, sir. He's in the laboratory with Jim O'Brien. Do you want me to call him and ask him to meet you in your office?"

"No. I'll go to the lab to talk to Dave before I come back to the office." As he walked to the lab, his mind raced. *Who the hell is Aldo Benot? How did he get Paul McKenna's name? Well, maybe Dave Brodski knows who this guy is.*

Mac turned into the laboratory. O'Brien and Brodski and a group of technicians were gathered around the director of the laboratory, Dr. Larry Holmes. Holmes was peering through the microscope. He looked up as Mac took a seat on the other side of the lab bench.

"What have you got, Doc?"

"More than any of you hoped for. We got a matched set of fingerprints on Asfour Riyad. No prints from Hamid Marid or Sami Aban. However, preliminary tests show that hairs taken from the van could be the same as hairs taken from Riyad, Aban and Marid. I think DNA tests will confirm that, but it'll take a little time. Nothing on Saqr Kharouf and Gadi Qasim."

"Don't sweat it, Doc; we've got enough on Qasim to execute him. We have motion pictures of him shooting an American during a skyjacking and shoving him out of the plane. We'll keep digging for solid evidence against Kharouf too." He turned to the INS agent and extended his hand. "Hello, Dave. I'm glad to see you."

Dave Brodski took the hand offered and slapped MacKenzie on the back. "Have you been playing cops, again?"

Mac laughed and the two men walked out into the corridor.

"Guilty as charged. We didn't want to scare Shakir and Najjar away, so I produced INS identification. I don't know why but people get scared when they see FBI identification."

"No shit."

"When I use the INS identification, I also use the name of Paul McKenna."

"That was what I thought when Aldo Benot came into my office, asking for agent McKenna. I knew it had to be you."

"Who the hell is Aldo Benot?"

"Damned if I know. I didn't question him. I just assumed you would know him. You want me to handle it?"

"No, thanks, Dave. I had Joan put him in my office. Stick around and I'll take you to dinner."

"Well, I figured if you were taking the name of INS in vain, the least you can do is pay for dinner."

"I'll catch you after I see this guy. Where will you be?"

"In Jim's office. If you need me, yell. INS likes to help you poor FBI guys."

Mac opened the door to his office and the offensive body odor assailed his nostrils. He didn't have to look at the man; the odor told him who it was. He walked around the other side of the desk.

"Mr. Benot, what can I do for you?"

"Hey, are you in tight with the FBI?"

"Sometimes. What's your problem?"

"You wanted Khalil Najjar. You still want him?"

Mac studied the balding head of the super and he could smell the bad breath across the desk. "What have you got?"

"A couple of hours after you left, I was outside of his apartment and I smelled something burning, so I banged on his door and like I told you, he wasn't home. So I let myself in with my passkey. He left food on the stove and it was burnt so bad you couldn't identify it. I figured he musta left in a hurry. I took the pot off the stove and opened the windows and turned on the exhaust fan to get the smoke out. There were some papers that blew off the table onto the floor. I picked them up and was puttin' them back on the table, when it caught my eye. When I was young, I was with army ordnance, so the papers really interested me. I think this guy was making a bomb." He took the papers out of his pocket and laid them on the desk between them.

"You want to take care of it, or do you want me to talk to somebody here in the FBI?"

Mac scanned the pages. "I'll handle it, Mr. Benot. Thank you for bringing this to my attention." He leaned across the desk and shook hands with the malodorous Mr. Benot. He sat back in his chair and watched the man retrace his steps into Joan's office then into the corridor. When the door closed, Joan rushed in to Mac's office and began opening windows and fanning away the odor of perspiration and dirt, with the use of a file folder.

"Mr. Mackenzie, how can you sit there with all that stench surrounding you?"

Mac shook his head and smiled. "Sometimes, Joan, the worst odors to one person can smell like roses to another. That smelly old man just handed me the salvation of New York City. He might smell like brimstone to you but he sure smells like roses from heaven to me." He leaped out of his chair, grabbed the papers Aldo Benot gave him and hurried down the corridor to Jim O'Brien's office.

"Jim, come into the conference room. You too, Dave." He pulled open the paneled wall partition to reveal a giant map of Manhattan and the surrounding boroughs.

"Where did I say the next hit would be?"

Jim looked bewildered but put his finger on a red flag on the map. "You said Abd al Jabbar was an obsessive compulsive that he liked things neat and tidy and for this reason he was working in a circle, the perfect geometric shape. No beginning and no end."

"Right, so the logical site for the next bomb would be the Empire State Building, right there, represented by the black flag. Note that it's inside a closed circle." He handed the papers to Jim O'Brien. "Take a look at these."

O'Brien looked at the neat Arabic characters and the painstaking detail of the drawings. "How did we get these? The sketches are obvious, but what do these characters mean?"

"Actually, the sketches are all we need but I faxed a copy to Peter Aziz in Washington for an interpretation. We should get an answer soon.

He looked at Dave Brodski. "Aldo Benot brought these papers to Paul McKenna."

Jim O'Brien frowned. "Who the hell is Aldo Benot?"

A slow smile spread across the square face of Dave Brodski, "Well, I'll be damned."

Jim looked from one man to the other. "Will somebody please tell me who the hell Aldo Benot is?"

"Remember the super at Khalil Najjar's apartment building?"

"The odoriferous one? Who could forget him? It took an hour to get the stench out of my nostrils." His eyebrows arched until they almost met his hairline. "He gave you these?"

"It looks like Najjar was in a hurry to leave the apartment and left these papers on the table. He also forgot to turn off the gas range and it was his burning food that forced Aldo Benot to go into his apartment. He saw these papers and recognized the rigging of a bomb. Thank God that Benot was with army ordnance, when he was in the service. Najjar even made detailed drawings of the sewer and the tunnel going into the building. Here's another sketch of the air conditioning system and he marked the spots with X's where the bombs are to be planted."

"But how do you know it's the Empire State Building?"

"Look at the diagrams of the sewer and tunnel. Up here," he pointed to small initials, "ESB. He even marked the manhole they would be using on Fifth Avenue. How much more could he have done? Make copies of these and return the originals to Najjar's apartment. If Najjar returns, tell Benot to say nothing to him. We don't want them changing plans at the last minute. Keep a couple of copies for us and get a set over to Jerry Mears by messenger. Call him and tell him the drawings are on the way to his office. Then we're going to the pub. Dinner and drinks are on me. First, though I want to call Peter to see if there's anything important in the writing that doesn't show up on the sketches."

As he talked to Aziz he scribbled on a pad. When the call was completed, he read his notes out loud.

"Merciful Allah, guide this miserable hand to detail the construction of the bomb that will destroy the Empire State Building and if it is your will, tell your unworthy servant what he must do to escape the death Abu Ammar has designed for him."

Mac picked up his jacket. "Gentlemen, let's get drunk."

CHAPTER 19

Washington, D.C.

Glenn looked at her watch. "We've been waiting for three hours. I'm starved."

Mike pushed his seat back to find a more comfortable position. "If our man turns out, not to be Bengal and we nab him, lots of nameless people will be grateful to you for giving up your dinner." He put his head back and closed his eyes.

Glenn sat up. "Car coming toward us, very slowly."

"Tony, get down," Mike said, as he reached for Glenn and covered her mouth with his until the car passed. It stopped about twenty feet away. The passenger door opened, a man stepped out and waved to the other occupants of the car. There was a second car that had not entered the motel parking lot but waited until the driver made a move. The first driver backed up and exited the way he came in. The second car outside the lot followed them. Tony concentrated his attention on the man who emerged from the car.

"We can eat now," Tony said. "That's Bengal. I wonder where they were."

"We can find out easily enough. CIA has been tailing the driver of that car. He's an American, turned terrorist. His name is Willie Jones. Now goes by the name of Omar Tarafah. Did you get a good enough look at your boy, Tony? You're sure it's Bengal?"

"Positive. I'll contact him if you want."

"No. That would be dangerous." He turned his attention to Glenn. "Where would you like to have dinner?"

The car phone buzzed. Mike picked it up and identified himself. "Helix," he said and nodded. "We'll be there as soon as we can, considering the traffic." He pushed the off button on the phone. "That was Ardell. He wants us back at the office, tout de suite."

Glenn frowned. "Not until I get something to eat. I'm not fussy; a hamburger will do just fine."

From the back seat, Tony Emerson could see the amusement in Mike's eyes, reflected in the rearview mirror.

"I understand you've known Glenn since you were children. Has she always had this, voracious appetite?"

Tony winked at Mike through the mirror. "I think she has a voracious appetite for many things, including food."

"Very amusing, now if you boys are finished being funny, let's get some food."

Mike shook his head. "Okay, there's a hamburger joint about a mile up the road."

When they arrived, Cliff Ardell was pacing in front of his desk. A sure sign that his frustration had exceeded his patience.

Mike thought, *It looks like all the possible leads he thought he had on finding Randy's murderer have come to a dead end.*

"I have good news and I have bad news," Ardell began. "The good news is that the New York group has a handle on their problems and will be closing in on that operation. The bad news is that all of our leads on finding Randy's killer have ended in zip. The only person unaccounted for is Boulus Qadir. One of our agents was on Qadir's tail but at a busy intersection, he was cut off by a Semi. When he was able to get beyond the truck, Qadir was long gone."

Mike asked, "What about Gabriella Russal? Where was she?"

"She and Karim spent the entire night at home," Ardell said, as he popped two antacid discs into his mouth.

"Where were our men posted?" Glenn asked.

"Where they're posted every night, on the street outside of the gates to her driveway." Ardell stopped his pacing and gave his full attention to Glenn. "There's another way off the estate, isn't there?"

"There are three cabanas in the pool area, for guests to change into swimsuits. Each of them has two doors. One leads into the pool area, the other leads to the inter-coastal waterway. They keep several boats tied up at their dock. It would be easy to slip away and go up or down river. Unless a man was posted at the dock, anyone could have left the house without being seen. The area is well hidden. I'm not saying that's what happened, but it's a possibility."

Mike admired the way Glenn handled herself. *Damn,* he thought, *she may be bleeding for her friend but she's not going to be fooled by her. Maybe she's not as fragile as I think.* Mike pushed his chair back a little, lit a cigarette and admired her long, beautiful legs, which were tauntingly crossed. He blew out a thin stream of smoke, directed at the floor.

"Mike, if you want to look at the lady's legs, take her swimming. Do I have your undivided attention?"

"I can give you my undivided attention, Cliff, and still admire a great work of art. You're a little touchy today. Are you afraid you're falling behind in your little contest with MacKenzie?"

Clifford Ardell's eyes narrowed. Anger and frustration showed on his face. "The only reason Mac is so far ahead, is because I sent Aziz to help him. If Peter hadn't been able to identify the kingpins, they'd be exactly where we are…nowhere. You've noticed, of course, we have not had any explosions in Washington?"

"Not yet. Would you send up warning flags if you were planning a big hit? Abd al Alim is trying very hard to make everything look normal in this area. He must have been very unhappy about the necessity of killing one of our men and one of his own at the same time. That aroused the attention he didn't want. If he was feeling safe that we weren't onto him before, we just lost our edge." Mike recognized the danger signs of pushing Ardell to the wall, so he changed the subject. "Incidentally, Tony identified Bengal. It's him, not a plant. At least we have an agent on the inside. What did you find out about the argument Blanche Cameron had with George Davet at the country club?"

"We questioned Mrs. Cameron and Mrs. Russal simultaneously. Mrs. Russal said the argument stemmed from the fact that Mrs. Cameron wanted Davet barred from the club dining room because he was hired help and not a paying member. She went from angry to furious when she was told Davet owned fifty-one percent of the country club. That was the display you and Glenn witnessed. Guess what Mrs. Cameron's reaction was, when we told her Davet was murdered?" He didn't wait for a response. "She said, 'Good, now I don't have to resign from the Club.'" Ardell shook his head. "That broad's got iron balls."

"What was Gabriella's reaction to Davet's death?" Glenn asked.

"Mrs. Russal's comment was, 'What a pity. For the first time in his life, George won an argument with substantial backing and didn't live to enjoy his victory. He was an excellent golf pro and well liked at the club by most members. We'll miss him.'" Ardell shrugged. "That was her reaction. No emotion. She acted like she didn't know him outside the club and we know that's not true. We found out that they met at the home of Karim's father, Mukhtar Abd al Bari Russal, in Saudi Arabia. It was on one of their trips to visit Karim's family. We have no idea if their trysts in Iraq were personal or if he was trying to recruit her."

Glenn shook her head. "I doubt that very much. Griad Basq was a very macho man. It would be beneath his dignity to recruit a woman for a man's job. I believe if they met anywhere, it was because he was trying to lure her away from the Russal family.

The have-nots aren't very happy with the haves, and Karim's family is respected and held in high esteem. It would have been quite a coup if he had succeeded. Basq had money but compared to the Russals he was a pauper. Their clandestine meetings open the door to a lot of speculation; odd…that the three of them should end up in Washington."

Glenn said, "Now that you mention it, I can't remember ever seeing Karim and Davet talking together. It was always Gabriella who talked to him…usually, when Karim wasn't around. I'm sure Davet was never a guest in their home."

Mike said, "The big question is…was it Davet that Gabi met at the Algonquin Club the day we followed her? We couldn't see the car or the man. Cliff, you saw the sketches she made of the table arrangements. We don't know if she gave any sketches to the man she met. Before we could get close enough, he was gone. In all fairness to her, she did nothing to arouse our suspicions. She said she was going jogging and as soon as he left, that is precisely what she did."

Mike turned to Glenn. "When you were in college, did she ever mention going hunting? To the best of your knowledge, did Gabriella know how to use a gun?"

"I think so. She said something about hunting in Africa with her father and brother, before she went to Paris. I know she was an expert with a rapier. She was the only girl on the fencing team. I don't think she ever lost a match. She said it gave her grace and poise. She was right. Look at the finished product."

Cliff Ardell asked, "How did she meet Karim Russal?"

"She met him through me. When she left Italy, she was despondent, depressed. That was unusual for Gabi. I was the liaison between my father and the managers of the Alexander Hotels. I was going to our newest hotel, in Kuwait. I asked Gabi to go with me. The oil barons were meeting at the hotel and Karim was there with his brother Musa. I had met Karim six months earlier in our hotel in Dallas. He was a very likeable person. We talked and that was it. I didn't think our paths would ever cross again. He recognized me and came over to talk to me. I introduced him to Gabi. The rest is history."

"When was that?"

"1987. They got married less than two weeks after they met. I was their witness. They were in my bridal party when I got married the following year. There was never a time when we weren't friends. Gabi and Karim have always been there for me, especially when my husband was killed in 1989. It's difficult to believe Karim or Gabi could be involved in anything as brutal as this. I'm not convinced they are." She bit her lower lip. "I know there's a lot of circumstantial evidence against Karim. He was at the Vietnam Veterans Memorial at the time the hired guns were there." She studied the expressions on the faces of the men present. "If they're guilty, I'll bring them in."

Ardell said, "We know that, Glenn. I'm sorry to have made it necessary for you to relive a painful time in your life. We had to know about the Russals."

Mike lit a cigarette. "Okay, Cliff, you can drop the other shoe now. You could have given us this information over the phone. What's the real reason for calling us in?"

"You know, Redmond, you should be sitting in my chair. You seem to know more about what I'm thinking than I do." He hesitated. "But you're right, there is another reason. Tonight, the Breckenridges are going to a dinner party at the home of Congressman Thomason."

Mike's eyes rolled up and his shoulders slumped forward. He made an honest effort not to curse. "The guy has a goddamn death wish."

Ardell ignored the comment. "You and Glenn are on stakeout. I want to know the identity of everyone going to or coming from that dinner, including the hired help. Some of our operatives have been assigned as a bartender and waiters, through the catering agency. Cameras, earphones, everything you need are set up in a telephone service van. I don't think we have too much to worry about, even though I agree with you, Mike, it's a stupid move on the President's part."

* * *

New York City

Jim O'Brien stood behind Duncan MacKenzie and studied the large detailed map of the Manhattan area.

"What are we looking for, Mac?"

"Abd al Jabbar is a creature of habit. We know there was a park where he lived before. Apparently, he was a frequent visitor to Christopher Park. I'm making book on the fact that he found another place also near a small park." He began putting white flag pins on the map. "Prospect Park in Brooklyn. McCarren Park and Monsignor McGolrick Park in Greenpoint; Cooper's Park in Williamsburg; St. Mary's Park in Mott Haven; Claremont Park in the Bronx; St. Catherine's Park in Yorkville; Col. Young Park along the Harlem River and DeWitt Clinton Park in the ship terminal area." He sat down and stared at the map. "There are more parks without names. Let's concentrate on the Harlem River, Mott Haven, the ship terminal area, and Yorkville. Get some men out there to the apartment buildings and hotel motels. See how many new tenants have moved in, within the last two weeks. He probably has new identification and has altered his appearance enough, so that he can't be identified easily by the picture in the papers. I'll send out another contingency to cover the Bronx. Concentrate on the areas nearest to the parks. We already have men posing as water department workers around the Empire State Building. Hell, we'll even arrange for a small water main break."

Mac rubbed the back of his neck and wished he could spend a little time with Sam Boyer. He found himself thinking about her a lot lately. "I hope we're not missing anything."

"Why don't you go home, Mac? You can do with some rest. I'll call you if anything develops."

"I guess I can do with a little shuteye. You can reach me at my apartment." He picked up his jacket and walked into Joan's office. His eyes met those of Sam Boyer. He was surprised to find his mouth still remembered how to smile.

"Hello, Sam, is anything wrong? Is Matt okay?"

"Hello, Mac. Matthew's fine. I came to talk to you about Franny Renzo. His mother is concerned that whoever killed Moose will try to get Franny because he talked to you."

Mac smiled again. *It was a feeble excuse,* he thought, *but it worked. She found the excuse I couldn't find.*

"Why don't we have coffee and you can tell me about it." He held the door for her and turned to Joan. "I'll let you know where I'll be as soon as I know." He drove to the waterfront and pulled into a parking lot. He punched a number into the cellular phone. "Joan, I'm at Maestro's restaurant." He walked around the car and opened the door. When Sam slid off the seat, it hiked up her skirt so that it was mid thigh. Mac's half veiled eyes never betrayed his increased pulse rate. He thought, *Peter Aziz would say, "great legs," to which I would answer, "great ass. Tits aren't bad either."*

Pictures of composers, musicians and entertainers lined the walls of the Maestro. "What time do you have to be home to get Matt to bed?"

"Mrs. Pierce said she would keep him overnight in her apartment."

"Marvelous," he smiled. "How about an early dinner? I missed breakfast and lunch."

"I worked through my lunch hour so that I could leave early. I'm hungry too."

A broad shouldered man in an expensive silk suit approached them and shook hands with Mac. "Buona sera, mio caro amico. Where have you been keeping yourself?" He eyed Sam and smiled. "Now I see where you have been keeping yourself." He bowed to her and she blushed.

"Giorgio, this is Samantha Boyer."

Giorgio kissed her hand. "My pleasure, Signorina." He sat them at an isolated table, covered with a white starched cloth.

Giorgio handed them menus. The food at the Maestro hit the crème de la crème rating.

Sam looked over the menu. "I'm not very familiar with Italian cooking. Would you order for me, Mac?"

He scanned the menu and made his selections.

Before the food came, a waiter brought over a bottle of Frascati wine. "Compliments of the Maestro, Mr. MacKenzie."

"Thank Giorgio for me," Mac said as the waiter uncorked the bottle. He smiled at Samantha. "Let's get the business out of the way, then we can enjoy our food."

"Mrs. Renzo," Samantha began, "is very concerned that the person who murdered Moose will come looking for Franny. I tried to tell her there was nothing to worry about, that you would protect him."

"Nobody knows we talked to Franny. I didn't mention his name in my report, nor will I. You can tell Mrs. Renzo that Franny is perfectly safe."

"She'll be glad to hear that. She doesn't want Franny to end up like Matthew." She sipped her wine "The picture in the newspapers, Abd al Jabbar, has he been apprehended?"

"Not yet, but it won't be long now."

"I'm sorry, Mac, I know I shouldn't be asking questions."

"You have every right to ask questions. A brutal murder happened next door to you, and you're concerned."

"But why Moose? He seemed harmless enough."

"When we broke into Moose Morrison's apartment, we found several assault rifles. We know he was working for a terrorist organization. He took part in the bombing of the Kryler Building. Unfortunately, the terrorists got to him before we did. Either way, the outcome would have been the same."

"I hear what you're saying. But you're telling me about a different Moose from the one I know. He was always kind to Matthew, even took him to baseball games. He treated Matthew no differently than he treated the other boys. After Matthew was shot, and I was able to bring him home from the rehab center, he needed a lot of physical therapy and it was impossible for me to handle it alone. Moose came every day and helped Matthew to exercise. Every Christmas, he took him to the stores to see the decorations and get him involved in the excitement of the season. On Sundays he took him to church."

She smiled, remembering the times Moose spent with Matthew. "In the summer, it was picnics in the park. In the winter, after a snowfall, he pulled Matthew on a sled. He opened up a world that would have been denied to him."

"What about your former fiancé? Didn't he do these things with Matthew?"

"No, he didn't like Matthew to be with us. Jack was always uncomfortable around him. I guess he resented my brother because he required so much of my time. Jack didn't want to share me with anyone. He began putting conditions on our relationship. Ones I couldn't live with...so, by mutual agreement, we went our separate ways."

"You would have had a terrible life with him if you had given in to his demands."

"I know. When it was over, I had a feeling of relief. I'm sure Jack did too. It was only then that I realized how much my relationship with Jack had affected Matthew. I hadn't noticed how he was withdrawing, not only from me but from the world in general. I guess I was too wrapped up in my own problems to see how unhappy he was. The Matthew you see today is much improved over the Matthew of a few years ago."

"What happened to your parents?"

"They were caught in a crossfire between rival gangs. Matthew was with them when it happened. They were killed and Matthew was in critical condition for months after the shooting.

I don't know if he has any recollection of our parents, it's almost like he withdrew into a cocoon and wove the opening shut, probably forever."

"What do the doctors say?"

"There was a portion of his brain that was destroyed by the bullet. They said he would be able to function but at a much lower level. They're doing amazing things at the center. But when Matthew is frightened, he forgets everything they taught him and he's five years old again. How do you stop someone from being afraid? He needs a lot of love, a lot of attention and a lot of reassurance. When Moose was killed, there was a noticeable change. Someone he loved was taken away…again."

Mac wanted to reach out and gather her in his arms but he did nothing.

"What about you, Mac? Tell me about your son."

"Todd? We're not very close. Don't get me wrong, he's a great kid, never gives me any problems. He's much closer to my mother than he is to me. It's only natural. He spends a lot more time with her."

"What happened to his mother?"

Mac was surprised to find the sadness, the emptiness, the loneliness, the longing were as acute as they were ten years ago. "A couple of days after Todd was born she complained about a headache. Hour by hour it got worse, so they took her down for a CAT scan. By the time they saw the aneurysm in her brain, it had ruptured. They got her to the operating room, but it was too late. They said the pressure of childbirth exacerbated the condition."

"And you think there were signs that you ignored or just chalked it up to pregnancy, right?" She reached across the table and took his hand. "There was nothing you could do. But all this time, you've been punishing yourself. Todd needs you every bit as much as Matthew needs me. I'm sure your mother is very good to him but that's no substitute for the love he needs from you." Her hand on his was warm and comforting and when she squeezed his hand, their eyes met. "Are you still going to take us on a picnic Sunday?"

He smiled. "Absolutely."

"Why don't you bring Todd along? I think he would enjoy a picnic too."

He felt like a schoolboy with his first crush. "Lady, it's a good thing you're on the other side of this table. If you were any closer, I don't think I could resist taking you in my arms."

She freed her hand from his, pushed her chair back and stood beside him. "There's no table between us now, Mac."

To Mac, they were no longer in a restaurant, they were alone on an island. He stood and took her in his arms. When their lips parted, he whispered in her ear. "You feel so good…it has been so long, so very long." Some movement across the room brought him back to reality. He held her chair as she sat down again. "I want you, Sam. Right now, I ache all over from wanting you…I haven't had these feelings…"

"I know. You haven't had these feelings for a long time. It's the same with me. I thought I was beyond all that. After Jack, I decided never again. Everything was under control until you came along. I started thinking about you. Then I couldn't get you out of my mind. I couldn't wait until Sunday, I had to see you today."

They left their dinners untouched. Mac dropped some bills on the table, picked up her coat and steered her outside. He unlocked the car door and held it for her. When he got behind the wheel, he turned to face her. Her lips were moist and slightly parted. Every fiber of her being begged to be taken. He pulled her to him and covered her mouth with his. There was no denying the thumping in his chest as he pulled her closer while his hands explored the exquisite contours of her breasts.

"I have an apartment I keep in town when I'm on a case. I can't promise I won't get a call five minutes after we get there. Say the word and I'll take you home."

Her hands did some exploring of their own and there was an audible gasp as he sucked in some air.

"There's your answer, Mac. We can't deny what's happening. My desire for you is every bit as strong as yours is for me."

He picked up the phone and punched in a single number.

"I'm on the way to my apartment."

CHAPTER 20

Washington, D.C.

The house across from Congressman Lyle Thomason had been built in 1788 and was being restored to its original Federalist period.

Mike was impressed with the masculine feel and comfort of the spacious room. "How did you manage to get in this house?"

"It belongs to my cousin, Bradley. He was the one who cut in when you were dancing with Sally. He's in China gathering information for his next travel book.

"He's…that…Brad Crawford."

"He asked me to look in, now and then; to be sure the restoration is going according to schedule. What time is it?"

"Six forty-five. The dinner guests should be arriving any time now. This is better than that stuffy van."

She handed him a snifter of cognac.

"Thanks. This is like watching the Redskins from the fifty-yard line. Here comes a limo." Mike focused his binoculars on the two figures emerging from the car.

"It's Senator Cameron and his bitchy wife."

Glenn suppressed a smile and turned on the two-way radio. "This is Raven. Helix and I are in place. Are the guests of honor here yet?"

"Negative. We've been here since sixteen hundred hours. Other than the catering crew, Senator and Mrs. Cameron are the first to arrive."

"Did you check out the caterers?"

"Affirmative, two waiters, Henry Levan and Drew Clever, will serve the dinner and clean up. Drew is one of us. Another of our agents, Tom Raulson, is bartender for tonight. The chef is Andre D'Arcy and his assistant is Adam Mandel, both have clearance. There was one man who drove the panel truck with the supplies. He unloaded them and left after the supplies were in the kitchen. The supplies checked out thoroughly and were verified by Raulson. Incidentally, Raulson is wearing a wire, so we should get some interesting conversations. Here comes another car. It looks like Mr. and Mrs. Blanding. Yep, that's who it is."

Mike wasn't looking at the Blanding vehicle; he was watching the slow moving car approach from the opposite direction. He adjusted his field glasses but the setting sun caused a glare on the windshield of the advancing car making it impossible to see the driver. "There's a car approaching from the east end of the street, driving very slowly. He's pulling over. I can't see the driver. There's a glare on the windshield. He's parked about three houses down from this one. Check it out."

A jogger appeared from behind the van and headed east on the north side of the street, so that he would pass beside the car in question. The driver opened the door, narrowly missing the jogger and mounted the steps of the house with the overgrown lawn.

"The driver was the only one in the car but we had better check him out," said the voice of the jogger. Peter Aziz watched the progress of the jogger from the van.

"According to surveillance teams sent out this morning, the man who entered that house is Carson Little. He works on Capitol Hill as an interpreter. He and his wife split about three months ago so he's living alone."

"There are other cars coming from the west end. It looks like the President's car sandwiched between two secret service cars."

Glenn repositioned herself at the window. "It's almost thirty minutes since the Breckenridges arrived. Do you think that's all of them?"

"Don't know," said Mike. "But I understand it's fashionable to be late."

"Not fashionable, just bad manners," Glenn said as she adjusted her binoculars. "A white Mercedes just turned into the east end. It looks like Gabi's car."

"How the hell does she get all these invitations?"

Glenn laughed. "I told you she knows everybody who is anybody in Washington. She's a much sought after guest and social climbers will do anything short of murder to be invited to one of her parties. Next to the President, she probably carries more political clout than anyone. She's a heavy contributor, as she said, to both parties. That assures her of continued status in Washington society, no matter which party gets in. Nobody plays the capitol quite like Gabi.

Mike said, "There's another car pulling up behind the Russals. The windows are heavily tinted. I can't see who's in there."

They watched the second car's slow advance. Glenn asked, "Blue, can you get a make on the second car?"

"Negative."

The car door opened and Anita Gregory and Paul Qadir joined Gabriella and Karim on the sidewalk. They spoke for a few minutes before they entered the Thomason home together.

Mike cocked his head to one side. "How the hell did Gabi arrange this?"

"I doubt if Gabi's responsible for this. Since the Kennedy years in the White House, it's considered quite chic to invite actors and actresses to a party. It's the 'in' thing to do these days."

Blue's voice crackled on the radio. "There's a taxi coming up the street."

It stopped in front of the congressman's house and a distinguished, white-haired man emerged, handed the driver some money and walked up the steps. His step was light and quick. He was impressive.

"Who was that?"

Glenn smiled. "That, Michael dear, is Clayton Alexander."

"Your father?"

"The one and only. I'll bet he flew in because Alden wanted him here. Let's sit in the van, I want to hear what's going on inside." It was almost dark when they climbed into the van.

Blue pushed a button and the chattering of people in the room sounded like the clucking of hens. As Tom Raulson carried mixed drinks to the guests, bits of conversation were picked up from the wire under his vest.

"Haven't I seen you somewhere, young man?" The crisp, brittle tones belonged to Blanche Cameron.

"It's very possible, ma'am. I'm a mixologist at the most important Washington gatherings."

Glenn giggled. "Good for you, Tom, that should put the old bitch in her place."

Raulson moved on.

"What the hell do you think you're doing, Alden? The goddamn Arabs are trying to pepper your ass and you're playing games."

"Clayton, they have a much better chance of getting to me if I stay in one place. I think I stand a better chance as a moving target."

"That's bullshit, Al, and you know it. You're just making yourself a more frequent target. A good marksman is going to hit his target if it's moving or not. That damned Iraqi madman is out for your..." The voice trailed off as Raulson moved on.

"Darling, I know you're in charge of seating at the fundraiser and I would like to be at one of the front tables near the dais. Those horrid outdoor speakers make it impossible to hear what's being said."

Gabriella laughed. "Darling, at functions like that you don't need to hear anything, all you have to do is write out a check."

"But, my dear, if we're seated at a front table, Matthew will be very visible. You know visibility is closely akin to success…especially in Washington."

"Of course, Blanche, if that's what you want."

"…truly a decadent society. Historically, it reminds me of the Roman Empire just before it fell. It's the people of simple means and simple beliefs who will triumph in the end."

"Would you like your drink freshened, sir?"

The voice of Karim Russal answered, "No, thank you, but I would like a glass of cold water."

"Of course. And you, sir?"

The voice that spoke about the simple things answered, "I'll have bourbon and water."

Raulson picked up empty glasses and wiped away the water rings on the Louis XIV table. He managed to stay in the area long enough to catch the rest of Paul Qadir's thoughts.

"Believe me, Karim; the world would never notice the demise of a nation such as this. Life for us would go on, peacefully, as it has for thousands of years. This democracy is just a little over two hundred years old, I doubt if anyone would notice its passing."

"Paul, you know absolutely nothing about the history of our people. When Arab nations weren't fighting other Arab nations we were fighting among ourselves. Wealth in our country is in the hands of a few and if you are born to it, all well and good, but if—"

Tom Raulson was out of hearing range.

"Ladies and gentlemen," said Lyle Thomason, "dinner is ready."

There was an obvious sound of movement and voices but nothing was clear until they were seated in the dining room and Drew Clever was within range as he placed food before each guest on one side of the table and Henry Levan served the other side.

"Clayton, darling," purred Gabi's voice, "how long has it been since I've seen you?"

"It must be two, two and a half years. You haven't changed, little one, you're as pretty as ever."

Gabriella laughed. "Clayton, you have always been one of my favorite people. Did you know I fell in love with you the moment I set eyes on you?"

There was an answering laughter in his voice. "If you fell in love with me, why the hell did you marry Karim?"

"Why, darling, I wanted you to live. You probably couldn't have survived my voracious sexual appetite."

"You know, Gabi, there's an old cliché about snow on the roof and fire in the furnace. We're not going to rush to the buffet and try to consume everything on it. We walk to the buffet, slowly and select only the choicest of what that buffet has to offer."

"Touché, darling, touché."

Dinner lasted for three hours and conversation went from political rallies to vacations and from baseball to sailing.

Alden and Marcia Breckenridge were the first to leave. Mike looked up at the second floor and saw a figure move away from the window.

"The front room of the second floor."

Peter Aziz saw the curtain fall into place. "Were you able to see who it was?"

"No," Mike said, "but somebody was interested enough to watch their departure. That says one thing to me; Abd al Alim was at that dinner party tonight."

CHAPTER 21

Washington, D.C.

The subdued light in the conference room gave the meeting an air of relaxation that belied the consternation that brought the group together. Clifford Ardell opened the file in front of him. "We have thirty-seven hours to find Abd al Alim. Thirty-seven hours and one dead agent. I think Randy Perry bought it because he uncovered something. Before he joined the company, he was an investigative reporter. A good one. I think he discovered the identity of Abd al Alim. Somehow, he left us a clue. We just haven't found it.

"The M.E. should be finished with the autopsy. Our men are sweeping the entire channel where the bodies were found." He lit a cigarette and studied the small group through the smoke. "Each of you has a copy of the material Randy gathered in Rome. Somehow, Gabriella Russal is involved in this plot right up to her pretty little neck. Each separate piece of information means nothing but when I put the pieces together I got more than a picture. I got a scenario. Let's take the pieces one at a time:

"Fact one: she lied about going to see her grandmother on her frequent trips to Rome. We know now, her grandmother, Concetta Renaldi, died in 1986.

"Fact two: she claimed she had nothing to do with her adopted brother, Salvatore, because he's always in trouble. Salvatore Cammeo died in 1985 when the car he was driving blew up.

"Fact three: we know Salvatore Cammeo was a member of the Red Brigade.

"Fact four: she was in love with him and gave birth to his child when she was seventeen.

"Fact five: at the time of the child's birth, Mrs. Russal was registered at the hospital as Maria Renaldi. She used her mother's maiden name. The child's name is Violetta Renaldi. Mrs. Russal's former governess, Philomena Lucca, cares for the child during school vacations and holidays."

He paused to allow them to digest the information. "I think Randy uncovered something else and was checking it out when he got killed…I think he found out Gabriella Russal was and is an agent of the Red Brigade."

Peter Aziz cleared his throat. "It would certainly account for her trips to Iraq and her contact with Griad Basq, alias George Davet. If Basq was the only person other than the Iraqi madman who knew the identity of Abd al Alim, then…eliminating him would have been an absolute," Aziz speculated. "What if Randy followed Basq to a prearranged meeting he had with Alim. We know enough about Alim to suppose caution would be paramount and any place of rendezvous would be reconnoitered prior to the face-to-face meeting. What if Alim spotted Randy, circled around and came up behind him?"

Glenn listened intently to Peter's theory. "What if we're wrong? What if she's not Alim? What if it's Karim or Paul Qadir?"

Mike shook his head. "Bengal said Qadir was sent as backup. I doubt that Qadir knows Alim's identity. We've had a tail on Qadir and Karim. At the time Randy and Basq were killed, Qadir was with Anita Gregory and Karim was at the country club. Gabi was to meet him there for golf. She was late."

"Gentlemen," Glenn said, "allow me to play the devil's advocate and point out that Gabriella Russal's habitual tardiness has been known for several years in Washington society. You've got to have more than that to bring her in."

Peter said, "Last night when we saw someone at the window of a second floor bedroom of the Thomason's house, only two people were missing from the group. Gabriella Russal and Blanche Cameron."

"Are you going to take Gabi into custody based on supposition? Remember her friends in high places. The first one to protest will be Alden Breckenridge. What if we're wrong? What if the danger is coming from within?"

Ardell took a deep drag on his cigarette and exhaled a thin steady stream of smoke before he answered, "Blanche Cameron."

"Why not? We heard her ask Gabriella to seat her and the senator at one of the front tables, supposedly so that her husband would be visible. We think it's to satisfy her political aspirations for his career—but are we sure that's the reason?"

"I hear what you're saying, Glenn, and we can't overlook even the smallest possibility but there's a lot of smoke coming from the Russal camp. We've got to see if there's also fire. If Mrs. Russal is an agent of Italy's Red Brigade, we're dealing with someone whose commitment to terrorism is fanatical. The Red Brigade has the most brutal record of all groups involved in terrorism. When Salvatore Cammeo was a student, he joined the Red Brigade and Gabriella was his adoring apostle. Randy told me he felt the reason Gabriella's father separated her and Salvatore was not because of the love affair…it was because Salvatore recruited her…for the Red Brigade.

"Just because that terrorist group isn't making headlines doesn't mean they've disbanded. They're dormant, like fleas in winter…waiting for the right conditions.

"As far as Mrs. Russal is concerned, I think it's a matter of being an assassin for hire. Not for the money. But for the high, the thrill."

Ardell opened Gabriella Russal's file. "When I was studying her dossier, I compared the dates of her trips to assassinations that took place throughout Europe and the Middle East. Eight of those trips coincide exactly with hits made in Israel, France, and Kuwait. Coincidence?"

"What's our next move?" asked Mike.

Ardell closed the file. "You and Glenn attach yourselves to Gabriella Russal like you were her second skin. Peter, you cover Paul Qadir. As backup, he may have to carry the ball if she fails. I've assigned men to cover Senator and Mrs. Cameron in case Glenn's suspicions are correct. We'll have a security entrance similar to the ones at airports. There's only one way in and the same way out. Our men and the FBI will be covering the periphery of the Algonquin Club. The FBI has men planted as waiters, busboys and bartenders. The FBI is working with us at the Lincoln Memorial too. Thanks to Bengal we know the makeup of the explosive, how the charges will be wired and where they'll be placed. We expect the terrorists will fight to the end. We'll try to get Bengal out of there before it goes down."

Ardell looked at Aziz. "Peter, what can you tell us about the New York contingency?"

"I talked with Mac on the phone today. He is convinced that the target area is the Empire State Building. The terrorists plan to enter through the air conditioning system and wire the explosives inside the system. Abd al Jabbar is running the terrorist show there. Unfortunately, they haven't found him yet. Mac and his boys got a break when one of the terrorists skipped in a hurry and left behind a schematic of the final explosion. It was like he wanted somebody to find it. The FBI picked up three terrorists at JFK airport. One of them was Abu Dawud. He looked at Glenn. Dawud's real name is…Gadi Qasim."

Slowly Glenn looked up from the file she held. A look of incredulity accentuated her large green eyes and she whispered the name, "Gadi Qasim?" She looked like she had been struck. "Qasim in New York?"

Peter smiled. "In New York and in custody. It won't bring back Philip Meyer but at least you know justice wasn't dead—just sleeping."

Mike Redmond watched the parade of emotions reflected in Glenn's eyes, suspicion, doubt, anger, hate and finally resignation. Mike's own thoughts took over.

Damn, she's a beautiful woman. Men want to hold her, protect her. She captivates and imprisons them in the depth of those green eyes. Got to give her credit though, she doesn't expect special consideration. She's a team player and she'll do her part even if she's torn apart inside. I wish there was some way I could buffer the hurt…Whoa, buddy, you sound like a guy with long-range plans. There's no room in your life for this nonsense. Another time, another place, another dimension but not now, not like this.

"Mac has done one hell of a job in New York." Peter Aziz finished his report and Mike brought his thoughts back to the meeting.

Ardell said, "Glenn and Mike, find a reason—any reason to be with Mrs. Russal. I'll have Chuck Appleby cover Senator and Mrs. Cameron. There's a good chance of crossfire especially if it looks like their backs are to the wall. Civilians could be hurt—or worse, taken hostage. Be sure that doesn't happen. The Secret Service will have their men scattered throughout the area." He stood up. The meeting had come to an end. Before anyone moved, he said, "We don't need dead heroes."

CHAPTER 22

New York City
May 18

Abu Ammar stood in the shadow of the trees across the street from his apartment. His animal instinct warned him there was danger nearby. He sniffed the air like a prowling tiger.

His instincts were never wrong.

He waited and watched. Two men emerged from the building and went directly to the black Buick at curbside and drove away.

Still Ammar waited and watched. Cautiously, he walked into the building. The door to Kurt Herrick's office was open and Herrick was working on his books, his perpetual rent books. He looked up as Ammar entered.

"What can I do for you, Mr. Badru?"

"I saw two men leaving. Was one of them Herman Tobias? I thought I recognized him. I used to work with him."

"No. You don't want to know those men. They're with the FBI. They're looking for a man called Abd, or Abu something or other. They showed me a picture of him. Poor guy, looked like somebody worked him over with a switchblade. They think this guy might be involved in the bombings."

Ammar suppressed the urge to smile. "Thank you, Mr. Herrick." He took the elevator to the second floor and approached his rooms cautiously. He checked the door before he ventured in. Slowly, his eyes scanned the room. Everything seemed normal. He hurried to the closet to check his suitcase. It was angled, just as he left it. The pencil line on the underside of the luggage was at the edge of the shelf. He took it down and opened it. The Kalashnikov AK47 with the folding stock was just as he had set it in place and the 9 mm Marakov was still in the holster. His hand caressed the pistol. He took it out and strapped it on, putting the silencer in his pocket. Rahman Isa, the former intelligence chief of ANO, had taught him well.

Rahman Isa had said to Jabbar, "Learn as much as you can about makeup. One day, a good disguise can save your life. It has worked for Abu Nidal on many occasions and a word of caution, stay away from whiskey. It impairs thinking and slows down reaction time."

Before Ammar left Iraq, rumors abounded about Abu Nidal's deteriorating mental condition. They said he went from hero to killer. Ammar remembered everyone praised the reckless daring of the idolized patriot. They said, "Somewhere along the way, power took the place of nationalism and absolute power destroyed the inner man."

Ammar said, "That won't happen to me. Once this mission is completed, I'll go home. I'll start a new life and put all this violence behind me. I'll..."

He knew he lied.

He was caught up in the same deadly power that put Nidal on the road to destruction. He enjoyed the feeling of omnipotence when he murdered Raymond Briggs. Killing Moose Morrison should have been a regrettable necessity. Instead it was an exhilarating rush of excitement. Even from a distance he had the power of life and death in his hands. He got a kind of sexual gratification from the fear he generated in others. It transcended anything he had ever experienced.

He glanced at his watch. It was time to meet Najjar and Shakir. Najjar's change of attitude puzzled him. He wondered, *What could have happened to negate Najjar's fear? Najjar couldn't be fool enough to think Ammar would relent and spare his miserable life. No. Khalil Najjar knew his impending death was inevitable. He also knew it would come at the hands of the man he once called friend. So, why wasn't he afraid any more? The reason for the lack of fear, couldn't have been because he accepted his fate, he was too cowardly. Could Najjar have betrayed the cause? Was that why the FBI was at the apartment house? He rejected that possibility also because Najjar never knew where Ammar lived. Not in the Village and not in Yorkville.*

Ammar boarded the subway. The ride to the garage took twenty-two minutes. *There is nothing to be concerned about,* he told himself. *Najjar is acting. When the time comes for him to die, he'll die badly. Death is the factory that makes cowards of the bravest men. I won't worry about him. He could never be like me. I am the new Paladin of my people.* But he couldn't shake off the feeling of impending disaster...and that concerned him.

* * *

Two men in hardhats were busy loading jackhammers into the city utility truck. Three others talked beside the hole in the street.

Ammar, Najjar and Shakir melted into the group of sidewalk superintendents with nothing better to do than to gawk at the city workers.

The one with the name Hastings printed on the front of his hardhat was barking orders to the other men. He held a dead stump of a cigar in his mouth, moving it from side to side with his tongue. "Get the rest of this shit on the truck. Move it." He looked around at the crowd. "The party's over, folks, you can go home now." He lifted his hardhat, scratched his head and replaced the hat at a jaunty angle. He growled at the men boarding the truck, "Be back here tomorrow morning at eight and clean up this mess." He slid behind the wheel of a small pickup truck and pulled forward into the slow moving traffic.

The sawhorses with flashing lights remained in place as a warning to motorists about the open hole.

The crowd began to disperse and within minutes all that remained were three terrorists, staring at each other. Khalil Najjar breathed a sigh of relief. At least the lives of the workers were spared. He murmured under his breath, "We'll put the bomb in the ventilation system and I'll visit my coffin." He looked at Ammar to see if his words had reached the ears of his executioner. Satisfied that they had not, he thought, *This is not the way I would have chosen to die. Few men get to choose the method and time of their deaths.*

* * *

They climbed into the van, changed clothes and donned hardhats.

"Shakir, bring the push broom and start cleaning up. Najjar, help me carry the packages and set them in place."

Ammar picked up a flashlight and checked outside before he opened the sliding door. Najjar followed him down the ladder into the sewer. The stench made Najjar gag. Abu Ammar smiled. "You'll get used to it." They went from the sewer into the tunnel that connected the system with the ESB and into the sub-basement. Najjar went first and Ammar handed him the blue plastic bundles containing the bombs, then followed him into the sub-basement.

Floodlights suddenly illuminated the entire area, stunning the two in a blinding flash. A voice from the behind the light shouted, "FBI, put the packages on the floor. Easy like."

Najjar put down the two packages he carried and put his hands over his eyes to protect them from the blinding light. Abu Ammar dropped his packages, fell to the ground and palmed his gun in one move. He took several shots at the voice targets behind the lights. There was rapid gunfire from everywhere outside the arc of light. The enclosed area became Baghdad once again for Abd al Jabbar. Once again he felt the blood puddle on his chest and gurgle in his throat. Once again he heard the screams of Rosha and Alula. There on the ground beside him, staring at him with lifeless eyes was Khalil Najjar. He turned his head and looked into the eyes of Duncan MacKenzie. A curse rose to his lips. He tried putting words to his thoughts but all that came out was blood. Copious amounts of blood as his unseeing eyes stared into eternity.

CHAPTER 23

New York City
May 18, 11:00 p.m.

Alberto Sanders sat in the chair with its front legs tilted and the back leaning against the wall. "I thought nothing could ever touch this city. I didn't think anything could bring New York to its knees. For a few days I thought the New Yorkers wouldn't get up. They wouldn't want to rebuild. But I was wrong."

Mac stood at the window of his office on the thirty-fifth floor and looked down at the sleepless giant, lovingly known as the Big Apple. "Never lose sight of the fact that when New Yorkers are forced to their knees, they're in the perfect position to attack the enemy. The groin is the most vulnerable spot. One thing's for sure; they'll never forget how a few men held this city hostage. There will be some subtle changes in this metropolis of musical comedy and drama; of ballet and opera; of museums and galleries. But some things will never change, it'll always be the city of lights and traffic jams, where cab drivers curse the bus drivers and bus drivers curse the traffic and the pedestrians curse everything." He walked to the desk and picked up the phone. "I wouldn't live anywhere else. This is my town and these are my people. New Yorkers are a dichotomous lot. They're spirited and apathetic, sensitive and vulgar, caring and impersonal, moral and licentious, mean and kindly, and sometimes, dangerous. But they always answer the challenge when you need them."

He punched in some numbers and waited. A sleepy Cliff Ardell answered the phone. "Yeah…what is it?"

"Cliff, it's Mac. We just tied up our loose ends."

The voice at the other end was suddenly alert. "You got Jabbar?"

"I've got more than that, Cliff. You might want to talk to Mike. Jabbar had many aliases one of them was Chisisi Badru, and he had the identification to verify it; now Mike can close the books on Catlin O'Hara's murder."

There was a long pause at the Washington connection. "Are you sure, Mac?"

"Reasonably. He was wearing the Badru disguise when we took him out tonight."

"Are you okay?"

Mac yawned. "Tired, but okay. We lost one man and O'Brien took a bullet in the leg and another in the shoulder. I'm waiting for the doc to tell me how he's doing."

"Then you were right about the target?"

"We were lucky. We had a lot of help from a few city dwellers who got tired of being terrorized. I appreciate your letting me borrow Peter. It would have taken us a lot longer without him." He hesitated. "Cliff, will you tell Mike about Badru, or do you want me to talk to him?"

"Thanks, Mac. Can you fly to Washington tomorrow? Maybe we can tell him together. His inability to get a lead on Chisisi Badru has made him question his effectiveness in the company.

"Okay. I'll get a flight out of here tomorrow."

* * *

The door to Mac's office opened and closed. He turned and faced the medical examiner. "Damn it, Mac, the doctors at the hospital told you to go home and rest. What is it; you think this organization can't run unless you're in this office?"

"Hi, Doc. I couldn't go home just yet. Not until I was certain we got the right man. The kingpin."

"You can go home now, Mac. You got the right man. Jabbar did an excellent job on his makeup. The scars were well hidden with a plasticized material. The blond head also had a brunette base and his blue eyes came out at night. The autopsy didn't reveal anything of a startling nature. The microscopic examination will take a little while but I doubt that it'll change the gross findings. Death was caused by a break in the aorta. He exsanguinated."

"Translation, please."

"He bled to death. His aorta was severed by a bullet and he bled out. Those are the hazards that go with the job."

"Speaking of hazards how's O'Brien?"

"He'll be okay. He took a bullet that shattered his knee, so he'll be in the hospital for a while. The bullet in the shoulder went right through without doing any damage."

The doctor checked the sling on Mac's arm. "And you took two bullets in the arm and shoulder. Like I said, what the hell are you doing here?"

"I put in a call to Cliff Ardell in Washington. I just finished talking to him so I can go home now."

Doc Levick shook his head and closed the door behind him.

Mac drove to the Mott haven district in the Bronx and turned into 142nd Street. He realized how tired he was when he climbed the brownstone steps. In the vestibule, he pushed the button for Sam Boyer's apartment.

"Yes?" she answered.

"Sam, it's Mac. I've got to see you."

The buzzer sounded the release of the door leading to the apartments. The door to her apartment swung wide as he neared the top of the stairwell. Her smile turned to fear when she saw his arm in a sling. She covered her mouth with her hand to stifle her gasp. "Oh, God." She reached for his good arm and led him into the apartment. "What happened?"

"Nothing serious." He devoured her with his eyes. "I had to see you tonight. I'm flying to Washington in the morning."

The alarm she felt registered on her pretty face. "Will you be gone long?"

He ached to take her in his arms. "I should be back on Saturday—in plenty of time for our picnic on Sunday."

She touched his arm lightly. "Do you think we should? Go on a picnic, I mean."

"Absolutely." He tried to smile, but couldn't. "Sam…I need you."

He held her with his good arm, answering kiss for kiss. She pulled him toward her bedroom.

"What about Matthew?"

"He's spending the night with Franny Renzo. There's no school tomorrow and Franny's mother told the boys she would take them to the zoo."

She unbuttoned his shirt and unbuckled his belt. He stepped out of his clothes, his excitement showed in his breathing.

She touched his wounded arm. "I'm afraid I'll hurt you."

He had a mischievous glint in his eyes. "Don't worry; I'm not a virgin anymore."

She muffled a giggle. "That's not the part I was worried about hurting…" The rest of her comment was lost in the wonder of his lovemaking.

CHAPTER 24

Chevy Chase, MD.
May 19, 1:00 p.m.

"Karim," Gabriella fussed over him. "Mon cher, are you feeling better?"

"I took some of that pink stuff," he said, "I think it helped. How was golf?"

"We didn't play. Instead, Mike and Glenn went to the club with me and I did all the last-minute preparations, so I'm free until this evening. I think I'll relax in the jacuzzi and get rid of the tension in my muscles." She opened the closet door and pulled out a new gown. Mint green organza with yards of material, that showed off her red-gold hair. The bodice was cut low, to emphasize cleavage of her ample breasts and the skirt billowed out in graceful folds. The long cape snapped at the base of the throat and folded back on itself over her shoulders so that when she walked, it looked like she was floating. The effect was dramatic. She watched Karim's reaction in the mirror.

"Do you like it, caro?"

"Completely sophisticated, completely charming and completely…Gabriella. Enchanting."

"I take it that means yes?"

"The dress does not make the woman. The woman makes the dress. It hides just enough to make it interesting." He touched a red-gold curl that fell across her forehead. "I love you, my Gabriella."

She pressed her body against him. A frown creased her forehead. She put her hand to his face.

"I think you have a slight temperature. Why don't you stay here tonight and I'll come home as soon as Alden delivers his speech."

"Certainly not, I'll be at that dinner if I have to drag along a port-a-potty. Get into the tub. I'll fix us a drink and you can tell me all about your morning."

* * *

Washington, D.C.

Duncan MacKenzie explained how they were able to lure Abd al Jabbar into the sewer. "All the workers were with the Bureau. We didn't know what Jabbar's disguise would be but we had pictures of Najjar and Shakir. Hank Sommers was acting as crew boss and spotted them in the crowd. When he raised his hardhat and scratched his head; that was a signal telling us they were there. At that point his crew went home. Our men were already in the sewer so we took the route they would have to take to the sub-basement of ESB. By the time Hank and his men left, it gave us enough time to get in place. Only Jabbar and Najjar entered the area. When they got to us, the floodlights went on, momentarily blinding them. Bullets went flying in every direction. I had to give Jabbar credit. He handled himself well. He didn't get flustered like Najjar. His shots were well aimed and all of this, when he was dropping and rolling on the ground. O'Brien took a hit in the leg and right shoulder. Len Garcia took a hit in his left side. He was lucky, the bullet went through without hitting any vital organs."

Peter smiled. "Jabbar must have liked you. He hit you twice."

"When the dust cleared, we had three down and they had two dead. It was strange because Najjar didn't have a gun. He had a knife but...the knife was still in his pocket."

Sally buzzed on the intercom. "There's a Doctor Levick on the phone for Mr. MacKenzie."

Mac picked up the phone.

"Hey, Doc." He listened for a few minutes. "No shit. Are you sure? No, that's okay. Thanks for the information."

Mac looked at the others in the room. "The other terrorist, Khalil Najjar, wasn't killed by our agents. He was executed by Jabbar. There were two shots in the back of his head. Both shots were from a Marakov PM. The markings matched Jabbar's gun. When the bomb squad disarmed the explosives, they found a hypodermic syringe taped to the side of one of the blue plastic bags. It contained the drug curare. Obviously intended for Najjar."

Mac put a cigarette in his mouth and fumbled for his lighter. Peter flicked his lighter and held it to Mac's cigarette.

MacKenzie continued, "The other man, Abdul Shakir, was lookout and was taken into custody. When he heard Najjar was dead, he kept mumbling something about karma. Thanks to Najjar, our deductions about where the final bomb would be placed were confirmed. I have no idea why he drew the diagram of the bomb and now we'll never know, but thank God he did. There was enough explosive charge in what we found to bring down at least half of the building."

"Come in," Ardell responded to a knock at the door.

Doctor Fenelli walked into the room, carrying a folder.

"Come in, Adam, come in." Ardell introduced the medical examiner to the group.

"I just finished the post mortem on Perry. He died of a single gunshot wound to the back of the head. There were no other marks on the body."

Cliff Ardell sat back in his chair. "Thanks, Adam."

Doctor Fenelli opened the folder he brought with him. "When we examined what was left of his head, he had this wedged between his upper teeth and his cheek." He handed the clear plastic bag to Ardell.

Cliff held it up to the light and turned the bag over in his hand. "Looks like a brass button."

Mike took the bag from him. "Let me see that." He stared at the oval brass button with a sailing ship.

Glenn looked over Mike's shoulder and gasped. The color drained from her face." Mike knew she recognized the button too. He said, "Gabriella Russal had a jacket in her car. The buttons were brass with sailing ships. The bottom button was missing." Mike fingered the button. "If Randy grabbed this button when he was falling to the ground after he was shot, then Gabriella was in front of him. That means somebody else shot him. Griad Basq?"

Ardell said, "Or was there a fourth person present?"

Glenn snapped her fingers. "Boulus Qadir. He's the only one not under surveillance at the time. Remember, we lost him when the semi cut off our men. If he and Basq had a prearranged meeting with Gabriella, it's possible he was late. Basq and Gabi could have been waiting for him. Randy couldn't have known there would be a third person. Qadir could have come up behind Randy. But, why he would kill Griad Basq too?"

Mike took a cigarette from the box on the table. "He could have been ordered to kill Basq."

Glenn said, "If he killed two people, as you suggest, there had to be a lot of blood spattered over his clothes. You just don't walk into somebody's house with blood all over you."

"No, but if you carry a warm-up, or a jogging suit in the trunk of your car, it's easy enough to change. Then all he had to do was dispose of the bloody clothes." Mike smiled at Glenn. "Can you furnish us with the rest of this scenario?"

"A plastic trash bag and a hospital emergency room."

Cliff Ardell cocked his head to one side. "Maybe I'm dense, but I don't get it."

Glenn continued, "When bad accidents or gunshot and stab wounds come into an emergency room, they usually end up by cutting off the patient's bloody clothing. The things are then put into a trash bag and sent to a common area for disposal. Sometimes the hospital incinerates such waste, other times it's picked up by a commercial hazardous waste service. Just a thought but it's a fast way of getting rid of bloody clothing."

"You might have something, Glenn. How did you find out about that practice?"

"When I was in college, someone very close to me was critically injured on an icy slope. I went to the hospital with him. He hung on by a thread. In the emergency room, they cut off his clothes to assess the damage. He didn't make it. I saw them put his personal effects, wallet, watch, rings, into a manila envelope, which was witnessed, sealed and registered. It went into the hospital safe. His bloodstained clothes were put in a plastic bag and tossed into a bin with hazardous waste material. Companies that pick up the waste material make the rounds of hospitals, the same as trash pickups. The bags go into closed trucks and are hauled away. If that's what happened, it's long gone."

Cliff asked, "How many hazardous waste dumps are there in the Washington area?"

Mike said, "Probably one. However, that doesn't mean anything. Some of these waste companies will truck the material hundreds of miles to other waste dumps. Probably as far as New Jersey or New York. Remember the barge that was bouncing around from port to port and none of the States would let them dock because they were carrying hazardous waste material? Well, that's not uncommon."

Cliff argued, "You're talking about radio active material like isotopes, we're talking about blood soaked clothing."

Mike shook his head. "Also hazardous material. The people at the hospital have no idea whether or not the victim had AIDS. In such cases, the material is considered hazardous waste and handled as such."

"Okay," said Cliff. "We're back to square one."

Glenn said, "Not quite. We were almost certain Gabi was Abd al Alim. Now we have the introduction of a fourth person at that execution. Was that other person Boulus Qadir? If so, is he Alim? Or is he really the backup as Bengal suggested. Both of them will be at the Algonquin Club tonight. It'll be interesting to see how they get their weapons into the area undetected." She paused. "And they will you know. Abd al Alim didn't get to the top of that profession without being innovative. Gentlemen, I think we've been watching the work of a master."

Mac said, "Even masters get careless." He was obviously uncomfortable about something. He described Jabbar's disguise. "We followed a lead we got the day of the bombing of the Kryler Building and the Federal Building. The man who came to us gave an accurate description of Jabbar. When we got there, the man known as Sakhim, actually Jabbar, had just moved out. We knew he had to change his appearance because the news media published his picture in the newspapers and on TV. Now we had no description of the man we were looking for and time was running out. Based on what we surmised about Jabbar's habits, we canvassed the areas near small parks. It paid off. The registry in one of the small buildings in the Yorkville district showed that an Egyptian had recently moved into an efficiency apartment...his name was Chisisi Badru."

Mike's hands coiled into tight fists and he seemed to have stopped breathing. He stared at his clenched fists, as though willing them to open. When he looked up, his deep blue eyes reflected the pain that had remained concealed since he found Cat O'Hara's body on the balcony in Beirut. In a hoarse whisper, he said, "Are you sure?"

Mac nodded. "We're sure, Mike."

Glenn wanted to take Mike in her arms. She wanted to rock him and croon to him as he did with her and as she had done with Clayton Alexander. Instead, she put her hand over one of his fists and the clenched hand began to relax. He shut his eyes and nodded. He said, "Another chapter, closed."

Glenn looked up at Mac. As though he read her thoughts, he said, "Gadi Qasim is in custody. I doubt that he'll ever make it to trial. They'll probably find that he hanged himself in his cell."

Mike's fingers wrapped around her hand. She looked into his eyes and was drowning again in that sea of blue.

Both were feeling the pain of a lost love.

Both were feeling the confusion of the uncertain attraction between them.

CHAPTER 25

Washington, D.C.
May 19, 6:00 p.m.

The tables were set farther back than the drawing indicated, leaving a larger area of empty space between the dais and the front row of tables. Cliff Ardell paced off the corridor between the rows of cherry trees from the patio of the Algonquin Club to the dais. Agents with metal detectors concentrated their efforts in the wide pathway for the third time.

MacKenzie adjusted his binoculars and slowly scanned the area in front of and beyond the staggered maple trees for several hundred feet. Occasionally, a brief flash of light could be seen as the setting sun reflected the metal of the infrared telescopic sights of agents' semi-automatic weapons. Snipers jockeyed for better viewing positions. Six agents from the Bureau crouched behind the bulwark on the club's roof, each covering a segment of overlapping arcs, for a full three hundred sixty degrees.

Mike Redmond finished his inspection of the kitchen. He found nothing. Peter Aziz came out from the men's room and stood beside Mike. "Nothing in there," he said, "except hand towels and discretely packaged condoms in the storage closet." They walked to the door of the ladies room and waited for Glenn to finish her search. She opened the door and shook her head.

"Nothing. I checked the stalls, towel holders and the toilet paper, sanitary napkin and tampon dispensers. The supply closet has sealed boxes of the items I mentioned."

Peter said, "We checked under every seat, every table, in every cooking vessel and food container. Every room inside the club was searched. As of right now, there are no weapons or explosive charges inside the club or in the outside area where the dinner is to be held. Whatever fire power is used, will have to be brought in." While he talked, he was studying Mike's reaction. "I know that look. What's wrong?"

Mike walked to the door leading to the outside tables and shook his head. "My gut reaction tells me we've missed something that should be evident."

Mac came in by way of the parking lot carrying a folded piece of paper and stood beside Mike. "I told Ardell our men are in place at the Lincoln Memorial, there shouldn't be any problem. Bengal laid it all out for us. Tonight, after this is over, Cliff and I want to talk to you and Glenn about the New York Project."

"Okay. I'll pass the word along to Glenn."

Mac unfolded a sheet of paper. "Secret Service just gave me the President's revised speaking engagements."

Mike read the schedule and handed it back.

Mac said, "Originally, Mr. Breckenridge was scheduled to arrive at eight o'clock, in time for the dinner. It looks like somebody pounded some sense into that thick head of his and got him to agree to stay out of sight until it was time for his speech. He'll arrive at nine-twenty-five and be escorted to the dais by Mrs. Russal. She'll introduce him. His speech was clocked at twelve minutes. By the grace of God, our President should be out of here by nine-forty-five."

Peter asked, "Where will I be sitting?"

Mac answered, "Near the club dining room, where Mr. Breckenridge will make his entrance. I'll be sitting at the table with you." He checked the table assignments. Glenn and Mike will be at the table with Mr. and Mrs. Russal. Mr. Qadir and Miss Gregory will be seated with Senator and Mrs. Cameron. These tables are in the front row."

Glenn took the table layout Mac was holding. "Mac, where did you get this layout?"

"From Cliff Ardell. Why?"

Glenn stood beside Mike, sharing the sketch with him. "Remember how the tables were set up this morning when we were here?" She pointed to the place where there had been an exit aisle. What happened to the aisle?"

"Damn," said Mike, "that's what was missing."

A light flashed near the parking lot.

Mac said, "That's the signal. The Russals just pulled into the lot."

Peter watched from behind the drapery. "Four, no, five more cars. It's probably the rest of the committee for this bash. Mac, didn't you say Qadir was escorting Anita Gregory?"

"That's what's on the guest list."

"Paul Qadir is alone."

Mac and Peter made their way outside to the patio. Glenn stood beside Mike, her ebony gown and matching full-length coat accentuated her green eyes and pale skin. Her hand rested on Mike's arm. She whispered, "You're very handsome in your tux."

His eyes took her in from top to bottom. He covered her hand with his.

"It's a pity we couldn't meet under different circumstances. A different time, a different life...We could have set this tired old world on its ear." He bit his bottom lip and turned to face Gabriella and Karim.

Glenn smiled a greeting. "It looks like it'll be another successful evening for you, Gabi."

"I hope so, darling. I think so."

Mike asked, "Where's Anita? I thought she was coming with Paul."

Gabi pursed her lips, displaying the dimple in her cheek. "I think they had a lover's quarrel. She called earlier to say she had a headache and begged off."

Mike laughed. "Blanche Cameron will be delighted. Now she'll have Paul and the senator to herself."

Karim excused himself and headed for the men's room.

Glenn asked, "Isn't he feeling any better?"

"He says he is, but I doubt it. I wonder if it could be a virus. A little while ago, I started with a crampy feeling. I hope I'm not coming down with it too. This is too important a night to come down with the bothersome trots."

Dinner was served. Gabi ate very little and Karim ate nothing.

Snatches of Blanche Cameron's conversation could be heard over the music. Drawing attention to herself made her feel important. Paul Qadir was trying unsuccessfully to be attentive. Gabriella made four trips to the ladies room in forty-five minutes. Each time Glenn accompanied her, under the pretext of wanting to be sure Gabi was all right.

"I think you're coming down with the bug. You look a little green."

"I'll feel better soon, I took one of Karim's anti-diarrheal tablets." She got up again to go to the ladies room. She put her hand on Glenn's arm. "Wait here, darling. If Alden arrives while I'm in the bathroom, you'll have to escort him."

Glenn sat down again.

It was nine-twenty.

Karim leaned over and whispered to Glenn. "I think there's something wrong with Gabi tonight."

"What makes you think so?"

"She's just not acting like, my Gabriella. She's nervous. I'm worried. Even Paul seemed upset. Don't you feel it?"

Gabriella took the small key to the supply closet out of her purse and quickly unlocked the door. She reached for the large box of sanitary napkins on the bottom shelf, locked the closet, and entered the last stall. Deftly, she opened the box, pulled out the top layer of napkins and piled them on top of the toilet tank. She removed the belt of plastic explosives, lifted her gown and molded the belt to her figure. She pulled the cape down so that the folds fell in front, thus covering her gown and the explosives. She checked outside the stall before emerging. She looked at herself in the full-length mirror and nodded her approval. She checked the time.

It was nine twenty-four.

Alden Breckenridge made his appearance and looked for Gabi. Glenn got up to greet him.

"Don't bother, darling, I'm here."

Glenn turned as Gabi walked past, her eyes focused on the president. She walked slowly, deliberately. Glenn noticed that the cape she wore now covered the front of her gown. The delicate material gave a hint of what was hidden under her gown.

"My God, Mike, Gabi's wired. She's going to kill Alden and herself."

Karim overheard her remark and his eyes registered fear. He bolted from his chair. Everything seemed to happen in slow motion. Karim screamed, "Gabi…No-o-o-o-o."

Mike saw the vacant stare that he came to recognize as the trance condition of a fanatic, performing a final ritual. He sprang to his feet, raced in front of Gabriella and pushed the President to the other side of the stand of trees, sending them both to the ground. He covered the President with his own body. Mac drew his gun from inside the sling on his injured arm and was about to fire when Karim reached her. The realization of his presence registered on her face just before he embraced her, only a split second before oblivion.

Mac was thrown into the open area between the trees like a feather blown by hurricane winds. His good arm twisted at an unnatural angle. Peter lay under the limbs of a tree, toppled by the impact.

It was just as Mike predicted, with no clearly marked exit to follow, people ran in all directions to escape what they thought was the end of the world. Matthew Cameron's body lay like a broken doll on the ground beside his table. Blanche Cameron screamed at him to stand up and get her out of there, while she clung to Paul Qadir. "Do something," she screeched. "Get me out of here."

Paul Qadir tried to pull her arms from around his neck. He opened his jacket and pulled out his revolver, shoved it between Blanche Cameron's considerable breasts and pulled the trigger. Her eyes registered disbelief. Her hands clung to his shoulders momentarily. She grabbed at her chest and felt the blood oozing from between her fingers. She opened her mouth to scream but the sound died somewhere in her throat. She fell to the ground like a marionette, released from its strings.

Alden Breckenridge was unconscious on the ground with Mike Redmond shielding him from attack. Qadir's eyes scanned the area looking for the President. He saw the still form on the ground and aimed at Mike's back. Patrick Dwyer fired at Qadir, narrowly missing him. Qadir turned in his direction and fired three shots, sending the Secret Service agent into an uncontrolled spin. Qadir smiled to himself and yelled, "Husam al Din, Husam al Din, Sword of Faith." His gun was pointed at Mike's back. "Infidel American pig," he screamed. Suddenly Qadir's body stiffened and blood gushed from an open wound where his right eye had been. He hit the ground, his face and body contorted. His body twitched slightly, and then was still.

Glenn stood over Paul Qadir. The gun held at her side. She saw the destruction around her, took a deep breath and looked for Alden Breckenridge. She saw Mike on the ground in front of the President, his revolver clutched in his hand. Mike waved, indicating everything was okay and confirmed that the President was stunned but unharmed.

She hurried to the still form of Duncan MacKenzie and carefully turned him over. When she touched him, he winced. She smiled at him. "Well, at least you can still feel."

"Oh, shit."

"What is it, Mac?"

"How the hell can I make love with one arm in a cast and the other in a sling?"

She laughed with the hysteria that comes when a crisis is over. "Very carefully, Mac, very carefully."

EPILOGUE

Glenn Alexander kicked off her shoe and rubbed her foot.

"I'll do that." Mike sat on the floor in front of her and gently massaged the arch of her foot.

She smiled. "Thank you. I can't believe that it's only midnight on May 19, it feels like it should be the end of fall…when everything dies." Momentarily, tears gathered in her eyes. "I'm glad Alden is okay." She looked around the empty conference room, fighting back tears. "I'm going to miss Gabi and Karim. It's hard to believe they're gone." Impatiently she wiped away the tear that dared escape from under her curled dark lashes. Remnants of other tears clung tenaciously to her top lashes and glistened in the reflected light before they followed the first tear.

"Glenn…I…" Mike started, but words got lost in the atmosphere when the door opened. FBI and CIA agents poured in like molasses running downhill. They sat in chairs around the conference table.

Cliff Ardell sat at the head of the table. He looked at the weary faces of everyone in the room.

"We were lucky. Everything went according to plan. SIS agent Bengal has a flesh wound of the head and is being sent to Britain. We owe him and SIS a debt of gratitude. The terrorists for the Washington contingency of the Husam al Din are all dead. They chose to fight to the end rather than fail in their mission. Willie Jones tried to escape when the bullets started flying. He was shot in the back by one of his own men."

Ardell continued, "Boulus Qadir paid with his life for his part in the attempted assassination. Gabriella Russal, alias Abd al Alim, sacrificed her life for a misguided cause. Her husband, Karim, in an effort to stop her, met the same fate. We found what Randy Perry wanted us to know. He asked another agent in Rome to follow up on a hunch he had. She has been a hired assassin since her days in Paris and she sold her services to the Iraqi Madman."

Duncan MacKenzie walked quietly into the room and took the last seat at the table. Cliff Ardell nodded to him. "The man of the hour is MacKenzie. Not only did he clean up the mess in New York but he came back here to help us. He took two slugs in New York and another in Washington." He took a small memo pad out of his pocket, and read from it. "Senator Cameron was killed by the percussion from the bomb. Mrs. Cameron was shot in the chest at point-blank range by Boulus Qadir and was pronounced dead at the scene. Qadir was backup for Abd al Alim. When Alim self-destructed, that put him in the position of carrying out the assassination. He would have succeeded, had it not been for Glenn Alexander. Her aim was swift and sure. Qadir is added to the casualty list.

"We lost two Secret Service men in the explosion. We have two wounded FBI agents from the shootout at the Lincoln Memorial; Peter Aziz was treated for a bullet wound of the leg and released. Fortunately for us, the tree that fell on top of him was a cherry tree and didn't do too much damage. And we lost Randy Perry. All of those casualties to save the life of one man."

He popped two antacids into his mouth. "Word will get back to Bin Laden and the others; there is no place in this world where they can hide. We'll find the scorpion and crush him."

When the debriefing was over, Mac waited for Peter at the door. "Can I hitch a ride with you to the airport?"

"It'll be my pleasure." He raised one eyebrow. "How the hell are you going to make love to Sam when you can't even take it out off your pants?"

"I'll manage." His eyes twinkled. "Of course, I'll have a lot of help from her."

Peter nodded. "It's about time you got your personal life off center. She seems like a terrific woman." He smiled at Mac. "Great legs."

Mac countered with, "Great ass. Tits aren't bad either."

* * *

Mike and Glenn drove to Alexandria in silence. When he parked outside her house, he turned to face her. "I owe you one. Thanks for covering me."

Glenn was uncomfortable. "All in a day's work." She shifted her position to see him better. The assignment is over; maybe we'll work together again. At least next time we know what to expect." She reached for the door handle.

"Wait." It was his turn to be uncomfortable. "I want you to know that I requested another assignment in the Middle East."

She avoided eye contact with him.

He said, "I have to get away from you, Glenn. You're beginning to invade the secret places in my brain and heart. I need to get away."

She pulled on the door handle and he grabbed her and spun her around. The pressure of his lips forced hers to part. He pulled back from her. "This is what I mean. I've got to get you out of the hidden recesses of my being." He shook his head. "I don't want to love you. I've got to purge you from my system."

She pulled away from him but both of them seemed to be having respiratory problems. "I know, Mike." To herself, she said, *You'll never be rid of me, Michael Redmond. I'm Alexander the Great. I'll follow you around the world. You'll see me in the most unexpected places; at the most inopportune times and I'll tug at your heart until you relent. Watch me, bucko, watch me.*

She stepped onto the sidewalk and waved. He saw the front door open as she approached and Templeton Osbourne stepped out to greet her.

Printed in the United States
87599LV00003B/295-297/A

9 781424 123988